Goodbye, Paris Nash

A novel

Barbara Fletcher-Brink O'Connor

Authors Note: All characters appearing in this work are fictitious, except Jim Shoulders who was a dear friend. Any resemblance to other real persons, living or dead is purely coincidental.

Brink Publishing, New Braunfels, Texas

ISBN-13:978-1480111295
ISBN-10:1480111295

DEDICATION

FOR MY CHILDREN, J.J. AND ALYSON BRINK

ACKNOWLEDGMENTS

Anyone who has ever tried to write a book knows the process is difficult. I thank my truthful friends who told me where I had gone off track. I thank my encouraging friends who told me I was brilliant and talented. I thank my family for their love and support. I couldn't have done it without any one of you. I especially thank my fellow writers in The San Antonio Writers Guild, the New Braunfels Writers Guild, and to my fellow artists at The New Braunfels Art League. Special thanks to River City Ink, my soul sisters plus one, Naomi Patterson, Alexandra Marbach, Joy Elkins, Manuela Stafford, Stefanie Daily and our plus one, Frank Kavanaugh.

Thank you Bob Rogers from KENS television for letting me tag along with reporter Fred Lozano years ago to get a feel for the television newsroom. Thank you, Robert Lopez Flynn, for your early encouragement.

To my proofreaders, Carol Kohl, Carolyn Pittman, Carol Lipscomb, Bethlee McLaughlin, Sharon Neumann, Susan Belken, Sherry Kelley, Carol Erwin, Lewis Sarkozi, Virginia Graham, Bette Holley, Jerry Harlan, Tonie Ogier-Bryan my daughter Alyson Brink, my mother Katherine Classen and my husband Philip O'Connor.

Prologue

The host of the talk show I was watching made a convincing plea, "If you'd like to come to New York and be on our show, check our website for upcoming themes." Out of curiosity, sitting in my big chair next to the fireplace sipping my second cup of coffee, I tapped the program's web address into my laptop and scanned the list of future topics.

Did you discover your husband had a gay lover? Yes, I did, but that was a very long time ago and I do not want to talk about it on national television. *Did your birth mother abandon you?* In a way, but it would do no good to fly to New York and discuss that subject either. *Did someone change your life, and do you want to thank him or her for it?* Yes, someone did and yes, I wish I could thank her.

The way I understood the program's process, interested viewers write about their life experiences, and the show's producers decide which stories best fit their agenda. The winning entrants get a free trip to New York, stay at a big name hotel, appear in a ten-minute segment on the *Dr. Lou and a New You* self-help program, and share their intimate stories with millions of television viewers.

Even if they chose my story, it would take much longer than a ten-minute segment to tell what Paris Nash did for me. It sounds trite, but is true, to say, "She gave me a life I never expected to have."

It has been more than twenty-five years since I first saw Paris Nash. Meeting her was a coincidence, as every important event in my life seemed to be. I would never have embarked on that life-changing journey if a flu epidemic and freak ice storm had not collided, forcing Bud Johnson to give me the assignment in the first place.

1986

Chapter One

I had only been working at the station for six weeks when the perfect storm hit. All but two of our on-air hosts were home in bed, sick with a yet unnamed flu. Ignacio Rivera, the station lothario and sports reporter, was the seventh of our on-air personalities to call in sick that week.

KWNK's receptionist, Maxine, kept up with the casualties and shared their progress. "The poor guy told me he is running a hundred and three degree fever," she told me. Maxine served as our matriarch, had been with the station for over twenty years, and her concern about the suffering employees was genuine. The rest of us, having to fill in and pull double shifts, were almost too tired to care.

Our noon anchor, the community service reporter, the afternoon show host, three other field reporters, and Tracy Brennan, our evening and ten o'clock anchorwoman-from-hell, had all succumbed, Tracy claiming a "relapse." Most of us thought she played to the drama and was getting way too much pleasure from receiving stacks of get-well cards from her devoted fans.

The morning show co-anchors, Bob and Juanita, our more robust on-air personalities, were doing all of the fill-in for their recuperating counterparts. The two of them embraced the entertainment business adage that the show must go on, and went. They were exhausted from doing noon news, evening news, late night, as well as their usual morning show, and had succeeded in elevating themselves to such importance that they could not be risked going on the assignment Bud gave me.

"He better not ask me to go out in this freezing mess to report on some stupid cow," Juanita threatened, her head swelling with new importance.

Everyone agreed with Bud, our brilliant station manager/news director. He could not dare put either of them in jeopardy, and surprised us all when he chose me to go cover the story instead.

No one was more shocked than I was when he called my favorite cameraman, BZ, and me into his glass-walled office and told us, "Siobhan, I want you to cover the judging at the Junior Livestock Show. They're picking the Grand Champion Steer today." He raked his fingers through his salt-and-pepper hair and added, "We need film for noon, BZ, so don't fool around out there. No telling who else will call in sick before you get back here."

It was the first time Bud said more than two words to me since hiring me six weeks before, and it was to deliver a major you-are-on-your-own assignment. Frankly, I was a little disappointed that he failed to give me more direction or a scintilla of encouragement, like "Go get 'em girl." Or, for that day, anyway, "Sorry you have to go out in this rotten freezing weather. Take care out there." However, Bud did neither. He gave us our assignment and dismissed us with inattention.

To his credit, when Bud gave me the assignment, he believed it was a breakthrough opportunity for me. I, the new hire, was getting to cover the kind of feature story he usually reserved for our anchor-diva. To me, though, it seemed more like an opportunity to suffer inevitable comparisons to Tracy Brennan, who had received, in the last three Nielsen rating books, the highest television-news-anchor name recognition in our market. I, on the other hand, had not acquired name recognition around our own studio and was still waiting for someone to tell me where they hide the extra coffee in the break room.

The one thing I did see in my favor that morning was that I had dressed appropriately for the unexpected assignment. Since KWNK adhered to the citywide request issued by the mayor's office to dress western during rodeo week, I was wearing boots and jeans, a plaid snap front shirt and a western-style duster I had paid too much for at the thrift store my friend Phyllis and I frequented.

Since the temperature outside was at the freezing mark and since I forgot to bring my Stetson with me, I decided to pull on the black knit cap I kept in my coat pocket, even though it would play havoc with my hair. At that moment, I simply wanted to stay warm and not make a total fool of myself on camera. My priorities were not complicated for the freezing February day.

I headed toward the parking lot aware of ricocheting advice colliding inside my head, pinging like sonar against my skull, everything I had learned from my grandfather, the professors at Tech, and from people at the station who, bless them, had spent time and energy helping me learn the ropes. A nausea wave, my own personal fight-or-flight mechanism, prepared me to get ready for *something*. I was too nervous to consider what that something might be.

When I got to the parking lot, I saw BZ waiting patiently for me in the neon yellow KWNK van, running the motor to warm it. Icicles dripped from the building overhang and as I slipped and fell on my butt, I noticed a thin sheet of ice covering the ground. Billowing exhaust fumes greeted me as I recovered, making me cough as I climbed into the front bucket seat. The cold vinyl chilled through my now-damp denim and made me shiver in my seat.

Waving my gloved hands in front of the vent, I asked BZ, "Is the heat on?"

He gave me a, "Do you think I'm stupid" look, rolled his eyes, and stepped on the accelerator. I gave him a "duh" shrug as we left to cover the selection of the Grand Champion Steer at the Alamo City Junior Livestock Exposition.

The long-standing event, San Antonio's homage to agriculture, was a well-intentioned attempt to educate our citizenry about where the food they eat originates. The exposition focuses on farming and ranching and gives city folk a chance to experience agriculture. People come, go through the barns, and look at the exhibits and the animals brought in by Future Farmers and 4-H members.

Most people come, glance at the animals and the proliferation of agricultural exhibits, and then rush off to get to their seats in the Coliseum where they watch the rodeo bull riders, calf ropers, steer wrestlers and Bronc riders compete for National Rodeo Association standings and prize money.

Most are actually there to see the mega-star performers that A.L.E.C., the Alamo Livestock Exposition Committee, introduced back in the early seventies to boost attendance figures. Now, most people do not remember much about the animals or exhibits, but talk about which star they saw perform in concert after the rodeo each night. They miss the heart of the event.

I do not blame our population for their lack of enthusiasm about agriculture. Few of them depend upon crops or herds for their livelihood. Most have lost touch with the earth and all it provides. Concrete and asphalt cover old-time fields, and subdivisions grow where cattle once grazed. San Antonio is no longer a sleepy little cow town. It is a big city now.

While BZ drove, I propped my feet on the van dashboard, rested my notebook on my knees and attempted to write copy for my assignment. Within the hour, I would report the names of the two hard working youngsters whose dedication would receive recognition at the judging for Reserve Grand Champion and Grand Champion Steer of the Livestock Exhibition.

Anyone living in or near San Antonio knows about the Grand Champion Steer. That animal receives as much or more attention as the concert stars. The Reserve is actually the first runner-up, an honor to be sure; however, the biggest prize goes to the boy or girl whose animal wins Grand Champion.

The Grand Champion Steer of the 36th Annual Junior Livestock Show is (blank) raised by (blank) from (blank) which is near (blank). Two shot: (Blank) has hand-fed his/her steer for the past (blank) months. The grooming of the steer is as important in the ring as is the steer's conformation. Note to me: If a girl wins, ask about the glitter, hairspray, and perfume. If a boy wins, ask about the precise hair cutting and whether he made the halter by hand or if he even considered glitter. Then one shot on me: The San

Antonio show is a terminal show, which in the simplest terms means that the Grand Champion steer will leave the auction next week on a truck headed to the slaughter house to be processed into whatever combination of freezer food is ordered by the winner of the auction, which will be held..."

I stopped writing to ask, "When are they going to auction off this unsuspecting animal?"

"It's the last Friday of the show," BZ told me.

"I know, but what is the day date? The fifteenth?"

"Let's see, today is Friday the seventh...," he counted off on his fingers, "...next Friday is the fourteenth, Valentine's Day. Until then they'll put the winner in that big pen out in front of the Coliseum so people can see what prime beef looks like before it hits the meat counter."

I winced.

BZ continued, "Last year I watched little kids standing at the grand champion pen, sticking their arms through the fence slats, feeding the steer cotton candy." He laughed and shrugged remembering the image.

I went back to writing my script.

...will be auctioned Friday, Valentine's Day, February 14. So, come on out and meet (blank) Grand Champion Steer of the Livestock Show and Rodeo.

BZ interrupted, telling me "We need to pick up a packet." He pulled up at the Coliseum public relations building and pointed to a door at the top of an icy outside staircase. He grinned at me.

I got out of the warm van and trudged up the icy steps while, from the interior of the cozy vehicle, BZ gave me thumbs-up encouragements every time I recovered from near slips. When I reached the landing, I stuck my tongue out at him and waved a rude hand gesture just as the A.L.E.C. public relations guru opened the door to hand me a media packet. He could only have been less friendly if he had used it to slap my face.

The unsympathetic man warned me in a stern tone, "You had better get over to the barn. KWNK is the last station in. The auction starts in fifteen minutes." He skidded down the stairs in front of me and headed to the cattle barn, puffing white in the freezing cold as he jogged away.

While BZ drove, I glanced through the media packet and learned that the Alamo City Livestock Exhibition is one of Texas' big three regional events. Houston, Ft. Worth, and San Antonio all award big prize money to winners in the junior livestock categories. At each show, the biggest prize bundle goes to the winner of the Grand Champion Steer competition.

In a small way, the selection of Grand Champion is similar to judging in championship dog shows. Each breed of cattle holds an independent judging and selects a champion to represent the breed. Then, those breed champions compete for Best in Show, or Grand Champion Steer in this case. That is where the dog show analogy ends.

Unlike those canine shows, where bloodlines are prized and improving the breed and selling pups are the goals, the livestock show entries are neutered beef cattle. They are non-breeding stock who cannot compete in multiple shows; they cannot win Grand Champion Steer in San Antonio and then get carted to Houston to try for big money again.

The steers, actually castrated bull calves, have a single life purpose: to become beef for the meat counter. The lives of the steers end when the event is over. The entries, like the first little piggy, go to market.

On the bright side, for the remainder of the San Antonio show, the Grand Champion Steer lives like a four-hooved rock star in a giant pen in front of the Coliseum where everyone who enters the grounds can see him. This is one important animal. It is upon its massive shoulders that college scholarships for deserving young Future Farmers and 4-H members rest.

The young people who plan to pursue careers in agriculture compete because they have a chance to win scholarships to Texas A&M or Texas Tech or some other college or university in the state where agribusiness is still venerated. The handler who shows the Grand Champion gets a full ride four-year scholarship from A.L.E.C.

A portion of the scholarship monies comes from big corporate sponsors who pay to have their name associated with the event, but A.L.E.C. raises the majority of the funds at the auction on the last day when local business leaders bid tens of thousands of dollars to win the Grand Champion Steer. The cost, if figured per pound for beef, is not a bargain, but to the winning bidder, the value in media coverage is priceless.

The high bidder at the auction gets front-page stories in both daily newspapers, and is interviewed on every local news program, both television and radio. Later in the summer, the company receives even more P.R. exposure when they either host a fundraising Grand Champion Barbeque or donate the beef to an orphanage or food program. The winning bidder gets a truckload of recognition for the tax-deductible bid.

We got to the barn as the Texas Longhorn Band struck up a deafening rendition of "The Eyes of Texas." Last week A.L.E.C. sent press releases saying they discovered that someone, in error, sent invitations to the two archrivals, the orange and white Longhorn band and to the military khaki clad Fighting Texas Aggies. Both had accepted.

The long standing rivalry between the two schools played out, and no one was surprised when the Aggies brandished their "Gig 'em" thumbs up gesture during the Longhorn Band playing "The Eyes of Texas" or by the Longhorns reciprocating with hook-'em-horns when the Aggies began "The Aggie War Hymn."

As BZ and I reached our reserved-for-media front row seats, the attending alumni of the schools exploded into such cacophonies, I feared the bleachers would collapse from boot stomping. When both bands joined to play the "Star Spangled Banner," hats came off to cover hearts and peace reigned once again in the auction barn. School rivalry be damned, few groups are as patently patriotic as the agri-business crowd.

While we waited for the judging to begin, my reporter's eye took in details of the scene, thinking how I might revise my script. BZ was busy capturing atmosphere shots to intersperse in the editing of my piece, scanning the patriotic bunting draping the raised stage and the colorful banner some brave soul had climbed into the rafters to hang above it. A podium, microphone, and folding chairs faced the crowd waiting for the judging to begin.

Hefty red, white, and blue velvet drapery panels hung heavily behind the stage and around the bleachers where we sat, creating a cocooned mini-theater inside the huge tin and board cattle barn. The scent of fresh damp earth mingled with the aroma of corn popping at the concession stand and the odor of Aqua Net, floating from behind the curtains where the young handlers were grooming and spray-netting their entries in preparation for the judging.

Contrary to what the PR person told me, the proceedings were late starting and the crowd was thankful when the bands stood together to play "Texas, Our Texas."

Hats and hands went over hearts until the state anthem ended when whoops and cheers erupted. From behind the stage, a Stetson levitated as we watched until it revealed itself upon the head of a small man wearing a dark blue western suit festooned with fringe and beaded appliqués. He glittered from cactus to Conestoga reminding me of a tiny, twinkling Porter Waggoner.

Local dignitaries and officials clambered up the steps behind the overly sequined man and made a path to shake hands with him before sitting. I overheard someone say, "The little guy is Eloy Grisham. He's the chairman of the show this year."

As if on cue, the chairman smiled and spoke into the microphone, "Welcome, welcome, welcome." Holding his arms wide like a beneficent Pope embracing the crowd, he intoned, "The hub of Texas welcomes all of you who braved today's inclement weather to witness the selection of the 36th Grand Champion Steer of the Annual Alamo Junior Livestock Show."

He waited for applause to start and then for it to stop again before he continued. "Joining me this morning…"

My mind wandered while the Chairman introduced the appointed commissioners from all adjoining counties. I zoned out while each of them gave a message of appreciation to the crowd for coming to support the fine young Texans who worked so very hard to prepare their steers for this moment. Then the Chairman introduced the county judges, elected officials not important enough to speak, who tipped hats when he called their names, each smiling bigger than Miss Rodeo Texas, who was there to place embroidered satin blankets on the winning steers. When the Chairman introduced her, she blushed, waved at the crowd, and tried to ignore the wolf whistles from the boys in the college bands.

Finally, it was time to open the gates on each side of the stage and allow fine young Texans and their well-behaved steers into the judging arena. After Chairman Grisham introduced the three expert cattle judges, identified by the wide black armbands they wore, they began their work. We watched them poke, pat and prod each animal, noticed the running of hands on flanks and butts, and saw them stand back like artists at an easel to study the conformation of each entry.

All the while, the young handlers attempted to coax their steer to stand in the perfect position to show its best features. Some of the handlers nudged at the hooves with long handled crooks, spacing heavy limbs to best advantage. Some used a wire bristle grooming brush to stroke the steer's broad back, lulling it to motionless tranquility.

For two years or longer, these animals learned to accept human touch. They had daily baths and brushings, had been hand fed, primped and polished, techniques to make them lose their natural instinct to flee. These unsuspecting animals expected to receive similar kind treatment forever and had no idea a slaughterhouse lay in their near future.

The docile breed champions selected at separate judging events the day before represented the best bovines in the show. The champion Polled Hereford, Limousin, Charolais, Brangus, Angus, Santa Gertrudis, Simmental, and Maine Anjou were striving to win the coveted Grand Champion Steer award.

The three judges finished examining the entries and huddled to compare notes about which steer each believed to be the superlative representative of Texas' best prime beef on the hoof. The confab lasted far too long for my short attention span and my eyes wandered to one of the handlers, a pretty young girl holding the lead of a sparkling Polled Hereford steer.

The girl had dark hair and fair unblemished skin, but her eyes were closed and she swayed forward and back, making me think she was going to faint. I tapped BZ's arm and motioned toward her. He slowly turned the lens of his camera in her direction.

The sound of applause brought our attention back to the judges, who were shaking hands with one another, smiling, patting each other on the back in congratulation and agreement. One of them took the official clipboard and paperwork and handed it up to the exceedingly confident, overly sequined chairman, who looked it over in preparation of announcing the winners.

"Ladies and gentlemen," Eloy unhurriedly ended the crowd's anticipation. "The judges have reached their decision. Your reserve grand champion," he announced the first runner-up "is Showboat, a Charolais steer raised by Lester Steubing of Winters, Texas."

A whoop went up from the gallery above us as redheaded Lester, so excited in the moment that his freckles disappeared into the flush of his face, received a second place ribbon and his steer Showboat got a shiny satin Reserve Grand Champion blanket positioned across his broad back by Miss Rodeo Texas. The judges stood with Lester for photographs, all smiling, none wider than freckle-faced Lester.

BZ was busy capturing those images while I kept my eyes on the swaying girl. When I noticed her knees begin to buckle, I punched BZ and he focused his camera on her chalk-white face barely visible beneath her wide brimmed black hat.

"Ladies and gentlemen, your attention please," the

chairman's voice boomed over the loudspeakers

All cameras, except BZ's, swung toward Eloy as Lester pulled Showboat away to make room for the Grand Champion. "Your 36th Grand Champion Steer is Charga, a Polled Hereford raised by Paris Nash of Kingsland, Texas."

All eyes turned toward the only Polled Hereford in the ring, but they were too late to see the swaying girl fall. She had crumpled to the arena floor at the hooves of her sparkling Grand Champion Steer. BZ captured the fall on camera, and I could hear our competitors groaning. They had all missed the shot of the day.

Chapter Two

Paris Nash lay in the dark, clumped soil, slight, not moving, her steer touching his muzzle to her cheek. Seconds later a wiry blond woman in boots and jeans climbed over the arena fence nearest her. As soon as the woman's boots hit the arena dirt, she began running a hand along the body of the steer, crooning, "Whoa, Charga. Steady boy. Easy now."

She grabbed the lead line dangling from the steer's halter and pulled it back toward the steer's thick neck, attempting to move the heavy animal away from the unconscious girl. She patted the steer's wide jaw and ducked, putting herself between the girl and the twelve-hundred-pound animal. I was certain she was the girl's mother.

Eloy shouted into the microphone, "Is there a doctor in the house?" In a less frantic tone, he said, "We've called for the paramedics and they're on the way." He pointed at the crowd of teenagers behind the fence pushing to see inside the arena, "Back away for the medics."

The judges helped disperse the gawkers by spreading their arms wide and herding contestants and steers away from the girl, shouting, "Get back. Move. Let her have some air."

I noticed a young man moving against the throng, swimming upstream, shouldering a path to the girl. Once beside her, he knelt and the older woman spoke to him, handing over the lead rope. He stood and pulled it, urging the steer to follow him. The gentle animal lumbered behind, then turned its head, and looked back at Paris Nash lying motionless on the ground.

"Be back in a minute, BZ." I ducked between panels of red and blue velvet, pausing momentarily to let my eyes adjust to the dimness on the opposite side of the curtains. The scent of raw hay, fresh manure and hair spray permeated, while dust motes floated lazily in shafts of light shining through cracks in the old wooden structure. When the big tin double doors swung open to let the ambulance enter, the lazy specks swirled rapidly on the rush of air and I began to sneeze.

I found myself in a sea of steers and handlers and looked over them to see a parting of the crowd as the young fellow leading the recently announced Grand Champion Steer walked to the back of the old barn. Miss Rodeo Texas shouldered after him saying, "Excuse me, please. Excuse me, please," until she caught up and, determined to complete her assignment, unevenly hung the satin Grand Champion blanket across the animal's wide back. She made a silly curtsy, said "Congratulations," and turned to run up the steps to the stage.

As the boy and steer walked away, another boy, wearing an FFA cap, called out "She all right, Charlie?"

Without taking his eyes off the ground, young Charlie

waved a hand over his head.

"Hang in there, Charlie, she'll be okay," a shrill-voiced girl encouraged.

The young man nodded, not looking up, and kept trudging. I caught up with him at the pen where I watched Charga standing quietly letting the boy remove his halter and the catawampus satin blanket. The boy pushed an empty coffee can into a sack of grain and scooped up oats, dumping it into a feed bucket hanging from a fence post. The steer did not hesitate to eat and as he began to chew, I watched the young man stretch his arms across the steers warm back and rest his face there. He began to sob.

I crept up quietly and waited until his sobs abated, then I cleared my throat, "Excuse me, Charlie?"

His head jerked up and at that moment, he looked much older than when I first saw him in the arena. His strong jaw jutted with defiance, defining the planes of his face, making him look more man than boy.

As he pushed his dark blue FFA cap back on his head, he wiped his sleeve across his eyes and a wave of compassion came over me. Some reporters I have known wait for this very kind of vulnerability, and use youthfulness and an upset emotional state as opportunities to take advantage for a story. That kind of reporter would jump in and begin firing questions, trampling emotions, demanding to know what had happened to the girl in the ring.

I was not that kind of reporter and hoped I never would be. One of my least favorite communications professors told me, "You are not there to feel sorry for the subject; you are there to get a story. If there isn't a story, make one. You have to fill air time."

My grandfather taught me higher ethics, something completely different. He told me, "They are called reporters, not storytellers. The profession is supposed to be the eyes and ears of the public, not the imagination. Your job is to give an accurate accounting, leave conjecture to novelists. If you cannot be objective, you are in the wrong job." Those thoughts flashed through my mind until Charlie growled at me.

"What do you want?"

"Are you okay? Can I get you anything?" I looked in my satchel and gave him a packet of tissue I kept there.

"No," he was abrupt, refused the tissues, and mumbled, "I got to get back to Paris." He wiped at his eyes with his shirtsleeve and started toward me, motioning me back out of Charga's pen.

"I'm Siobhan O'Shaughnessy with KWNK," I spoke quickly. "We are here covering the judging. It looks like you're part of team Charja," I smiled weakly as I backed away from him, adding "Congratulations," probably too brightly.

He corrected my pronunciation. "It's Char Ga, not Ja." He turned away, padlocked the pen gate, and started walking toward the arena.

"Charga," I corrected my pronunciation using the hard G, trying to match his long stride as he walked ahead of me. "Has she been ill? The girl Paris, I mean. The flu's been rampant in the newsroom where I work and I thought maybe she had it or was getting over it or something?"

He did not answer me. He kept walking and I quickened my steps to keep pace, clearly chasing this story. I took one of my official KWNK business cards from the dozen or so I kept clipped to the back of my notebook and held it out to him.

"If there is anything I can do, please call me." Then I faltered, "I mean I don't know what I can do, I'm really raw at this business, but I'll do whatever I can to help."

He turned and we made eye contact. He reached for the card, slid it in his hip pocket, and then he loped off toward the EMS ambulance, reaching it as technicians rolled the gurney carrying the girl through the wide back doors. With little effort, he climbed in behind it and sat beside the blond woman, who moved over to make room for him.

I stood for a minute, wondering about them, supposing he was the girl's boyfriend. Then I realized he could be a relative, a cousin or adopted brother, maybe. Perhaps they were stepsiblings. I wanted to find out more.

Bud's admonition to us about getting back for the noon news surfaced in my mind and I went to find BZ so we could finish up and get back to KWNK with the story. He was where I'd left him, standing at the fence all alone since the crowd had dispersed. The spotlights were off and trampled earth and chairs askew were the only evidence that the steer judging was completed.

"What do you think?" I asked as I approached him.

"I think you went to pee," BZ answered with a smirk.

"No," I swatted him with my notebook, "about the girl."

"I think she got overcome that she won," BZ's voiced faked falsetto, "Like a girl."

I made a fist and punched his bicep, "Chauvinist!"

He laughed at me, and when I pulled back to thump him again, he ducked and weaved so I could not land another hit.

"You're getting violent on me, Oshun."

"And you, the father of *two* daughters! I'm gonna' tell your wife." I thought the threat of that would be torment enough. I changed the subject to the work we needed to finish. "Let's get the one-shot over with and head back to the station."

21

"I think you might want to check the mirror before we start filming, talent," he grinned, an eyebrow raised, motioning to my head.

I had forgotten about the knit cap. I pulled it off and felt the static electricity make my hair follow. BZ laughed and pointed at me.

I saw a girl wearing an FFA jacket walking close by and, I ran up to her. "Want to make your hat a television star?" I asked.

She stared blankly and I explained, "May I borrow your hat for a minute?" I pointed the wide brimmed felt hat she wore and then to my flying tresses and to BZ holding the camera. "I'm going on camera and well." I gestured to my head.

She took off her hat and handed it to me, "I see what you mean," she giggled.

I tucked my hair under the hat and smoothed the sides as she watched and nodded approval. BZ shouldered the camera and gave me a three-finger countdown. I looked into the lens, smiled one of my long practiced, slightly unhappy smiles, and began. "There has been additional drama today at the judging of the grand champion steer at the Joe and Harry Freeman Coliseum. What is usually a celebratory event has become one of great concern about the condition of the young handler who showed the Grand Champion.

"Paris Nash of Kingsland, Texas, collapsed to the arena floor as her Polled Hereford, Charga, was named 36th Grand Champion. We will keep you updated on the girl's condition. In a more pleasant development, Lester Steubing of Winters, Texas, won Reserve Grand Champion with his Charolais steer, Showboat. Both animals will be on display in front of the Coliseum until the auction next Friday. I am

Siobhan O'Shaughnessy reporting for KWNK news from the 36th Annual Junior Livestock Show at the Joe and Harry Freeman Coliseum. Y'all come on out and see Charga and Showboat, now, ya' heah'." I gave one of my much-practiced upbeat, happy smiling closeouts. BZ nodded and winked; his version of KWNK's greatest praise. The FFA girl reached for her hat.

While BZ radioed the station to tell Bud we were on our way, I asked the girl, "Do you know her, the girl who passed out in the arena?"

"You mean Paris. Not really, around you know?" she shrugged.

"Has she been sick all week?" I attempted to start a conversation to get more information. "These barns aren't the best place for someone trying to get over the flu."

"No, she hasn't been sick, but she's been kind of quiet. Her and Charlie Garza, her boyfriend; they've been keeping to themselves a lot. I don't really know them," she explained, "Just from some other FFA stuff. But, come to think of it, she did look kind of paler and skinnier to me."

The little information she gave me did not satisfy, but at least I learned that the boy was the girl's boyfriend.

We got to the station faster than it took to drive to the arena. The weather was typical February Texas. The sun was out, strongly claiming supremacy over the ice left by the freezing rain. I searched inside my everything-satchel for sunglasses. City crews had salted the bridges, and as we passed over one, the gritty sludge crunched beneath the van tires.

I spent the drive checking my notes about the girl against her bio in the media packet. "Hmmm," I murmured.

"Yo?" BZ asked.

"Thinking," I answered.

"About?" He glanced my way.

"The girl. She's only fifteen, a sophomore at Kingsland High School. You ever go up there?"

"To water ski and fish," he said, "on Lake LBJ close to Horseshoe Bay, not as far down the lake as Kingsland."

I nodded. I remembered water skiing on one of those lakes when I was in high school, but wasn't sure if it had been at Lake L.B.J. or Marble Falls. I thought I remembered where Kingsland belonged in that part of the Hill Country.

"She's fifteen?" BZ asked. "She looks a lot younger than that to me."

"Did you hear what the girl said? The girl who let me borrow her hat."

BZ shook his head.

"She said Paris looked paler and skinnier. I wonder what that means. Where do you think they took her? What hospital?"

"Well, let me see." He paused, "Ft. Sam is closest, but my bet is Children's Hospital downtown."

"I want to follow up on her," I told him. "She looked so little out there on the ground next to that big steer. Did you see the way Charga looked back at her when the boy led him away? I think that animal really cares about her."

I started to tear up and BZ, in an annoying singsong cartoon voice, said, "Not for long. In another week he's gon' be hambur-ger."

Chapter Three

When we got to the station, everyone had already heard about the fainting girl. They were waiting for us, hoping we could fill in details. Maxine, the receptionist, already made up her mind about what was wrong. "She's probably pregnant!"

Jim Draken, the weatherman did not agree. "She's probably coming down with the flu, what with the weather being so unpredictable."

The weekend sports anchor thought she had food poisoning, "Did you ever eat out there, man? It's Ptomaineville."

I had finished pouring myself a fresh cup of coffee when I saw Bud motioning me into his office. "Nobody else wants to venture into a hospital." He gestured at my Kleenex wielding co-workers at their desks outside his glass-walled office. "Want to do a follow up on the girl?"

It appeared that my robust health was giving me an

edge over the rest of the staff. I rushed back to my desk and started looking up hospital phone numbers. On our way back to the station, BZ suggested they probably took her to Children's Hospital, so I started there.

The admissions clerk answered and, on her first search found no patient registered under the name Paris Nash.

Then I told her, "She came by ambulance."

The voice informed me, implying I should have given her that piece of information in the first place, "She's probably still down in the emergency room. She may never even be admitted to the hospital."

"Is there a way you can check for me?" I stood firm, refusing to let her unpleasant attitude intimidate me.

She seemed annoyed with my request, but said, "Yes. Hold. I'll check for you."

I put the phone on speaker so I could hear her return and motioned to BZ that I wanted to speak with him. He and Scott, the noon news producer, were watching his tape of the judging, both beamed with satisfaction. I knew Scott must have complimented BZ on the piece by the blush on BZ's face. After Scott finished editing the story, it would be tight and concise, might end up running a minute, maybe a little longer. I, however, did not care how long or short it aired because I had accomplished one of my goals. I actually covered my first feature story and as it turned out, it was a story with follow-up.

BZ glowed with excitement as he headed toward my desk. "Scott liked the piece." His wide smile showed how happy he was. "Scott thinks we are the only crew to get the fall as it happened. It really is dramatic, want to see it? The girl is falling and in the background you can hear Eloy announce her as the winner."

"Nope, not right now, I'll catch it later. I'm on hold, waiting for Sister somebody to check ER for the Nash girl."

"Children's Hospital?" BZ guessed.

I nodded. "Bud gave me the go-ahead to follow up on the story." We high-fived, slapping palms to celebrate.

BZ sounded positive when he told me in a superior tone, "Odds are she's pregnant."

"Yeah, that's Maxine's idea, too. I don't think so though," I shook my head.

"Are you going for the flu, food poisoning or the excitement of winning?" He acted out spiking a football, doing a goal line fist clench. BZ was in a very good mood.

"No, I don't think it's anything like that. Something more serious, I think. I noticed real sadness when I talked to the young man, her boyfriend as it turns out, he seemed...," I searched for the right word, "morose, worried...about her."

"Aha," BZ beamed. "I might win a bet! Sounds like a dude with a pregnant girlfriend to me."

My phone spoke, "Hello?"

"Yes," I fumbled with the receiver. "I'm waiting to see if you have a patient in emergency named Paris Nash." I listened and replied to let BZ know the outcome of her search. "You do?" I nodded to BZ. "Will she be admitted?" I shrugged. "Okay, I'll call back later."

I rushed into Bud's office, interrupting his conversation with our sports expert. "I found her. She's at Children's Hospital."

Bud nodded, "Go see what you can find out."

"Should, could," I corrected, "BZ come with me? In case?"

Cary, the sports anchor, shared his opinion about the girl. "My money's still on food poisoning. Don't ever eat out there," he warned.

BZ was sitting on the edge of my desk, watching for a signal and when I gave him a thumbs-up, he went to gather his gear. I stopped at my desk, grabbed my canvas satchel, took a couple of sips of coffee, and headed to meet him at the van.

The vehicle, for the past hour, had been sitting in the sunshine, baking in the parking lot out back, felt warm and toasty when I climbed inside. Almost too warm and toasty, I thought, waving my hands in front of the vents, so I asked BZ "Is the air on?"

He gave me one of those, *do I look stupid* expressions. I shrugged, raised my eyebrows at him, and we were off.

The weather's about face played havoc with the warm layers I needed earlier in the morning, my heavy sweater made me too warm so I dug in my bag and pulled out a grey knit vest I had put in my satchel for just such a circumstance. I unfastened my seatbelt, squirmed out of my coat, and pulled my bulky sweater over my head.

I left the black cotton turtleneck on, put the grey vest on top of it, and tugged at some of the more prominent pills that had grown on it. I refastened my seatbelt, burrowed in my bag again searching for my make-up pouch and mirror. I propped my feet on the dashboard, clenched the mirror between my knees, and touched up my lipstick, blush and mascara. Then I ferreted out my hairbrush, a cloth-wrapped rubber band, and prepared to put my hair in a ponytail.

BZ leaned to tried get a look inside my bag, "Got any tacos in there?"

I laughed at him, realizing we had not eaten anything all morning. "Let's get something to go at Taco Cabana, I'll buy," I told him.

We ordered our food, and as we waited in the drive through I managed to make my hair look fairly decent, considering it spent the morning under a knit cap, flew beneath a Stetson, and been roughly raked by my hairbrush. I smoothed it into a ponytail and managed to fluff my bangs into something other than flat against my forehead. BZ nodded his approval as he passed me the paper Taco Cabana sack. I handed him his coffee, black, and his favorite taco, *Carne Guisada*. I nibbled on my Bean and Cheese between sips of cold orange juice and tried not to spill anything down the front of me.

"You know," BZ frowned, wadding the foil wrapper from the now eaten taco, tossing it into the empty sack, "I think Sylvia's cousin is a nurse over there."

"Where?" I looked out the van window for a doctor's office.

"Children's." He picked up the radio microphone and keyed the hand piece. Maxine answered and he asked, "Maxie, can you do a favor for me and do a patch through to Sylvia?"

"I sure can," Maxine, answered.

They disconnected but BZ held the handset as he drove, waiting for the callback. "If Sylvia's cousin is still working at Children's, she might be able to help us. Sylvia will know what name that woman is going by now. It's Maricella something." He mocked whispered to me, "She keeps getting married and divorced."

Only a second later Maxine called with the patch to Sylvia. "*Hola, mi Amor,*" BZ's wife purred.

BZ blushed and alerted her. "I'm here with Oshun, and we're headed to Children's Hospital. Does your cousin Maricella still work there?"

"Last I heard she does," Sylvia said. I could hear the shrug in her voice.

"What's her name now?" BZ asked.

"Maricella Rodriguez, the last I heard. She doesn't give up on matrimony!" They laughed at the family joke, and Sylvia changed the subject. "While I have you on the phone, what do you know about the girl at the Rodeo?"

"You mean the one with the winning steer, right?"

"Yes, the girl that passed out. The story has been on the radio all morning, and everyone in my office is talking about it. Most of them think she's *embarazada*."

"Maxine and me, too," BZ laughed. "I've got a bet on it. Siobhan doesn't think so, though." Then he told his wife, "We covered the judging, and I shot the film," his chest puffed. "Try to catch it at five. It is good if I do say so myself. We're going to the hospital now to follow up on her. I'll keep you posted if I learn anything."

They ended their conversation, and BZ dropped me at the entrance to the emergency room at Children's Hospital while he parked the van in the lot across the street where our competitors parked theirs. We were not the first to discover the location of the girl. I counted five different vans from local radio and television stations, all painted with their station logos and call letters.

I stepped inside the waiting room to find it full of competitor talent; the gaggle of egos did not notice me as I slipped by them on my way to the information desk.

"Is Maricella Rodriguez working today?" I smiled as sweetly as I could at the white-clad woman.

She frowned and turned away to speak to someone I could not see, "Is Maricella Rodriguez still on three?"

A voice came from between racks of patient files, "The last I heard that's where she was."

The woman looked up and shrugged. "You can check at the nurses' station on the third floor."

I thanked her and turned to see BZ coming through

the double doors. The gaggle welcomed him. "The man of the hour. You got that damn shot didn't you? I knew it," one of the egos said. Another commented, "Eagle eye, man, eagle eye." BZ beamed and joined their circle. When he glanced at me, I motioned with my thumb to adjacent double doors.

Slipping from the waiting area into a long hallway, I planned to begin my search for elevators that would take me to the third floor. Along the corridor, I saw a sign for the cafeteria and decided I needed a cup of coffee or something with caffeine. My energy level had dipped so I followed arrows pointing to the cafeteria and headed there to get coffee, following several turns down more hallways, arriving just as a uniformed employee placed a stanchion sign in the hallway. The sign said: "The cafeteria will re-open at 3:00 Vending machines left."

I searched depths of my bag for the small red leather change purse I always carried and approached the vending area, my mind so occupied with the task that I almost bumped into a young man standing in front of one of the shiny soda machines. He fiercely punched the coin return button.

I looked up and could barely believe the coincidence. I had practically collided with the girl's boyfriend, Charlie Garza.

"Stealing your coins?" I asked, pretending I did not recognize him.

"Yeah," he pushed the change return button as if it was a stubborn doorbell.

"Here," I shook my change purse. "I've got plenty of coins."

"Thank you," he told me as I handed over quarters.

He moved to the next machine and fed my coins into

it, pushed the Big Red soda button and waited until he heard thumping down the chute. Then he looked up at me. I thought he might remember me from earlier, but he did not.

"Thanks again," he nodded and walked over to one of the small café tables set up in the adjacent alcove, sat in a white plastic chair, and stretched out his long legs. He stared unblinking at the tip of his scuffed boot.

I loaded my coins into the machine, glancing at him from the corner of my eye I punched the Coke button and waited for the can to drop. I casually walked to where he sat and asked, "You're Charlie aren't you?"

He squinted up at me. His expression did not change. He obviously did not recognize me and I could not fault his memory. The knit cap was gone, the coat and sweater replaced, my hair slicked back in a ponytail. I didn't look like the same woman who had talked with him earlier.

"I met you in the auction barn earlier today. I'm Siobhan O'Shaughnessy from KWNK. I gave you my card?"

His eyes widened, "I don't have anything to say." His lips tightened and he pulled his legs back, preparing to stand.

"Please don't leave. I really don't expect you to tell me anything." I shrugged. "I'll have to talk to her family, or her, before I can report on the story."

"She won't want to talk to any reporter," he assured me in a scornful tone, "her folks won't either," he added as if trying to save me the trouble of further sleuthing.

"Well, I've got a boss who won't let me get off that easily," I laughed. "I've got to try to talk to them." I changed the subject from the girl, "Do you live up at Kingsland, too?"

He nodded, did not look at me, stretched his legs, and studied the toe of his boot.

"All of your life?" I kept attempting to engage him in conversation about anything other than his girlfriend.

He shook his head. "Not until two years ago. I transferred up there."

"From where?" I saw progress.

"Robert E. Lee," he answered.

"High School? Here?" I grabbed onto that topic.

"Yep, that's the one."

His answer puzzled me. I knew a little bit about Robert E. Lee High School. It was once the premier school on the north side of town, known more for athletics than agriculture. Now, it was definitely inner city and I doubted it would have a Future Farmers of America chapter.

"Do they have Future Farmers or 4H at Lee?" I pointed to his FFA cap.

He snorted, "No."

"So you moved from here to Kingsland? Why Kingsland?" I tried another subject to draw him further.

"Because my mom died and my father works on a ranch up there and I have to live with him." He made eye contact with me, a challenging, defiant expression on his face. I felt he had purposely made the comment more harsh than necessary so I would give up on him and go away.

"I'm sorry. I apologize." I studied the mottled floor tiles where his booted feet rested. "I didn't mean to pry."

"It's okay," he used a softer tone, looked up, and the defiant look was gone. He was a wounded child.

"It's not okay," I squatted beside him, feeling maternal. Keeping my gaze even with his, I said, "I am very sorry. I'm trying to make conversation with you to get you to tell me something about Paris. Your life is none of my business. It was rude of me. I am very sorry for your loss. I'm new at this. This is my first feature story, and I really don't know what to do in this circumstance. I'm sure it isn't easy having me ask you questions when you're trying to protect Paris and avoid saying anything to the media." I kept jabbering. "You're entitled to be upset." I finally gave up trying to explain my motives, stood, and then paused before I turned to walk away. "But I told you when I gave you my card, if I can do anything, let me know."

He nodded and lifted the Big Red soda can in a salute, "Thanks for the loan."

"It's a gift, the least I can do." I retraced my steps down the echoing hallway, leaving him alone.

I decided not to go up on the third floor to try and find Maricella by myself; instead, I went to see if I could find BZ. He was still standing with the other media people and when he saw my expression, raised his shoulders and eyebrows, communicating curiosity. I shook my head, and he left the group, came to me, and listened as I told him what had happened with Charlie. He decided to go with me to the third floor in our search for Sylvia's cousin.

We left after learning Maricella was on a rotation schedule and had the day off. The nurse on the third floor did tell us they had admitted Paris Nash, put her in an isolation area, and was restricted from having visitors. I felt defeated, but BZ told me not to let the setback get to me.

"You win some, and you lose some," he patted my shoulder the way I thought a big brother might.

"I had high hopes. I'm not giving up. I'm disappointed because I don't like leaving anything unfinished."

"There's always tomorrow," he encouraged.

We left the hospital to go back to the station, and all the way back to KWNK, I had visions of our competitors getting the jump on the story I wanted so badly to finish.

I had been at my desk for only a few minutes when the phone rang, my friend Phyllis calling to remind me about the plans we made to go out for dinner that night and then dancing at the Stampede. The date, made before the ice storm and before I got the assignment to cover the judging, was for our Friday girls night out.

I yawned and forced my mouth to form words. "I'd better not go, Phyl. I'm so tired." The extremely hectic day was catching up, and I felt exhaustion overtaking me.

"You have to eat," she cajoled, "Let's go for dinner," she said, making a statement, not asking a question.

"All right," I caved. "I'll go to dinner, but Phyl I can't dance a step. Let's not go to the Stampede."

"No problem. I'll pick you up at 7:00, alright?" I could never argue with Phyllis's logic. I would go and eat.

I stayed at the station to watch the five o'clock news with BZ in Bud's office. Bud had four televisions mounted on the wall behind his desk, one large screen, three smaller ones. Our engineers had set up the system with recording units on all the screens. That way Bud could compare our news presentation to our competitor's and use the tapes to compliment and criticize our delivery at weekly meetings.

The big screen was always tuned to KWNK, and on it, for just a second, I saw my face up close. The three smaller screens showed our competitor stations, and since none of them captured Paris Nash's fall, their lead story was about the previous night's ice storm.

My appearance in the piece pleased me. Even with all of my worry about my hair, I looked poised and professional. The borrowed hat did wonders toward that goal, and BZ's interspersed photography captured the sights and sounds of the event in a continuity that told the story with effects so complete, my closing invitation was only marginally necessary. Viewers would be sorry they missed seeing the judging in person and would probably go out to the grounds to see the steers.

Our competitors ran the judging story third in their rotation, showing only Eloy announcing the winner and then shifting to the girl lying in the dirt. BZ was the only photographer who captured her swaying and slipping to the ground as Eloy's voice, from the background, announced her steer the winner.

Bud grinned and pumped BZ's arm, "Congratulations, my boy," he said. "That is a great job!"

I could have kissed BZ when he motioned to me, "She's top drawer, Bud. It was her that pointed the girl out to me."

Chapter Four

I left the station in a great mood, thrilled about my day. The compliments Bud gave my story made me feel very proud, and if my grandfather were still alive, he would be proud of me, too.

When Phyllis arrived closer to 7:30 than to 7:00, I did not mind. Her lateness gave me time to shower and wash my hair. By the time she rang my bell, I had gotten a second wind, and was rethinking my decision about skipping the Stampede.

"You look cute," Phyllis complimented me when she walked in my front door.

I did not deserve her praise, because unlike my good friend, I was not dressed to the nines. Presentable, yes, my jeans were clean, and my periwinkle western-cut shirt looked brand new. My shiny boots and magenta suede-fringed jacket made me feel attractive, until I stood next to my friend.

Phyllis was wearing black velvet jeans, and a vest covered in rhinestone and sequined horses that rivaled the suit Eloy Grisham wore at the auction earlier in the day. On Phyl the look worked. The legs of her skintight jeans, tucked into her red stovepipe boots, showed off her curvy shape.

It took confidence to wear an outfit like that, and confidence is one thing my dear Phyllis has enough to share. Even when we were gawky sixth-graders, she never showed the least bit of self-consciousness. She could go anywhere, dressed any way, make friends with anybody, and never, ever, show the least discomfort. I always wished I could be more like her but copied her instead. I faked it, hoping to make it, but ended up shyer and far less confident than she.

Phyllis's gregarious personality worked well in career choice. She owned a day spa that catered to an elite clientele in the 09 zip code and for the past four years received the *Best Day Spa Award* in the newspaper's annual *Best in Town* contest. I believed her sincere friendly nature gave her an edge over any competitor. Her sweet, carefree, yet fearless attitude masked an extremely perceptive businessperson.

I asked her, "Where did you find the sparkly vest?"

"Resale," she gushed. "Ten bucks." Nothing pleased her quite like a bargain, especially a bargain at the resale shop. She practically bought out *Too Good to be Threw* helping build my wardrobe when Bud hired me at KWNK.

On the way to dinner, she wanted me to, "Tell about the girl. I saw the news. Loved you by the way, you were great. You didn't tell me you were going to cover that story. Wait, first I want to know about the girl. What happened to her? Why did she faint? Nerves, you think?"

"I really don't know," I admitted. "I'm trying to find out. Our best bet is BZ's wife, Sylvia, actually her cousin, who is a nurse at Children's Hospital. Sylvia is getting her to find out something for us. We went up there this afternoon to see if we could learn anything, but the cousin was off today. Bud asked me to do a follow-up, and I was so excited. I couldn't ferret out a single bit of information about the girl."

"That's too bad." Phyllis commiserated, listening to me, but squinting at approaching street signs.

"I did get to talk to her boyfriend, at least the young man who is her boyfriend according to the girl I borrowed the hat from for the closing of my piece."

"Cute hat by the way." She complimented as she turned into *Maggie's* parking lot, "Could she be pregnant?"

"I don't know. I didn't ask the boy if they'd been intimate," I couldn't resist a hint of sarcasm. "But the betting money in the newsroom is on her being in a family way. The boyfriend isn't talking about much of anything, and I've spoken to him twice today. Once at the judging and then when I ran into him at the hospital. He's extremely protective of her. I like that about him."

During dinner, we discussed her business and my work. She, sharing her plan to do a little renovation and remodeling at the spa, and I talked about my hopes for following up more completely about Paris Nash. With our good dinner, my energy level stayed high and she convinced me into going to the *Stampede* for "a couple of dances for the exercise value."

My second wind kept blowing and as the evening progressed, we both consumed Lite Longnecks and danced with good-looking cowboys who were in town for Rodeo week. Even though I got home later than anticipated, my mood remained buoyant, until I played the message BZ left on my answering machine earlier in the evening.

"Call me. Sylvia's cousin found something."

I knew better than to call his house at one o'clock in

the morning. He would kill me if I woke the baby, especially since I'd overheard him tell Maxine they'd just gotten her to start sleeping through the night.

The first thing I did in the morning was call BZ.

"The girl is still in isolation, and they're running tests," he told me. "Maricella said everyone is being more closed-mouthed than usual. No one will talk about her because the media keeps prowling around, trying to find out what's wrong with her. Mari said they wouldn't be running those particular tests if she were pregnant, so I guess I've lost my bet."

"Did Maricella say what she thought it might be? I mean, what do they usually run those tests to find out? Did she say?" I asked.

"She couldn't talk much when she called," he said, "but whatever it is, it's serious. Whenever the family leaves the room, they've been crying."

On my drive to the station, I thought about how different everything would have been for the Nash girl if she had not fainted in the judging ring. We would be seeing her smiling face on every front page, heard her name mentioned in lead stories on every television and radio rodeo broadcast, and would hear interviews with her until the auction at the end of next week. Then the publicity would begin again. Only then they would ask about how much money the steer netted. No one would be trying to guess if she was pregnant.

I kept thinking of ways to get Bud to let me continue covering the Paris Nash story. For a reason I could not explain, I felt drawn to her, or more realistically, since I had not even met the girl, to the mystery surrounding her. All I knew about Paris Nash I learned in the few minutes I watched her sway during the judging, from her brief biography in the A.L.E.C. press packet, and from her boyfriend, Charlie. Whatever the reason, I did not like the idea of anyone taking over my story.

I walked into the newsroom prepared to talk with Bud, but from the moment I stepped off the elevator, I realized what I wanted would never happen. Inside Bud's glass office, he sat in deep discussion with Tracy Brennan, the ever-smiling newscaster, miraculously recovered from her relapse with the flu. I'd never seen the woman waltz in before one-thirty in the afternoon, she rarely graced us with her presence before two, yet there she was, sitting in Bud's office, all puffed and buffed to shining glory at seven in the morning.

I suspected her return to work and early arrival had something to do with yesterday. If the judging had been like every other year, she would have been the one covering the story. If it had gone like every preceding year, she would not have cared about missing it, but this year the judging had real drama that sustained viewer curiosity. She undoubtedly wanted in on the glory train.

I would love to know how she reacted when she watched the news yesterday and learned she had missed being in on what turned out to be a major public interest story, her miraculous healing taking place so she could come in and take over. Right now, she was probably convincing Bud that *she* was the one who could get the scoop on Paris Nash.

I saw Tracy lean forward and plant her elbows on Bud's desk, smiling and outright flirting with him. The smiling was no big deal; Tracy smiled at everyone, all the time. When I first started working at KWNK, I thought she suffered from perpetual pleasantness. At our initial meeting, she made me think she was one of those perennially cheerful people I *admire* for always being in good spirits but *distrust* for the same reason. I do not believe any right-minded person can be eternally cheerful. Tracy proved me right the day I caught her telling off one of the other talking heads.

"Go to hell, you freaking idiot," snarling at poor mild-mannered Jim Draken, the wimpy weatherman while managing a smile like Miss America. I admit I tried it in front of the mirror, the snarling and smiling simultaneously, but couldn't do it. However, after that day, I never trusted her disarming show of friendliness again.

Even though I knew there was nothing I could do to change what was happening in Bud's office, I was extremely curious about the outcome of the conversation. However, instead of sitting at my desk, tormenting my psyche, I called down front and asked Maxine if there were messages for me.

"I'll say," Maxine, told me, "You got great response to the story you did yesterday. You have about sixty calls from viewers wanting to know about the girl. They want a follow-up story on her. Your friend Phyllis called early this morning and she wants you to call her back. And, there's another wanting a call. Do you want his name or do you want to pick up the slips?"

"I'll be right down." I stepped on the elevator, looked wistfully over my shoulder to Bud's office, and poked the down arrow. I knew, even as the elevator dropped, Tracy was still grinning at Bud.

When I got to the lobby, Jim Draken was waiting to go up. He nodded, and we switched places, as Maxine slid a neat stack of message slips across the slick grey countertop toward me. The top one was from Phyl. I flipped to the second slip and saw Charlie Garza's name. I grabbed the rest of the stack, and ran up the fire stairs instead of waiting for the elevator to come back down to the first floor.

My heart beat twice as fast as it should have by the

time I got to my desk. It had to be *the* Charlie, Paris's Charlie. My fingers dialed the number and I was elated when the operator answered the call, "Children's Hospital. May I help you?"

"Room 326," I responded to the soft-voiced question, reading from Maxine's neat block print.

"Hello." The answering voice sounded weak and distant.

"Is Charlie Garza there?" I asked, even as I realized the voice must belong to Paris Nash. For a split second, I thought about talking directly to her, but since Charlie had been the one to call me, I would wait to speak with him. I did not want to do anything to inhibit my progress.

"Can Charlie call you back from another phone? My doctor is here." She sounded very tired.

"Let me leave a number where he can reach me," I offered.

"It's okay," she said. "You are Siobhan, right?"

"Yes, I'm at my desk now."

"He's on his way to the payphone down the hall," she told me.

I hung up the phone and sorted through the stack of messages trying to look busy so no one would stop to chat. I glanced back toward Bud's office, Tracy was gone, so I rose from my chair and scanned the newsroom trying to see where she went, I wanted to be available to speak freely when Charlie called back. I didn't want her listening. When the phone rang, I immediately plopped down and jerked the receiver to my ear.

"Hello, Siobhan O'Shaughnessy here." I answered in a way I hoped sounded professional.

"I told Paris what you said," Charlie Garza began, "'if *there's anything I can do*,' remember?"

"Yes," I liked his directness. "If it's in my power, I'll do it," I added the caveat I should have tacked on to my initial offer.

"Even if helping us might border on being illegal?" He sounded seriously solemn.

"How close to that border?" I laughed, suspecting he might really mean unethical.

"Paris and I want you to help us save her steer. We need to save Charga from the slaughterhouse."

My grip on the receiver tightened, "I beg your pardon. Did you say you want me to help save her steer?"

"Paris wants to meet you and explain in person. It's a long story. It might be better if I talk to you first."

"I don't know what's on the assignment board today," I explained as I squinted to read the board on the wall across the room. "Can you call back in five minutes? I'll be able to set a time to meet. Okay?"

"I'll call back."

He hung up and I sat holding the receiver to my ear, listening to the dial tone, wondering what the two of them thought I could do to help save her steer. As I understood the A.L.E.C. rules, the animal stays at the exhibition until the auction and then it immediately goes to slaughter, and all of that happens in six days. For as far back as I could remember it worked that way.

I was only marginally aware of BZ coming up behind me. He tapped my shoulder and I jumped, slapped the receiver down on its base much harder than I meant to and looked up innocently.

"What's going on?" He asked.

"Nothing," I smiled brilliantly, trying Tracy's big teeth maneuver.

"Yeah, right." He didn't buy my ploy. "I walked right

in front of your desk, and you didn't even blink. Your eyes were darting left and right like the warning lights at a railroad crossing while you were holding onto that receiver like it was a lifeline. Nothing," he mimicked my fake smile.

"Okay. Nothing I can talk about right now, is that good enough?"

"Okay, okay. Later." He gave up good-naturedly and walked off toward the break room while I headed to the assignment board to discover I'd been scheduled to report on the thrill of quilt making at the Family Life Hall on the Coliseum grounds. I scanned the list and saw Tracy's name next to the assignment: follow-up on Paris Nash.

I turned and marched toward Bud's office. He saw me coming and I noticed him sit taller in his chair. He reminded me of something I read in a hiking magazine, *How to Protect Yourself from Bears. Look as large as possible,* the article said. That was what Bud did. He sat up straighter than usual, squared his shoulders, and rested his palms on the edge of his desk. He did look larger, and if I had been a bear, I might have been intimidated.

"Bud." I tried to sound indifferent as I tapped on his door. He motioned me to enter his space. "I see you have Tracy following up on Paris Nash."

"Yes," he said and launched into an unrequested explanation, "Since Tracy is back at work and anxious to get back into the swing of things, it seemed only right that she step back into her spot."

"Umhmm," I nodded.

"I know you might have some investment in the steer story..."

I nodded in agreement with his observation.

"...but you've only been..."

I finished the sentence with him, "...here six weeks."

"Jinx. You owe me a Coke." He used the children's taunt to joke with me and seemed pleased I stayed calm.

Accepting what Bud told me did not mean I liked it. I did not want Tracy to follow up on *my* steer story. While I did not have a choice in the matter, I felt no compunction to help her with it, either. My conversations with Charlie Garza were my business and I did not plan to share anything I learned with Tracy.

I had not been at the station long enough to acquire influence. My paycheck was the last written, and I was still within the ninety-day probationary period. Tracy, the six-year veteran and five-year anchor, carried all the weight.

I went back to my desk, pulled the media packet out of my drawer, and started doing research on past winners of the Quilting Competition. I attempted to absorb something about double eagle and wedding ring designs while I waited for Charlie to call me back. I looked up from my reading long enough to watch Tracy leave the newsroom. She waved her notebook, smiled at no one in particular, held her head high, and glided as if she was on a fashion runway.

Good luck, Smiley-face, I thought feeling slightly spiteful. If my grandfather had lived a few years longer, things would be very different here at KWNK. I felt my eyes and lips narrow and surprised myself with my rancor. It made me realize I had not really dealt with all my negative emotions about the betrayal brought about by my grandfather's premature death.

"Ready to go cover the quilts?" BZ interrupted me.

Sounding begrudging, I looked up at him and snapped, "Wouldn't you rather go with Tracy?"

"Nah, I got out of it. Sitting around the hospital all day with the grin-meister sounds like a terribly boring day. Besides, Maricella says nobody is going to get a story out of that family anyway."

I started to mention my conversation with Charlie Garza. I wanted to brag, but was superstitious enough to stay quiet from fear of jinxing my good fortune. I didn't want word to get back to Bud lest he insist I give Tracy any information I learned from Charlie.

BZ interrupted my thought. "Since the weather is nicer today, I thought going out to the rodeo grounds would be a much better option. You mind?"

"No, I'd rather work with you than anyone else," I admitted to him.

He assuaged my resentfulness of Tracy by what I assumed was a show of loyalty to me. Early on, I knew I liked working with BZ because he was the only cameraperson to offer constructive criticism to me and give me compliments on the work I'd done well.

"Do you mind waiting for a couple of minutes," I asked. "I'm expecting a phone call."

He checked his watch. "No problem. We have time. Signal when you're ready."

On a steno tablet, I organized the questions I would want to ask during the Quilt Exhibition interview, however; my mind kept looping back to what Charlie Garza said. He and Paris Nash thought I could do something to help them save that steer.

The phone rang, and I answered, expecting Charlie. Instead, my friend Phyl's bright voice asked, "Didn't you get my message?"

"Oh, I'm sorry, Phyl. It's been crazy around here; I've been waiting for a call."

"This will only take a minute. I know you'll want to know this," she insisted talking over my explanation. "Sarah worked late last night. She had a walk-in right at five."

Phyllis kept explaining and I kept half-listening; glancing at the clock on the wall, hoping Charlie wasn't on purgatory hold waiting for me to take his call. Phyllis was talking about the new masseuse at the spa who worked late last night, and I could not imagine why she thought I would be the least bit interested in that.

"It was her aunt," she concluded breathlessly.

I waited for the punch line, decided to play along. "Okay, so Sarah's aunt comes in…"

Phyllis interrupted me, "You aren't paying attention. It was the girl's aunt. The girl from the judging. The girl who passed out. The girl with the steer," she was obviously agitated at my slow up-take.

"Paris Nash's aunt?" Her insistence suddenly made sense. I sat at attention.

"Yep, the girl's aunt, and guess what? The aunt is a talker. Do I have news for you! Oops, we'll have to talk later, my next client just walked in."

I could hear her singsong voice, saying "Well don't you look wonderful…" as she hung up the phone.

Replacing the receiver, glancing at the clock again, I waited. The phone rang, and I grabbed it. This time it was Charlie.

"I'm going out to the Rodeo to do a story on quilting," I told him right away. "Can you meet me out there? In the Family Life Hall?"

"Sure, I've got to go out there to feed Charga in a little while. What time will you be there?"

"We should be there in a half hour. The interview will only take a few minutes."

"Okay, I'll meet you at Family Life, and if I get there earlier, I'll take care of Charga first and then meet you. Wait for me if you finish first. I won't be too long," he volunteered. "We really want to talk to you."

"Me too," I understated and hung up the telephone.

I caught BZ's attention and motioned with my hand, "Let's go."

He nodded and grabbed van keys from the hook on the wall.

"Let's go cover quilts," he shouted a pun at me.

He drove while I got out my green tablet and made two columns on the top sheet. In the first column, I rewrote the questions I wanted to ask the quilting experts in the interview. *How long does it take to make a fine quilt like this? What is the name of this pattern? Are the colors you chose of special significance?* In the other column, I wrote, how do you save a Steer? Can't Paris pull the animal from the auction? Shouldn't her parents be helping with this? Lastly, I asked myself, Siobhan, why are you doing this?

Chapter Five

I wanted to tell BZ about the appointment I'd made with Charlie Garza. However, I first wanted to get a sense of where his loyalty lay. I thought when BZ found out about the call from Charlie, he would want me to turn everything over to Tracy since she had the assignment. I didn't want to have that argument before I went on camera at the Quilt Exhibit.

The confusion I felt about the girl made it more difficult for me to sort out what was more interesting. I wasn't sure if it was from a personal or a professional point of view. My training told me I should make my decision based on the merit of the story, not how I felt about it. However, that concept only made sense if I were actually doing the story. Now that Tracy had it, I no longer had a reason to be logically professional. It had gotten personal on yet another level.

I hoped Charlie Garza would be able to tell me more about what had happened to the girl at the judging. If I knew more, the information would help me decide if I wanted to stay involved or if I should encourage the Nashes to talk with Tracy. Since Charlie would be joining us soon, I needed to let BZ know the young man was coming.

I decided to wait until he parked outside the Family Life Hall to say anything. However, before I could begin my explanation, Maxine called on the radio, and that changed everything. Phyllis needed to talk to me ASAP, she told me.

I looked for a pay phone and saw one attached to the outside of the horse barn across the street. I dug in my everything-bag for my change purse, and watched where I stepped as I crossed the gravel roadway to the phone. The grounds around the horse barn were a field of manure-mines, and I did not want to step in one and reek while I did the quilting interview.

I dialed the spa number, sure she wanted to tell me the rest of the story she had started on the phone earlier that morning about what the masseuse heard from Paris Nash's aunt. As soon as she answered I said, "Hi, Phyl."

She launched into an urgent whisper. It sounded as if she said, "Okay, Siobhan. She is dying."

"Who's dying? I can't hear you very well, Phyl, I'm on a pay phone next to the horse barn out at the rodeo grounds."

"Sarah told me when Paris Nash's aunt was here, she told Sarah she's dying." Phyllis' voice was frustrated insistence.

"Paris Nash's aunt is dying?" This did not make sense to me.

"No Siobhan, Paris Nash is dying. Hold on." She spoke away from the phone then told me, "I need to go. I have another client. I'll call you back later," and she hung up. I stood staring at the receiver, not believing she had left me like that.

I was clicking the receiver back in place when BZ rushed toward me.

"Are you finished? I need to make a call."

I nodded and stepped aside. He grabbed the receiver, clicked the disconnect lever a couple of times, put change in the slots and told me, "I got a page to call Maricella ASAP."

I knew what she was going to tell him. "Paris Nash is dying," I said.

He put a finger to his lips as he spoke into the phone, "Extension 303." While the call transferred, he asked me, "Who's dying?"

"It's what Phyl called to tell me. Paris Nash is dying."

BZ held his hand up to silence me. "Maricella Rodriguez, please," he said to the phone. Then he covered the receiver and asked me, "What? Is it on the news or something?"

"No. Phyl…" I began before I got the shut-up sign again.

"Maricella, its BZ."

He spoke to the phone sounding as confused as I had been when Phyllis told me her news. I watched his expression change and knew Maricella had told him the same thing Phyl had said to me. It was not yet on the news. Like every important event in my life, I had learned it by coincidence. Out of all the places in San Antonio to get a massage, Paris Nash's aunt chose to go to the spa owned by my closest friend.

BZ put his hand over the mouthpiece of the phone and mouthed, 'How did you know?'

I mouthed back, making both syllables a distinct mouth motion, "Phyl…liss."

"Okay, Maricella." He nodded at me. "Thank you for letting me know. I've got to call this in." He hung up and started searching his pockets for change.

I stood by, shuffling thoughts like a deck of familiar old cards. I could see Tracy taking over this news wearing a semi-serious smile and saying, "In a story just in, the young girl from the steer judging…" I did not want to see that happen.

"Have you got a quarter?" He held out his hand. "I need change."

"No." I lied, holding my bulging change purse behind my back.

He started to step away from the phone, "I've got change in the ashtray," he started toward the van. "Hell, I'll use the radio."

"No. Wait. Don't," My voice level increased with every word.

He looked back over his shoulder at me, "What are you talking about?"

"Don't call." I pleaded. "Wait. Let's think about this."

"Are you crazy? We have to call this in to Bud. He'll need to let Tracy know."

"That's what I mean." I walked toward BZ and hoped my intense eye contact would convey the importance of what I planned to say to him. My total focus on BZ kept me from watching where I walked, and I stepped squarely in the middle of a nice plop of horse dung.

"Oh shit," I muttered.

"That's what it is," he laughed.

I reached out and grabbed onto BZ's shoulder, leaned heavily on him, and scraped my boot on the gravel road.

"Please, BZ, don't call it in," I begged. "This story isn't a matter of public safety. It's not some scoop on world events. We don't even have any real proof that what we heard is accurate. This could be a rumor. And, besides, no

54

other station has it yet."

His eyes met mine, "Maricella heard it from one of the nurses in the isolation ward, so I doubt it is a rumor, and if Maricella heard it, someone else already knows it, too, and we will get scooped. Paris Nash has melanoma cancer, and it has spread all over her body. Maricella says if it is true she only has months to live."

"See, she said *if* it is true. Maybe it isn't."

When Phyllis called, she didn't say why the girl was dying. In my imagining, I hadn't considered anything like melanoma. Sadness began building, and tears started filling my eyes.

"BZ, can we at least wait until we talk to Charlie," I begged.

"Call him. I'll wait," he acquiesced.

"He'll be here in a minute." I looked over BZ's shoulder hoping to see Charlie striding toward us.

"Here?" BZ frowned, "When did you find that out? I thought the last time you talked to him was yesterday at the hospital."

In the few minutes it took to walk to the Family Life Hall, I explained about my conversation with Charlie that morning. I'd just uttered the words, ". . .and they want help saving Charga," when I saw two women rushing toward us. They had to be the names listed on the press release as contact persons.

Mae Louise Graham and Lillianne Schotz Ohlrich scurried toward us, ready for their interview about prize winning quilts. The two were entertaining, unlike many people who get stage fright at the sight of a camera and microphone. These two looked like Dorothy, Rose from "The Golden Girls" series, and had props ready to go. They had even set up a quilting frame so we could get film of them demonstrating the intricacies of quilt making.

"We are both cut-ups," Lillianne quipped, holding up small swatches of cloth. They showed how those small pieces fit into a larger pattern.

"We keep each other in stitches," Mae Louise giggled, holding up a large threaded needle.

The two women showed us a completed quilt face, a calico Lone Star, and placed it on top of the batting they had already stretched on the frame.

Mae Louise said, "The quilting business is quite a yarn." She showed us how to position the three layers: fabric, batting and backing, and then demonstrated how to sew them together to form a quilt.

Lillianne revealed the trick she used when binding the quilt edges in a way that, she said, "keeps it from coming apart. It'll last for centuries!"

Mae Louise pointed out examples of quality heirloom quilts that were on display in the exhibit hall. "That one is well over 150 years old and is still holding together beautifully," she said as she pointed to a star patterned one.

I asked the right questions, nodded and smiled appreciatively at the appropriate moments, building my closing on the pun BZ said at the station before we left. I ended the interview with a bright smile, saying, "This is Siobhan O'Shaughnessy with Mae Louise Graham and Lillianne Schotz Ohlrich at the Family Life Hall where we are covered in quilts."

BZ started in on me as soon as we were out of earshot of the two women. He lectured me as he loaded the camera equipment into the van. "You know, Bud expects us to share information anytime we find out something like this, don't you?"

"Duh," I answered. Then I argued, "If a big accident

shut down the interstate or if PETA started marching on the rodeo, I'd be the first to phone Bud." I glared, "But this is totally different, BZ. Think about it. What if the little girl in the hospital was your Angie? Then what would you want? Would you want her death to be the topic of coffee shop gossip? Do you think Sylvia would want everyone to know about it before she could deal with it herself?"

There may have been a fairer way to make the argument, but I was short on time and not in the mood to worry about how fair I was being. My interest in the story ended when Phyllis told me the girl did not have long to live.

I could not forget seeing Paris Nash sway in the show ring, so slight and pale, and watching her fall at the feet of her big gentle steer. I kept remembering Charga walking away, looking back at the crumpled girl lying in the dirt and the image of her mother kneeling, tears streaming down her face. I would never forget Charlie hiding his face on the big steers back, ashamed to be weeping. All of it haunted me.

As BZ argued, I realized I'd broken the cardinal rule of broadcasting. I'd let myself become emotionally involved with my subject and lost my objectivity. I heard my grandfather's voice again. This time he challenged me, "How do you plan on handling this situation, young lady?"

I'd been standing with my head bowed. BZ, standing with his hands on his hips, a disapproving expression on his face, was still trying to make me agree to call the news in to Bud. I looked up, thrilled to see Charlie walking toward us. I waved at him, but he did not acknowledge me and kept walking toward us taking long strides. With every second step, looked left and then front like a swimmer taking air.

I walked to meet him, saying "Hi Charlie," extending my hand. He took my fingertips hesitantly, gently, barely moving my hand at all.

We walked back to the van, and when Charlie saw BZ, he stopped. "Who's that?"

"That's our cameraman BZ. He did the taping at the judging the other day. He's the one who captured Paris falling in the ring," I added as a reference. "He's interested, too." I did not lie. BZ was interested.

"I'm not doing any interview," Charlie stopped and started to turn away from me.

"Oh no, I know," I grabbed his arm and reassured him. "BZ was here for the quilt piece, that's all. Remember? I told you?"

I started to introduce Charlie to BZ and realized that I did not know BZ's proper name. "Charlie Garza, this is...BZ...what the heck is your name?"

BZ blushed, reached out to shake Charlie's hand, and said, "I am Buenaventura Antonio de los Santos Zuniga," he clicked his heels and gave a dignified courtly bow, "call me BZ."

I raised my eyebrows. "That's one impressive moniker, my friend."

"Bud started calling me BZ," he told Charlie. "Bud is our boss, and if he likes you, he gives you a nickname. Sometimes he calls Siobhan, Oshun."

That surprised me. I did not know my nickname held special importance. I was suddenly flattered at having been given one. I wondered if Bud had one of those nicknames for Tracy.

Charlie smiled, "Well, I'm just Charlie."

"Okay, Charlie," I said, "You told me you want help to save Charga? What does that mean, exactly?"

He looked toward BZ and hesitated to say anything. I reassured him, "I've told BZ everything. You can trust him."

Charlie nodded and began explaining. "It isn't me.

58

It's Paris that wants it."

BZ motioned to a table shaded by an awning, "Let's sit there in the shade. I'll go find us something to drink."

"Great idea," I agreed, and Charlie and I moved toward the table while BZ went to search for refreshments.

Charlie sat, took off his FFA cap, wiped his brow on his sleeve, and put the cap back on his head.

I took the opportunity to tell Charlie what we learned from Phyllis and Maricella. "We heard a few minutes ago that Paris is seriously ill…" I hesitated, hoping he would cut me off so I'd know he was already aware of his girlfriend's prognosis. His silence made me worry. Maybe he hadn't been told how serious her illness was, maybe he was ignorant about the melanoma, or maybe he was unaware the girl would die.

He stayed quiet a minute or more before he finally spoke, "You mean that they are telling us she's dying." His eyes brimmed with tears. He looked down, and then off into the distance.

I was relieved that he already knew. It didn't make it any easier to talk about, but at least we were all working from the same information.

I put my hand on his arm to comfort him, "I'm sorry," I told him, aware this was the third time in two days I'd watched this young man cry.

We sat quietly waiting for BZ, allowing Charlie to regain his composure. BZ finally came around the corner of the Family Life Hall carrying three small plastic cups of lemonade triangled in his hands.

I reached to take one and BZ said, "They aren't terribly generous with their lemons."

He apparently had already sipped the watered down beverage. I sipped mine and made a face. BZ got eye contact with me and nodded toward Charlie. I frowned back at him, hoping he would notice my meaning and wait for Charlie to speak to us. He did not.

"I don't mean to rush you," BZ said, "but we have about an hour to get this film back to the station."

BZ sounded slightly aggravated to me, and I knew it was because I had stopped him from calling Bud with the news about Paris. I also knew he had not given up on telling Bud what we learned about Paris's illness. I feared he would fill Bud in as soon as we got back to the station unless Charlie and I could change his mind first.

"I'll make this quick," Charlie hadn't missed BZ's urgent tone. "See, when all this started, this steer raising business, Paris was sure she would be all arm's length, you know." He held his arms out straight in front of himself. "She wasn't going to get attached to the animal. All she wanted was to get enough money to go to college at A&M. Her big dream is being an Aggie, going to their vet school, being a large animal veterinarian."

Charlie paused and took another sip of lemonade before he continued, "Now, everything's different. Paris knows she's dying, knows she won't go to college, hell, she knows she might not even be here for Christmas." Tears rolled down his face and he wiped at them with his shirtsleeve, but kept talking.

"Her parents," Charlie tried to regain his composure, "keep telling her there isn't anything they can do about Charga. They're more concerned about her than they are about the steer. They say, '*you knew when you entered the show that Charga wouldn't be coming back home.*'"

"So," I interrupted, stating the obvious for BZ's benefit, "she doesn't want Charga killed?"

"Right," he nodded. "She knew this show was

terminal, but she didn't know how sick she was when she entered. She could have tolerated letting Charga go if she'd stayed well because when she signed the contract *she* believed *he* knew his purpose."

He stopped and said, "Before you tell me none of this makes sense, I already know it doesn't. But see, ranching is a different kind of life. You raise living things to kill them. The Nashes have had that ranch over a hundred years. Her father learned ranching from his father and his father learned from his. From the time they're babies, they teach the kids not to get attached to the animals. It's something I've been trying to understand, but I still don't. Living in the city the way I did most of my life, we went to the grocery store for our meat; we didn't raise it and then go kill it."

I thought about the cattle Grandfather kept at the little ranch he had on the Guadalupe River. I had loved the cows and the calves, but I never knew we were selling the calves for slaughter. I think I thought they were going to new homes like adopted dogs and cats. I never experienced the reality of what happened to them. As an adult, I finally knew what happened. I liked steak. I understood the process, but I never thought about eating an animal I knew.

"See, now that she's dying, she doesn't want Charga to die, too." Charlie dropped the bombshell

While I processed the information, logical BZ asked, "Why did she enter Charga in the show for judging if she knew all this? Why didn't she keep him out of the competition in the first place?"

"Because, like I said, she didn't know. They didn't tell her she was dying until yesterday in the hospital. Her folks knew already. They found out a week ago. They'd been taking her to doctors here for the last month or so and kept telling her they thought it was mono or something like that."

I listened to Charlie tell us the sequence of events. He said Paris had become tired and listless over the past few months and that her mother worried that maybe she had gotten mononucleosis at school where it was going around. They went to the local doctor in Kingsland, and he took blood. Then when they got the results back, he sent her to see a hematologist in San Antonio.

That doctor ran more tests and the results came back a week before the stock show. The doctor told her parents, as soon as he had a diagnosis, that their daughter had terminal melanoma, but they kept the truth from her because they knew how important the show was to her. They planned to tell her after the judging was over, but when Charga won Grand Champion, everything changed.

"Why won't A.L.E.C. let her take the steer back home? Haven't her parents asked?" I wanted to know.

"She had to sign release papers when she entered him in the show," Charlie said turning his palms upward, a gesture of futility. "This show is a big deal here, you know. I've lived in San Antonio most of my life, and I know how they play up the Grand Champion thing and what a huge honor it is to raise the Grand Champion, and how the businesses bid shit-loads, oh sorry," he blushed, "of money on it and get their picture on the front page. It's a big deal and they make sure you know it when you enter the show. They tell you if you don't want your animal to go to the slaughter house, you don't enter it in the show."

"So, Paris sent the steer to slaughter before she found out she was dying, but now she can't bear to do it?" I wanted to make sure I understood.

"Yeah, as soon as she found out how sick she is she swore she couldn't do that to him. She put her foot down and said '*no way is Charga going to slaughter*'."

"And where do we fit in?" I could not think of a thing I could do to help.

"You said you would help us if you could," he countered, looking straight into my eyes.

"Do you have something in mind, Charlie?" I made a mental note to avoid making such a broad offer to anyone again.

"Could you make it a story on the news? If enough people hear about it and understand and get upset about what those A.L.E.C. guys are doing, maybe they'd force them to make an exception to the rules or something."

BZ interrupted him. "That's something the newspapers do better than we could, Charlie. This is a complicated story. They have time to tell it."

I interrupted to explain. "We get a minute-thirty tops in our business. The newspapers are slower to act, but if they decide to do it, one story in print makes a bigger difference than a one minute story on our news would."

"Since the auction is next Friday," BZ said, "I don't know how we can get the paper interested in doing a story that quickly. Do you know anyone at the paper, Oshun?"

I shook my head. "What would happen if Paris took the steer out of the show anyway? What if she just did it? Then what could the stock show committee do about it?"

"They'd sue," Charlie, answered. "As soon as Charga won Grand Champion, he became the property of A.L.E.C. In reality, they own him already."

BZ asked, "Have the Nashes tried to talk to A.L.E.C. about breaking the rules, just this one time?"

"Yes," Charlie answered. "Mr. Nash talked to Eloy what's-his-name, and the little guy said '*Well, the money you make at the auction ought to help you folks with the hospital bills, don'cha think?*'"

63

"What a jerk," BZ muttered.

"My sentiments," I agreed. Then I asked Charlie, "Have the Nashes considered holding a press conference? There is a lot of local media interest in what happened to Paris. Everyone would be able to do a story. You could get publicity that way."

"Yeah, those reporters are camped out at the hospital," Charlie said. "I walk right by them because no one has figured out about me and Paris except you," he smiled at me. "Yesterday a lady from the hospital told Mr. and Mrs. Nash that she thought they should make some kind of statement so the media will leave. They are in the way all the time. That's all anybody's said." His eyes pled, "Could you talk to Paris's parents, Miss Siobhan? Maybe you could give them ideas about what to do. And, you could meet Paris."

"When?" I did not hesitate.

"Today? After you get off work?" He suggested.

I nodded enthusiastically, but BZ did not. I could not tell what he was thinking.

Charlie said, "I'll talk to Paris's mom and dad about it. If they don't want to meet, I'll call and let you know." He sounded hopeful.

"I can't make it tonight," BZ finally spoke. "My girls have gymnastics practice."

"BZ, I don't think we can postpone the meeting," I said. "We don't have enough time as it is. I'll go to the hospital and meet them. I'll call and tell you everything that happens."

BZ nodded, and I told Charlie, "I'll meet you by the vending machines where I saw you yesterday."

"I'll be there." He stood, shook hands with BZ and me. This time he took my whole hand in his and squeezed it hard. I believe he had decided we were trustworthy.

Chapter Six

On the way back to the station BZ cautioned, "You know Bud's going to be pissed off, don't you?"

I nodded. "Do you think it would do any good if we talked to him first?"

"I think if we do, he'll send Tracy to talk with the Nashes first thing."

I did not like that idea. "I can't imagine phony Tracy covering this story. I'm sure she'd try to look a little less cheerful than usual while talking about the dying girl's last wish."

BZ also grimaced at the thought of Tracy being involved. "It would turn into 'The Tracy Show'," he agreed.

"Let me talk to the Nashes tonight, and I'll call you afterward."

"You'd better call me," BZ warned. "No matter how late it gets."

I'd gotten him to change his mind about telling Bud

right away. I needed to take advantage of the reprise.

Charlie waited near the vending machines where we met the day before and jumped up from the table when he saw me, saying, "Mr. and Mrs. Nash are waiting to meet you in one of the family consulting rooms on the second floor."

He led me to the elevator, and on the way up, told me, "They are nice people. You'll like them."

I did like them. Paris's mother, the same woman who climbed the arena fence the day Paris collapsed, was lovely. She reached her hand out to me and said, "I'm Paris's mother, Cardiff Nash."

Mr. Nash was a tall slender man, and he removed his felt hat, revealing his rancher-tanned face. "I'm Paris's daddy, Franklin." He seemed shy to me.

"I'm Siobhan O'Shaunessy with KWNK."

We stood awkwardly for a moment until Charlie asked, "Do you want me to leave so you can talk?"

"Of course not, Charlie," Paris's parents spoke in unison.

"This is your idea, son," Franklin Nash added, resting his hand on the young boy's shoulder.

Charlie blushed. "Miss Siobhan works for the television station. Like I told you, she's the one who came back to see me after Paris fainted at the show and said she would help if she could."

Charlie added, "When I told Paris about it, she thought it would be a good idea if we talked to Miss Siobhan to see if she had any idea how we might go about trying to save Charga."

Mr. Nash said, "Let's cut to the chase, then. Has Charlie told you what Paris wants?"

I nodded, "Under the current circumstances, I understand why she feels the way she does."

"Well, I can't," he spoke plainly.

Mrs. Nash wiped her eyes with a tissue and said, "Franklin, it is her wish."

Mr. Nash had no answer to that. The lifelong rancher whose daughter won the prestigious Grand Championship award at one of the biggest shows in Texas simply shook his head. He was a man of pride and tradition and, I thought, must be unused to sorrow.

"I understand you've spoken to A.L.E.C.," I prompted him to speak.

"Yes, I spoke to Eloy Grisham and the little prick..."

Cardiff elbowed him in the ribs.

"...oh, sorry, ma'am," Franklin apologized. "Anyway he said the steer would bring a good price and wouldn't even talk to me about letting us pull the damn thing out of the auction next week."

"Charlie told me about that. I'm sure you were disappointed by Eloy's reaction." Franklin nodded and I continued, "Charlie also told me that he and Paris think getting the story out to the media might generate enough public sympathy for Charga that A.L.E.C. might feel the pressure and make them change their minds. Do you think public opinion would help?"

"I don't know." Franklin shook his head. "That bunch of little shits are damned determined to abide by their stupid damn rules. Every one of 'em I talked to in person agreed they couldn't do a damn thing. They say the whole idea of these terminal shows is to teach what ranching is all about."

He went on, explaining to me what they meant by that. "Ranchers raise cattle to sell them to packing houses. Hell, if the damn thing had stayed a bull, we wouldn't be here at all. We could breed him, and then he'd have a purpose. But he's a steer for Crissake." Franklin's agitation made his wife uncomfortable. Her eyes kept up with him as he paced. "All he can do for the rest of his life is eat and sleep and..."

"That's enough, Franklin," Cardiff interrupted. "Forgive us, Siobhan. We are under a great deal of strain."

I assured her they did not need to explain or apologize and spent the next thirty minutes gathering enough information to present to Bud. I explained why that would be necessary. "My boss will have to approve anything I do."

I did not know what Bud would think about me getting so deeply involved with the Nash family. I couldn't guess whether the station would support a story with its root being to change an observance like the Livestock Exposition. The agri-business crowd is not only patriotic but also staunch in its support of tradition in all things. This would not be a story with a predictable outcome. Our actions might effect change, or might tick-off our viewers. I couldn't get the station involved without Bud's blessing.

"Have any of the local newspapers tried to reach you?" I asked.

"Hell, every one of those media types tried to reach us; they're like a bunch of vultures sitting on a limb waiting for a body to drop."

Franklin Nash alternated between being a man concerned for his family and a man angry at the world because his child is dying. He knew the ranching business, he knew how his family operated, and he could operate within those two arenas with absolute assuredness. Hospitals, illnesses, and the media were outside his purview and he felt impotent against them.

"Sir," I asked him, "What do *you* want to happen?"

Tears welled in his eyes as he said, "I want to go home with my family and love my little girl to death. I want her to be happy for the rest of her life, whatever she's got left of it. But I know she won't be happy unless we can keep the damn steer from going to slaughter." His angst heightened with each word he said.

Cardiff rubbed her hands along Franklin's arm and pressed her face to his shoulder. He reached down and touched her hand, the fear they both felt for their daughter and the absolute love they had for one another were indisputable. I knew, when we came to a decision, there would be no second-guessing, blaming or finger pointing, even if what we attempted to do failed to work. They were a family united, and later when I had a chance to think about them, I wondered what it would have been like to grow up with parents like Franklin and Cardiff Nash.

I did not get to meet Paris that evening. I was disappointed, but everyone agreed it would be better if her parents had a chance to talk with her before she and I met. We agreed that the next morning would be a better time for her. I promised I would be back at the hospital before I went to work.

I had a lot more questions to ask, but I needed Paris to answer them for me. The public would want to know how a young girl her age could have come down with a fatal skin cancer, apparently without earlier symptoms. I did not know much about melanoma cancer, but wanted to know more, not only for myself, but also so I could answer the questions I knew Bud and our viewers would want answered.

On a whim, on my way home, I went out to the Coliseum to see Charga. My press credentials gave me access to the grounds and to the *Reserved for Media* parking spaces near the front entrance. The Grand Champion and Reserve Grand Champion steers shared a common fence in their luxury accommodations, portable pens set up near the ticket booth where everyone who entered the grounds could admire them. When I got there, Charga, the center of this dispute, was methodically rubbing his huge head against the top rail of his pen.

Carnival noise blasted full force from the adjacent midway, and I noticed lights and music whirring in a syncopated frenzy. A whiff of cotton candy made me want to find a concession stand. Screams from the daredevil rides reminded me of how terrified I had been when Grandfather let me ride the Devils' Death Loop for the first time.

Couples walking hand in hand across the wide concrete expanse leading to the Coliseum building were oblivious to anything but each other. Fathers and mothers ushered children away from the rides, toward the six double-door entrances, rushing so they would not miss the opening rodeo performance. I noticed there were no security guards posted near the two championship steers; in fact, I did not see a single uniformed person inside the grounds. I was glad to see padlocks on the gate to each pen and I wondered who had the key to the lock on Charga's pen? My guess was Charlie.

I climbed up on the low railing of the enclosure and leaned over the top rail as Charga lumbered over where I stood. I reached to scratch the curly white topknot on his head and the big animal leaned into my fingers, welcoming my touch. He jerked his head upward a couple of times as if trying to land my fingers where he most wanted scratching, and I complied, talking as I rubbed, "You know, you're causing quite a problem for Miss Paris," I told the gentle steer.

His huge head turned toward me when I said Paris's name. A large pale blue eye looked directly at me, and his reaction interested me. I thought I probably imagined it and continued talking to Charga, petting his back until he picked up a wad of hay to chew.

"She wants to take you back home. Paris changed her mind about all this hoopla." I reached further in to reach his wavy red neck. "I'm going to talk to Paris tomorrow," and he did it again! He rolled his head up and twisted it until a pale blue eye looked at me. I believed the steer knew exactly what I'd said; I believed he missed Paris Nash.

When I got home, I called BZ to tell him about what happened at the hospital, at the Coliseum and about my plan to meet with Paris before work the next morning. He said he would talk to me more about it over coffee when I got to the station. As soon as I hung up from talking with him, Phyllis called.

"I've got so much to tell you. I'm bringing pizza," she told me, instead of asking.

I put on my sweats and fuzzy slippers, washed my face, poured two glasses of cabernet, and set out plates and napkins. By the time, Phyllis made it to the house, I began to look as tired as I felt. It hadn't been easy keeping fatigue at bay the past few days, and weariness was overtaking me.

When I opened the door, Phyllis breezed in with the aroma of hot pizza and scent of gardenia coming with her. Still in her very high heels and wearing the suit she wore to work, she looked beautiful.

"You," she said pointedly to me, "need to make an appointment at the Spa."

"That sounds so much nicer than 'You look terrible'," I said.

She took over my kitchen telling me, "Go. Sit."

Exhaustion made me numb, and I could not think, much less maintain a conversation with her. I sat at my kitchen-nook table and listened to her talk.

Between bites of pizza and sips of wine, Phyllis said, "So, while Sarah worked on the aunt. . ." She told me what she had started earlier while I stood outside the horse barn.

"The aunt loves to talk and is, according to Sarah, a drama queen. For a while, Sarah admitted to me, she wasn't paying attention. It took some time for her to realize the woman was talking about the girl who fainted with the steer. The aunt kept saying, 'my niece' this and 'my niece' that and how sad she only had months to live."

I bit into a hot slice of the basil-spiced pizza, pulled at the melted mozzarella cheese, stretched and looped it around my finger, then plopped it into my mouth.

Phyl ignored my unorthodox technique and continued telling me, "It wasn't until the aunt said something about *Paris* loving the steer so much that Sarah made the connection because Paris is an uncommon name. Then Sarah started asking questions and got the aunt to backtrack to get the full story."

"It's true she is dying, you know," I said. "BZ got a call right after I hung up from talking to you today. His wife's cousin works at the hospital, and she told him the same thing you told me."

Phyllis took a sip of wine. "I'll have to tell Sarah the aunt's story is valid."

"Did the aunt tell Sarah how it happened? That's one of the things I want to find out. I've been curious about how it started ever since I heard."

I helped myself to another slice of pizza, eating from tiredness rather than hunger. Phyllis sipped her wine and sat back for a minute before she continued.

"If I remember correctly, now this is according to Sarah," she began, "it started after the girl got her first bra, when she was twelve or thirteen years old. She felt a sore spot on her back where the bra wrapped around and hooked closed. She told her mom about it. Her mom thought that maybe the bra had chaffed the virgin skin where nothing had touched. She put a Band-Aid on it. A while later, when the sore didn't heal, the mom decided they'd better have a doctor look at it. They took her to the local physician, who must have been the oldest living doctor in the state, and he made a little incision, called it a cyst. . ."

I interrupted her, "So, they've known for a long time how serious it is?" I felt irate that they hadn't done anything about it sooner. "Surely, the doctor told them she needed additional treatment."

Phyllis shook her head, took a bite of pizza, swallowed quickly and said, "Nope. Don't get mad at her parents. Get angry with the doctor. He said it didn't look like anything and to stop worrying about and keep it covered with a Band-Aid and don't go swimming until the incision healed completely. They forgot about it."

She stopped for a minute and inhaled the pizza's spicy aroma. "This is so good!" She closed her eyes.

I used her rapturous moment to think about the woman who climbed the fence at the judging. I thought she must feel very guilty, and I wondered if my own mother would feel that way if she heard I had received a death sentence because of something her neglect caused me. I doubted she would care.

I thought back to the old doctor. "Didn't he order a biopsy?"

"Apparently he did not."

At that moment, I noticed the time and interrupted her.

"Hold that thought, Phyl. I want to turn on our news and see if there's anything about Paris."

Tracy Brennan's smiling face filled the screen and behind her, projected on a blue screen, was a capture from the film BZ shot at the judging. It showed Paris lying at Charga's feet.

"I've got to hear what Tracy's saying. I hope no one else knows how serious the girl's condition is."

I turned up the volume and cringed as Tracy attempted to appear less detached than usual.

"…a source at Children's," Tracy intoned, "reports that Paris Nash, the young Grand Champion prize winning steer handler, is in stable condition. Our sources tell us the family may hold a press conference tomorrow to answer questions about the young girl. Cary, what's new in sports tonight?"

I pushed the mute button and apologized to Phyllis, "Sorry I stopped you. I didn't want to miss anything she said. You see how miraculously she recovered from her relapse and came back to work just in time to come take over my story."

"She's no fool," Phyllis countered.

"Yeah, but she's guessing about a press conference at the hospital tomorrow. The parents don't know what they want to do, at least not when I talked to them earlier," I said.

"You talked to the parents? Then you already know this stuff?"

"No, I didn't know about what caused it. I just know what they are trying to accomplish now. Tell me everything you know, and I'll fill you in on what I learned today."

"Okay, about two months ago the girl, started getting tired, sleeping more and didn't have her usual energy. She was losing weight and her mother got worried. They didn't think about the cyst incident. They thought she had mono because apparently mono had been going around her high school. They took her to the new doctor in town. He did blood work, discovered she was anemic, put her on B-12, and drew a bunch more blood to send off to the lab."

I poured more wine into our glasses.

"When he got the report back, the alarm bells went off. He talked to Paris's mother and told her they needed to take the girl to a specialist to have more tests done. I don't know when they found out how serious it is."

"Charlie told me they found out last week," I told her. "It was a few days before the livestock show. They were going to tell her right after the judging. They wanted to let her have the experience because she worked so hard with her steer."

"That's what the aunt told Sarah, when they got all of the test results, the doctor, and her parents decided to wait to tell her until after the judging. And, then she won, she collapsed, and now its gossip. I think I'd have done the same thing if she were my child--not told her, I mean," Phyllis said. "The doctor came right out and said the melanoma had metastasized, and there's no treatment for melanoma cancer."

"So, the family made an emotional decision to wait. I can't imagine," I shook my head.

"Her parents wanted to get her back home in familiar surroundings before they told her how seriously ill she really is," Phyllis added

"But, they didn't know the steer would win."

"Right," Phyllis agreed. "Winning messed up all their plans for privacy. When she collapsed in that arena...well, you know the rest."

I nodded. "They were trying do what they thought was best for their daughter. They didn't expect anyone else to know about the cancer until they were ready to talk about it with her. When I met them today, I almost asked them how she'd gotten to this point. Now, I'm glad I didn't ask. Her mother must feel terribly guilty."

Phyllis sighed, "Imagine. That poor woman. What she's going through."

"Yeah," I agreed, "but, she's the rock in the family. I liked both the parents. They are fine people, but neither is equipped to deal with this kind of circumstance. The dad, Franklin, is teetering on an edge." I made hand motions to show a fall. "The mom, bless her, keeps reining him in. He's one of those strong men who doesn't deal with his emotions very well. He thinks he's supposed to fix everything, and he is way out of his element in this situation."

Phyllis shook her head at the futility.

"And, get this, Phyl, you don't know this part. Paris doesn't want the steer auctioned next week. She doesn't want the steer to die."

"Well, why does he have to die? Why don't they take him back home?"

I explained the terminal auction rules A.L.E.C. enforces and about their unwillingness to make an exception to their policy for Paris.

"I'm no psychologist," Phyllis said, "but do you think she's knows she can't do anything to save herself, so she's going to focus on saving her steer instead?"

"Probably. That makes sense. I know her boyfriend, Charlie, and her parents, all believe she won't be happy unless her steer gets to go home with her. They want me to help."

When the news signed off and Johnny Carson came on, we realized how late it had gotten. Phyllis said, "I'm going to let you get some sleep. But if I can do anything to help, you know I will."

"You may be sorry you said that," I laughed,

remembering I had offered Charlie the same thing.

After she left, I retrieved a half pint of Blue Bell Butter Pecan ice cream from the freezer, got a spoon, and collapsed onto my big leather chair and pulled up the ottoman. I reached for the old quilt from the basket beside my chair, pulled it up around my shoulders, and closed my eyes, intending to rest them for only a moment.

I woke the next morning, still in the big chair, snuggled under my old blue quilt with a carton of melted ice cream in my lap.

Chapter Seven

My clock was set for five so I could get ready and be downtown before the morning rush hour. I wanted to be able to spend more than a few minutes with Paris before I went to work.

The early morning traffic flowed easily and the drive reminded me of how much I loved this city. The invigoratingly cool, crisp, early morning temperature made me hungry. I stopped at the new Taco Cabana I discovered on my way, ordered coffee and a bean and cheese to go, and headed to the hospital, munching as I drove.

I passed roads named for old time farm and ranch families, and wondered what the Maltzbergers, Huebners, and Classens would think about what had happened to the land they purchased in the early 1800's.

After the end of the WWII, many of them sold property to local developers who planted houses and strip malls on the land. Dairy farms near Wetmore disappeared, became rooftops from the sky. The Classens deeded land through their ranch to the state for Highway 281, and it had grown from a rutted road to four lanes of continuously blazing neon lights heralding restaurants, gas stations, and auto dealerships.

I drove onto Loop 410, an asphalt moat that surrounded the city, separating the old from new, lined with an array of businesses. Tall towers lined the roadway on the posh side of town, creating our unique linear skyline. Unlike the cluster of towers in other big cities centers, San Antonio has LoopLand, a tiara with its glitter facing the richness on the north side of town. My grandfather had watched the city change, contributed a great deal to it, and thinking of him made me feel grounded and serene.

When I reached the hospital, Charlie waited for me in the lobby and guided me to the nearest bank of elevators. As we waited for a car to descend, I shared with him the conversation Phyllis and I had the night before. When the elevator doors opened, we stepped inside and Charlie punched the numeral two on the panel.

"Her aunt's okay, just a little too dramatic for my taste," he told me, and he added, "They've moved Paris into a private room so it'll be easier for us to talk."

When we reached the second floor, he led me to Room 285. I paused outside the door, adjusted my purse on my shoulder, and took a deep breath before we stepped inside. I had prepared myself to meet a pallid, weak, limp, little patient; however, the girl who greeted me looked anything but ill. I flashed a questioning glance at Charlie. He was smiling at the girl.

"Miss O'Shaughnessy, this is Paris Nash." He said it with a flourish of his hand.

"Well, you look simply wonderful, Miss Paris." I

reached my hand to her. "Much better than the last time I saw you." She looked nothing as I'd imagined she would. "I don't know what I expected to find here, but you aren't even close to it."

She smiled and her sweet expression made her even prettier. "I know. I'm surprised myself at how good I feel. They've been giving me fluids and B-12 since they brought me here. They say I collapsed because I wasn't drinking enough water." She looked up at Charlie, "Sometimes I think they've got this whole thing flat out wrong." She laughed and reached for his hand. He sat on the edge of her bed and Paris motioned me close. "Sit here," she pointed to a straight-backed chair next to the head of her bed.

I asked, as I pushed the chair closer, "Is it a possibility? Could they have this all wrong?"

"Not according to Dr. Doom." She laughed and rolled her eyes. "He says this disease is crazy weird." She pulled her long dark hair back from her face and neck and showed me small stitches, dark threads, spaced at even intervals down each side of her neck. "Here's the reason," she pointed to them. "Stage three melanoma."

I frowned, not understanding the classification.

"It means," she explained with furrowed brow, "my lymph nodes all have cancer cells in them, and the way Dr. Doom tells it, my organs already have cancer cells, too. So, even if I did have chemotherapy, it wouldn't help in the end. I might live a month or two longer, but I'd feel, and this is a quote from the doctor, '*like shit*.'"

I did not know what to say. I shook my head.

"He said," she continued. "I'd be sick for the first part and too weak to enjoy the last part. So, I said screw it, I'm not going to do it. If I'm going to die anyway, I'd like to at least enjoy the life I have left." Her chin jutted out, and defiance

81

flashed with the intensity of a flare.

She seemed too well adjusted to accept pity, too mature to want drama. I am certain I never used, or heard anyone else use, the word stoic to describe a fifteen-year-old girl, but that was the word that came to mind as I listened to her talk about this illness.

A tap on the door interrupted our conversation, and a screeching falsetto voice shouted, "Man on the floor."

For my second surprise of the morning, one of the handsomest men I had ever seen walked in the room. He belonged on the cover of a romance novel. His dark hair, flawless skin, and double rowed eyelashes reminded me of Cary Grant or that cute George Clooney on E/R.

"Hi, Dr. Doom," Paris said. Charlie stood and shook hands with him.

I did not say a word. I watched the interaction between Paris and the gorgeous doctor standing at the foot of her bed. I stood and pulled my chair away so he could get by to examine Paris more easily.

"Sit," he pointed at me and then grasped the footboard of the bed and shook it forcefully. "Still feeling wonderful, Miss Paaariss?"

"Yeah, until you showed up," she folded her arms across her chest and pouted like a petulant child. "So, what have you got planned for me today? Any special beverages you want me to drink or radioactive slime you're planning to shoot into my veins?"

Their banter continued with not-so-subtle put downs about how he was so old he didn't even know Adam Ant was a great talent, and how could she call herself an American knowing next to nothing about Elvis Presley.

I watched, listened, and decided I liked her doctor. Not only was he a handsome man, but he had the perfect bedside manner for dealing with a teenage girl.

I had an impression I knew him from somewhere, but I could not remember ever meeting him before. It was not a professional visit, I was sure, and I thought he might have been in one of those public service announcements, *Dr. So-and-so recommends an annual colonoscopy after age forty* type things. I tried to read his nametag and could finally make out the name Hardwick. *Hardwick,* I tried to force a memory, but nothing came.

Paris introduced me to him, "This is my new friend, Siobhan O'Shaunessy."

He surprised me when he asked, "Didn't you go to school at Tech?"

His question took me completely by surprise. It did jog my memory. "Yes." I slapped my forehead. "I remember now. You were one of my first interviews. On the university channel, you, and another doctor." I felt foolish for not remembering before.

"You did an interview with me and Dr. Duncan about blood clots and birth control pills because your friend Alyson had pulmonary embolisms."

"Right, right," I answered enthusiastically, standing to shake his hand.

I'd suggested the interview to my communication professor because Aly was spending a week in intensive care because of that problem. The university set it up and the two doctors came out in scrubs to do the interview with me.

"We decided she got the blood clots because she used birth control pills and, I think, had been on a long road trip, and drove her Jeep for hours at a time without getting out to walk."

I nodded. He remembered perfectly.

He continued, "We talked about the risks of the pill

and smoking and not sitting for extended periods without stretching." He had a good memory. "Siobhan," he extended his hand, "It's nice to see you again. You were my first interviewer."

"Dexter Hardwick," I said shaking his hand, "It's nice to see you again. You were my first interviewee."

He asked, "So, are you still reporting?"

"Yes," I said, "At KWNK, now."

"Oh, sorry," he apologized, "I should know you. That's the station I usually watch when I have time. I did watch the piece you did with Duncan and me back in Lubbock, though. Good work," he complimented.

"Thank you. I'm glad you liked it. I got an A+ on it."

We laughed, and I felt surprised by how much his compliment pleased me.

"You've gotten married?" He asked with a raised eyebrow.

The question perplexed me. "No," I wriggled my ring-less fingers. "What makes you think I got married?"

"Your name wasn't O'Shaughnessy back then. It was Tabbard wasn't it?"

"You, Dr. Doom," I said, adopting Paris's nickname for him, "have an exceptional memory. No, I did not get married. I changed my name."

"Good," he smiled.

I did not know if he meant *good* you did not get married or *good* you changed your name, but I hoped I would have the chance to find out.

When he left the room, Paris asked, "Isn't he gorgeous?"

"Hey," Charlie scowled and pulled his arm away from her.

"I'm pretty sure she's talking to me," I joined in. "I

think she has an ulterior motive here. You know, he wasn't that cute back in Lubbock."

Charlie looked wounded, and surprised me with his impressive acting skill. If I had not known better, I would have believed his feelings had really been hurt.

"Awww, Charlie, I'm sorry." Paris reached out and stroked his face, and the IV tubing attached to her hand reminded me of her illness and the fun moment was spoiled.

"I know she thinks you are much better looking than Dr. Doom," I continued the teasing. "Am I right, Paris?"

"Absolutely! You, Charlie Garza, are much better looking. But you, Charlie Garza, are taken, and I'm not crazy enough to point out how gorgeous you are to any other woman!"

Charlie blushed. He leaned toward her and she wrapped her arms around him. She kissed his cheek in an attempt to assuage his hurt feelings. "I'm trying to set them up," she stage-whispered, smiling at me.

I laughed, "If you do, I'll have to start calling you little Phyl."

She looked at me with a quizzical expression. "I'm a little pill?" She and Charlie frowned at each other.

"No, my best friend, Phyllis." I laughed. "She's always trying to set me up, too."

"Don't you already have a boyfriend?" Charlie seemed ready to defend any man in my life against Paris's plotting.

"No. No boyfriend," I sighed, placing my limp hand to my forehead, blatantly dramatizing my dilemma. "I'm married to my work."

They laughed, and then Paris asked, "Were you married back then? I mean the different name thing Dr. Doom asked about, or is your name a pseudo name or whatever they call it?"

"A pseudonym? No. I did it for my grandfather." I hoped that would suffice. I did not want to talk about myself. I was there to learn about her, and besides, I hated talking about my life. Of course, that was what she wanted to know.

She looked at me with wide eyes, "Tell me why you did it. I've never known anyone who changed their name before."

It took me a minute to get comfortable with the idea of talking about my wealthy grandfather, my mother's wild lifestyle, my divorce, my breakdown. I rarely spoke about those things with anyone I did not know well. But that was what was so different. I felt I did know them well. I wasn't ashamed of my life. The past had been a painful catalyst, which forced me to come to terms with the low expectations I had set for myself. I felt safe sharing with them.

"Okay," I took a deep breath, "I was married and divorced, but that isn't the name change Dr. Doom meant."

They looked to one another and waited for me to continue.

"I was christened Siobhan Blayne Tabbard, my father's name was Tabbard, and he died when I was two years old," I began.

Paris said, "Oh, how sad."

"Yes, thank you. It is sad, isn't it, but I don't remember him, and I was too young to know him. My grandfather, who I adored, wanted me to take over the station one day. He never had a son and my mother had only me. He told me one day he regretted not having a boy so his name could stay with KWNK, so I changed my last name to his so it would. I did the interview with Dr. Doom before I changed it."

"So your grandfather owns the television station where you work?" Charlie asked. "He must be rich."

"He was. He was the owner and he was rich. He

passed away a few years ago. He was a brilliant self-made man. He owned a lot of businesses, but KWNK was his favorite."

"So do you own the TV station now? Or does your grandmother?" They asked.

"No, I don't. I don't remember my grandmother. She died before I was born, when my mother was a baby. Grandfather's wife Six inherited KWNK and she sold it."

"He was married six times?" Paris was incredulous.

"Well, he was a great businessman, but his personal life was a mess."

"Yeah," Paris agreed. "He must have loved the last one if he left everything to her."

"Well, not really," I disagreed. "Did you ever watch that Disney movie, *Bambi*?"

They nodded.

"Remember when the bunny says Bambi is twitter-pated? Well, that was my grandfather. Twitter-pated."

Paris said, "I'm that way about him." She play-punched Charlie's bicep.

Charlie asked me, "So what happened about the marriage?"

I hoped they would let that go. "Well I was too young. It was my junior year in college. I married a guy I had a huge crush on. I didn't know what love really was. His name was Andrew Messier. My married name was Siobhan Messier."

Paris made a "y*uck*" face.

"Yes, I know. Not great for on-air, huh? However, the marriage didn't last long, to no one's surprise. We did it on a dare in Mexico."

"Another woman?" Paris wanted to know the reason for the divorce.

"No. Another," I put emphasis on the word, "person."

"Oh." Their eyes widened as the realization dawned about what happened to my marriage.

"So who owns KWNK?" Charlie changed the subject.

"A conglomerate bought it from Six." I used the derogatory reference that made me feel better when I talked about her.

"That doesn't make any sense to me," Charlie said.

"Well, apparently Grandfather talked her into marrying him by telling her she was his soul mate, and that he didn't need a pre-nup agreement. So, Six inherited almost everything."

I did not mention the trust fund he'd left me, a lot of money I would inherit when I turned forty-five, nor did I tell them about the little ranch on the Guadalupe I inherited upon his death.

"What about your mother. Didn't she get mad?" Paris's good heart did not like the unfairness in my story.

"My mother got her trust fund a long time ago. She didn't want to fight."

She nodded, "I guess that's okay then."

"Did you change your name before he died? I mean did he know you did that for him?"

"Yep. A few days before his last birthday I told him, I had a special present for him. When he got the papers with the name change, he cried."

"So did he hire you at the station?" Paris wanted to know.

"No, I interviewed and got the job on my own."

"I bet your mom was proud of you." Paris said.

I shrugged. "I don't know. I haven't talked to my mother in years."

The conversation was making me uncomfortable. I

decided to change the subject. "Wait just a doggone minute here. I'm the reporter, and I'm supposed to be doing the interview."

A tap on the door interrupted again and a nurse came in to take Paris's vital signs and check the IV solution level. She took blood pressure, temperature and said, "I'll be back with a new bag in a few minutes."

After the nurse left, Paris surprised me when she said, "You've lived a really hard life, haven't you?"

Her question took me completely by surprise. I did not know what to say. I always thought my life was easy, a life of privilege. I'd gone to private schools, got a new baby blue Mustang convertible as soon as I could get my driver's license, had an American Express Card of my own at sixteen, and dragged the prerequisite oversized Louie Vooey throughout high school. I'd always thought the *things* Grandfather gave me made my life happy. Yet, from Paris Nash's perspective, my life had been difficult.

Paris gazed adoringly at Charlie. "I've been really lucky." She squeezed his hand. "Not only him," she smiled at me. "But everything really, up until now, has been wonderful for me. I mean I spent my whole life on a ranch."

"It's a great ranch," Charlie interrupted. "It's on the lake."

"It used to be on the Lower Colorado River part," Paris corrected, "until LBJ made the chain of lakes." She rolled her eyes, "Grampa never forgave Johnson, and never voted Democrat again. He complained about it until his dying day. Now we live on a lake," she mimicked a crotchety old man's voice, "'with six hundred Gol-Damn acres under water'.

She went on, "And, I've got a big family, two brothers, and two sisters. Rome and London are my brothers; Ireland and India are my sisters." She noticed my bewildered reaction to their names. "We are all named after places," she explained.

"Interesting," I said. "There must be a reason?"

Paris said, "Yep, it started with my grandmother. She was born in Wales and named my mother after her hometown because she figured she would never get to go back there. She always said, 'If I can't see Cardiff again, I can re-visit it every time I say your name.' That's how Mom got her name, and that's where Mom got the idea to name her children after places, except she decided to name us the places she would love to see some day but is sure she won't be able to."

"What an original idea." I admired her creativity.

"Names are important," Paris said and glanced up at Charlie. They smiled at each other, sharing a secret. "That's why I named Charga after him, Charlie Garza."

Charlie blushed.

"So, even when Charlie isn't around, I can go talk to Charga and feel close to this guy," she fake-punched his arm.

Charlie looked away, blushed again, and cleared his throat. He looked at his watch and reminded me, "I guess we should talk about him?"

I glanced at my watch and nodded. "I cannot believe we've been talking all this time. We do have to discuss Charga, though, so if I'm going to get to work by eight I'll need to leave pretty soon."

"I don't want Charga to die." Paris folded her arms across her chest in a protective motion and her mood went through a dramatic change. "I don't have a choice about dying, but, I have to keep the promise I made to Charga when I got him. I just have to keep it."

I reached over and touched her arm.

Tears flowed down her face and she cried. "I told him

he would be the way for me to get an education. I know this sounds so crazy," she sobbed. "When I first got him, I never lied. When I picked him out of the herd, I told him 'I'm going to make you a champion, Charga, and you will be the way I can go to college and make something of myself. I will love and care for you until the end.' Of course, all that time," she looked at me ruefully, tears overflowing, her voice so constricted I could barely understand the words, "I thought it would be his end, not mine."

I could not listen any longer. I put my arms around her shoulders and held her while she cried. I felt maternal toward her. Tears filled my eyes as, even while in typical reporter mode, I tried to distance myself from her pain, thinking of ways I could convey her feelings to A.L.E.C. How could anyone tell this girl, no? I wondered if her father's stoicism had worked against him when he tried to talk to Eloy about removing Charga from the auction. Maybe Eloy interpreted Mr. Nash's directness as a half-hearted request, or maybe Franklin Nash's inability to understand his daughter's need to keep the steer alive interfered with him being able to successfully convince Eloy Grisham how important saving the steer would be to her peace of mind.

Fortunately, she had Charlie as an ally and now she had me, too. Peace in her final days was what she needed, and if keeping the promise she made to the little steer was what it took, I was going to help her get it. The only question remaining unanswered was, "How do we do it?"

I was thankful when Cardiff and Franklin Nash arrived. Cardiff immediately saw her daughter's tears and came to her bedside. I stood and let her take my place. Franklin removed his hat, and in his direct, no-nonsense way, extended his hand to me.

"Have you got any ideas about what we talked about,

Miss Siobhan? We had to be rude to those people downstairs again this morning. Every time we come up here, all them media people, they want to know how," he used his Stetson to gesture to Paris, "she is doing."

"It might be a good idea for you to make a statement to the media about Paris doing well and being almost ready to go home, just to satisfy them. I wouldn't say anything about her wanting to save Charga," I paused and looked at Paris. "Not yet, anyway." I winked at her.

"Well, I don't cotton much to lying," Franklin admitted, "and Cardiff won't be able to talk to those people." He pointed the hat to Cardiff. "She'll cry."

Cardiff nodded, and Paris wiped her mother's tears. Franklin went to the bedside and put his arms around them both. I wondered how it felt to have two parents who loved you so much.

"Ask Dr. Hardwick if he could do it for you," I suggested. "He knows how to give limited information. And, reporters," I confessed, "don't usually mess with doctors. Doctors use complex medical terminology, and most of us get lost and look foolish trying to get a statement, so we back way off."

"That's a good idea, Daddy." Paris looked up at her father, her blue eyes surrounded by long wet lashes.

"Why can't you do it for us, Siobhan," Cardiff asked from Paris's side.

"I wish I could, but it wouldn't be best for you guys if I did. First, I have to get permission from my boss before I could do anything. If he said okay, I could but then other stations in town wouldn't air my statement because it came from a reporter on a competitor station.

"It's a legal issue, a credibility issue, and a timing issue," I explained. "We don't have time to fool around, and we need to get the story in front of the public as quickly as we can. I am flattered you trust me, and I do want to help, but I think I can be more helpful behind the scenes. I'll write out a suggested script for Dr. Doom to use if you like. Whatever we do, though, it's just between the five us, and Dr. Hardwick."

"Don't forget BZ," Charlie reminded me, remembering BZ's offer to help.

"Six of us then, and Dr. Hardwick." I explained about BZ. Afterward I asked Franklin to retell me the conversation he had with Eloy Grisham. I wanted to know exactly why the show chairman rejected Franklin Nash's request to allow Charga's withdrawal from the auction.

Paris's emotional state made me realize I needed to get an appointment with Eloy as soon as possible. Then I would have to get A.L.E.C. to meet with me and get them to agree about releasing Charga from the auction. Everything I could learn about how the man's brain worked would help.

I thought I could prepare arguments to change Eloy's mind and then the minds of the A.L.E.C. The plan I was creating focused on the amount of positive publicity they would get if they let Charga go home with Paris.

Her story would be a heart-warming human-interest tale that couldn't help but make the A.L.E.C. members appear as altruistic and compassionate. I hoped Eloy Grisham would have the rules amended for this one instance only. I knew it would not be easy to accomplish this feat. The agri-business crowd is notoriously stubborn.

Chapter Eight

There was little traffic on I-10, and I reached the station a few minutes earlier than I originally anticipated. There I found BZ huddled with Johnny Resendez, another outside camera operator. BZ caught my eye, raised an index finger acknowledging that he saw me, and mimed "I want to talk to you." I nodded and called down to the front desk to get messages from the front desk while I waited for him.

"Good morning, Miss Benjimina, anything for me?" I asked the part-time receptionist.

"Only a couple of people wanting to know how the girl is doing. I gave the slips to Mr. Johnson." It was apparent to me that everyone at the station already knew I was off the story.

I asked Benji if the "epidemic" had claimed any more victims. She laughed, "Not today. In fact, almost everyone who was out has called in to say they'll be back to work Monday. But," she cautioned in a whisper, "Keep washing your hands. There are sneezers about."

BZ came over, sat on the corner of my desk, and waited for me to hang up. "So?" he asked when I did.

I saw movement behind the curtains in Bud's office and gestured so BZ would be aware Bud might step out. I did not want Bud to find out what we were talking about until I was ready to ask him for his permission to be involved with Paris's quest to save her steer.

"Bottom line?" I suggested, BZ nodded, "She doesn't look the least bit sick, BZ. If Charlie hadn't taken me to her room, I would have thought I was in the wrong place. Take away the IV and the crummy hospital gown, she could be any teenage girl anywhere. By the way, I really like her young man, Charlie."

BZ nodded, "He seems like a stand-up guy."

"Paris made it clear to me, BZ. She definitely wants Charga to survive. I'll fill you in on all those details later."

I followed his glance toward Bud's office and watched our boss sit down behind his desk and reach for the phone. I relaxed.

"Well, that makes it easier." I continued telling BZ about Paris's wish. "Her parents are going to ask her hematologist, who I knew from Lubbock by the way, to make a statement for them. The Nashes are scheduling a brief press conference where they will tell the media how Paris is doing, thank the media for their interest, and explain she'll be discharged in a few days."

"Will she be?" BZ asked me.

"Discharged in a few days? As far as I know, she will. She told me she's refusing to have chemo; she's a strong willed, mature-for-her-age young woman. I don't think I've been that mature in my whole life."

"Nothing like a terminal diagnosis to bring out the

grownup in a girl." His wry comment was typical BZ.

"I'm going to try and reach Eloy Grisham to convince him that A.L.E.C. needs to bend the rules. If I make a strong enough presentation about the amount of positive publicity they could get, I might be able to sway them in Paris's favor."

BZ raised his eyebrows and rolled his eyes. "Humph, good luck on that one. Didn't Charlie say her father already tried talking to them?"

"Yes, but he didn't tell Eloy all the details. Eloy doesn't know how sick Paris actually is. He probably thinks, the way you did, that she's pregnant or has some minor ailment."

"BZ, Oshun." Bud's voice boomed from his office doorway and my body did a guilty jump.

He waved his hand and motioned us to come into his crystal palace. I went in and sat down, while BZ leaned against the doorjamb.

Bud took his time telling us what he wanted. I, of course, hoped he was going to tell us Tracy had re-relapsed and that I was getting the Paris Nash assignment back.

"You two have really pulled out all the stops, filling in over the last few weeks the way you have. It's good to know I have dependable backup." He smiled gratitude to each of us. "Neither of you have had a day off in three weeks. Now everyone is back in place and as of this morning, no one else has called in sick. We have what looks like a healthy crew, so I'm giving you a few days off. Go spend time with your family, get some rest, whatever you want to do, go…go." He shooed us out without further discussion.

"Hot damn," I whispered to BZ under my breath. "I needed that."

BZ suggested, "Let's go to Tristan's."

I gathered my notebook and the packet from the

A.L.E.C. public relations office, dumped it in my everything-tote, and headed for the elevator.

I told BZ, "I'll meet you there but, if you beat me, please place an order for *Chilaquiles*." My mouth watered at the thought of my favorite food.

From the first time I ate there, Tristan's became my favorite restaurant. He served the best Tex-Mex food in town, and by us getting there this early on a Sunday morning, we would beat the church crowd that usually filled the place. BZ had introduced me to Tristan's soon after I started working at KWNK. He'd been introduced by his cousin, Luis, who'd found out about Tristan's when a co-worker of his at the beer distributorship down the street took him there for lunch.

Tristan's did not advertise, depended upon work of mouth, and frankly, was not the kind of place most people would try on their own. I'm certain I would never have gone to the tiny hole in the wall if BZ had not taken me there.

The first thing I did on my first visit was check out the kitchen for cleanliness. I found it spotless, in complete contrast to the dining area, which was a decorating nightmare. Everyone teased Tristan about the way the place looked, and he always answered, "I mop the floor every Friday whether it needs it or not."

Actually, pretty much everything was clean, but while Tristan was a brilliant chef, good restaurateur and all around nice person, he knew little about ambiance. He knew what his loyal customers expected, knew most of them by name, and spent a lot of time greeting people and shaking hands with them. He inquired about their jobs, their families, and talked about the Spurs with them. However, the man could not decorate.

His restaurant boasted a huge collection of neon

signs, the most I'd seen in one place, representing brands of beer and ale, many I'd never heard of and a few I didn't think were brewed any more. I found their presence perplexing, since Tristan did not have an alcoholic beverages license and did not serve alcohol of any kind. The collection of neon signs had been up for a long time, I could tell, because layers of dust clung to their brightly colored bent glass rods.

Tristan once told me he purchased his dining room tables and chairs at yard sales. He was indiscriminate in his purchasing. He bought every conceivable cracked ice color choice of Formica dinette to fit his 1950's "theme." He had peach, turquoise, yellow, green, and silver. Most of the chairs came with duct tape patches that covered tears and cracks, and, after ruining several pair of pantyhose, I made a practice of checking my seat cushion before I sat.

The hand-lettered sign, long ago painted across the front window, was faded, and the edges of the T curled away from the glass but still delivered the message, "Tristan's, Home of San Antonio's Best Mexican Cuisine."

When I arrived, BZ was already sitting at a peach-colored table, sipping a tall glass of iced tea. I could tell he had helped himself to the complimentary chips and salsa because dribbles of it trailed across the tabletop to him. He pushed a silver-patched turquoise blue chair away from the table with his foot so I could sit and told me, "I ordered your *Chilaquiles.*"

Tristan brought the steaming plate to me as soon as I sat down. The eggs were scrambled with pieces of fried *tortilla*, chili pepper, and onion, with the most sumptuous *queso* I had ever tasted generously poured over the top. This dish was my newest food fetish. BZ had ordered his favorite, *huevos rancheros*, and after Tristan brought his plate to him, we ate like ten-day trail hands. After I swallowed my last bite, I dabbed the corners of my mouth with my napkin in a genteel, well-mannered way.

"So good," I purred.

BZ laughed at my charade before he asked, "Finish telling me about the girl?"

For the next thirty minutes, I filled him in on everything I had learned during my visit with Paris. "I want to get an appointment with Eloy Grisham." I concluded, "Since we have time off, maybe we can get in to see him today to explain how allowing Paris to take Charga out of the action could generate positive publicity for A.L.E.C."

"Count me out," he made a slice in the air. "What do you think the man will say?"

"Probably something similar to what he already told Franklin Nash. *The whole purpose of the show is to teach young people about ranching, not making pets out of farm animals,*" I mimicked. "But I have to try and convince him. Maybe, if he thinks there's something in it for A.L.E.C., he'll relent. This is a unique set of circumstances, and I think the story about Paris could bring a new level of interest to the Stock Show Committee and their mission statement."

"You're preaching to the choir. It all sounds good to me. Any chance it'll work on him?" His voice sounded doubtful.

"I don't know, but it is worth trying. BZ, if you'd been there to hear that girl tell why she wants the steer to live, you'd be more invested in this."

I had noticed something in BZ's attitude that started bugging me. His sudden reticence was not apparent the day before. His lack of genuine interest was grating on my nerves and he knew it.

"Okay, so I'm not as wrapped up in this story as you are." He dismissed my comment by adding, "Johnny

Resendez agrees with me. I have this little thing called a *family* to support. I prefer to stay employed."

"What does this have to do with your job? It will not make a difference if we let Bud know what we are doing. Besides, it's on our own time."

"If you remember, Sweetpea, we also kept knowledge from our boss," he reminded me. "We didn't tell him we found out about Paris's illness yesterday, and frankly, I can see this whole thing heading in a direction that will either bring notoriety to *yo*," he said pointing to his chest, "or *usted.*" He pointed at me. "It will get us either praised or fired. We need to talk to Bud before we do anything else."

"Exactly what I told the Nashes." I was glad he still used the collective we. "I'm half afraid Bud's going to say, 'Stay out of it'."

BZ, agreed. "He might."

I could not imagine going back to Paris to tell her there is nothing I can do to help. "I'm going to talk to Eloy, before I talk to Bud. That way I'll have more information. I need a convincing argument to prove that Paris's story is worth our time. Are you sure you don't want to come with me?"

"Yep, I'm sure. I'm going to go home and get some sleep. Sylvia took the girls to Pleasanton to visit her sister, and I know what to do with a few hours in a quiet house." His head rolled forward and he pretended he had fallen asleep.

"Be prepared, because I'm going to call you as soon as I leave the chairman," I warned, even more determined than before to meet with Eloy.

"Fine, I'll be there to listen." He assured me with his eyes half closed.

"Answer one question for me, BZ. Is the job thing the

real reason you're suddenly reluctant to help Paris? Yesterday you seemed much more interested."

"It's only the job thing." His bravura faded and he told me, "Sylvia and I discussed it for a long time last night, and then when I spoke with Johnny this morning, he told me there's talk about laying- off some of the camera crew. Last night Sylvia kept reminding me that we have two kids of our own to worry about, and as much as she sympathizes with Paris and her parents, she can't buy into doing anything that might jeopardize my job. We need both our salaries to make ends meet. It's probably because she works for a lawyer. She knows we could get into legal trouble if we don't watch out."

"She hasn't said anything about this at her office has she? We're trying to keep it quiet, right?"

"No, she hasn't said anything at the office. She is not stupid. She's only talking to her cousin, Maricella, and me. She's worked at the firm a few years, you know, and has seen people get into crap worse than this when they let their emotions rule over common sense. I'm trying to be practical is all."

"I'm disappointed you're pulling back," I told him, "but, I understand."

"I'm sorry, Oshun, honest, but unless Bud gives us a go-ahead, I'm staying low key on this." He shrugged. "You get his okay for us, and it's no holds barred."

I left BZ at Tristan's and drove to Phyllis' day spa to use her phone because it was closer than going home. I knew she was there today, overseeing the work for the remodeling, and she would not mind if I made calls from there.

Phyllis's business, The Spa that Loves Me, was in Alamo Heights, only a ten-minute drive from Tristan's. While I drove, I mulled over the conversation I'd had with BZ about his change in attitude. I had to admit, for a brief time, he made me start to worry, too. According to the rules of the trust my grandfather set up for me, I had to pay the taxes on the ranch when I got a job. This was the first year I would have to pay them. Actually, when I got right down to it, I could not afford to lose my job either. Getting Bud behind us, having him invested in Paris's story, was the only way both BZ and I could feel secure that helping Paris would not cost us our jobs.

Phyllis's signature gardenia scent greeted me when I opened the door. She was sitting at the front desk working on the schedule book, and I could hear hammering from one of the client treatment rooms down the hall. My drop in visit surprised and pleased her.

She jumped up and grabbed me in a bear hug. "I'm so excited to see you. Come see what I'm doing."

She showed me the changes the carpenter was making in the massage therapist's room. He had finished adding a wrap-around counter that I admired.

"I just made a fresh pot of coffee. Want some?" I nodded. "Joe?"

The carpenter shook his head.

"And, I've got some great blueberry muffins from the Basketry," she added.

Joe was not tempted, and as much as I loved Basketry baked goods, I too declined.

"Are you headed back to the station?" She asked.

"Nope, Bud sent BZ and me home today. He gave us a couple of days off," I beamed.

"You deserve some. You haven't had a day since you started working there! And, on your first day away you came to see me. How sweet." She fluttered her eyelashes.

"Actually, I came to ask if I could use the phone in

your office." I fluttered my lashes back at her.

"So, I guess I know where I rate." She laughed and walked me down the hallway to her office. I sat behind her desk, a utilitarian surface, and she told me, "I need to stay out front. Joe might have questions. I'll leave you here alone."

"I'm going to try to find Eloy Grisham so I can make an appointment to see him. I hope sometime today. Do you want to go out to the Rodeo with me?"

"Boy, I'd rather do that than stay here, but I have to get the remodel done, and the painter is due here in a minute," she said.

"I could use your help with Eloy. We could double team him."

"Just remember, treat him like a string. You won't be able to push him around, so pull him along."

"I hope I get the chance," I said.

"Piece a cake." She shut the door behind her.

I knew very little about Eloy Grisham. I had heard about him from his mother, Graciella. She had been a good friend to my Grandfather. In fact, they had dated a little in-between his marriages. Grandfather's fourth wife did not like Graciella at all and told me the old gossip about Graciella Grisham and her notorious past.

Apparently, Graciella Luna was the eldest daughter of one of our first Hispanic families, part of the original Canary Islanders who helped to settle the city. Her family accused her of insulting their ancestry when, back in the early fifties, she eloped with a Yankee pilot trainee. She'd only known him a short while, had met him on Houston Street while he was on a weekend pass from basic training at Lackland Air Force Base. The marriage caused a lot of gossip, which only got worse when she announced her pregnancy right away. Freddy Grisham had to leave to go to Korea and became a casualty months before baby Eloy's birth.

The things I remember from that long ago always amaze me. Perhaps they are the things I can't forget. Why that stuck in my mind, over other events from my lifetime, is a mystery to me.

In one of the lower drawers of Phyllis's desk, I found a telephone directory and searched through the yellow pages until I found store numbers for each location of Eloy Grisham's business, a small chain of grocery stores called *Comida y Mas.* I doubted anyone at the store level would be helpful in getting an appointment with the chairman, so I changed my approach and found multiple listings in the white pages. I tried the main office number just in case someone was there, and got a recorded message that offered an emergency number. I decided to try the number.

A woman with a beautifully accented voice answered. "May I help you?"

"Oh, I do hope so," I was my most charming self. "This is Siobhan O'Shaughnessy, from KWNK," I threw in a reference to the station hoping it would carry weight, "and I'd like to meet with Mr. Grisham later this afternoon. Do you think it would be possible?"

"I will check," she answered abruptly. "Please hold."

At least she had not hung up on me. While I waited for the woman to return, Phyllis tapped on the door.

"You know who came in again yesterday? Lannie White."

I should have paid more attention to her, but BZ's new reluctance was on my mind. I told Phyllis, "BZ may be dropping out on me. He's getting cold feet."

"What? Why? From what you told me the other night, he wanted to be involved."

"He said he was worried. I think his wife made him

think about possibly getting fired."

She nodded and said, "You know, I understand that. BZ has two kids and a mortgage."

"And no trust fund," I added.

"Well, you don't either, at least not for now," she reminded me.

I pulled my face into an exaggeration of an older me. "Not until I'm old and gray."

"Don't do that," Phyl chastised. "Your face might stick. Then what would you do? Besides, forty-five isn't that far away. It's only about, what? Seventeen years?"

I groaned and I heard a distant voice calling me back to the phone. "Mr. Grisham says he would take you to lunch today. It is possible?"

"Yes, I'm free. Where should we meet?" I smiled up at Phyl, and she motioned to her watch, mouthed 'I have to go,' and slipped out the door.

"He is working from the Coliseum for the run of the event," the woman told me in her unique precise wording. "Will you meet him at The Cowboy Club?"

Her voice seemed familiar to me, "Yes, I'll be happy to meet him there. When, what time?"

"At one o'clock, when the crowd is not so much?" She suggested.

"Of course, that will be fine." I could hardly contain my excitement.

"And, how is your mother, Siobhan?" The voice surprised me with its question.

"Is this Mrs. Grisham? I am so sorry. I should have recognized your voice. I didn't expect anyone, much less you, to answer the phone; I'd heard you retired from the business."

"I have retired, but I am helping Eloy while he is out

for the duration. In the nicest way he asked me to fill in for him. I could not refuse. I am happy to help him because he has more to do there than here for the next month. Someone needs to be watching the stores." Her voice was full of pride in her son.

"Thank you for arranging this for me. I'm sure your influence helped me get the appointment."

"I may join you. Would it be troublesome? I do not wish to intrude."

Her question left no room for any answer other than, "No, please, I'd love to see you again."

"Goodbye then, Siobhan. I will see you at one o'clock at the Cowboy Club."

I replaced the receiver and tried to figure out how I really felt about her joining us. I did not know if it would help Paris's cause or not. Certainly, another woman's voice could not hurt, especially if that voice landed on the side of the dying girl. I went to find Phyl to tell her I had succeeded in getting an appointment with Eloy.

She smiled and wiggled her index finger at me. "Come with me, darlin'."

When I left the spa, I looked and felt considerably better than when I went in. There was no time for a Moneypenny Massage or a Boldfinger Manicure, but the Licensed to Kill Haircut made my day. Phyllis worked magic with her shears, shaped my hair, blew it dry with a big round brush until it fell smooth, shiny and sleek. Then she gave my face a couple of passes with a blush brush, insisted I try one of the new mascaras she had started carrying, and sent me off saying, "Go get 'em girl. Call me later and let me know what's up."

Chapter Nine

When I was a child, my grandfather insisted we take the stairs to the Cowboy Club during Rodeo, and leave the elevator to the elderly. I knew he and the older men preferred walking up the narrow staircase, and, until I was in my teens, I thought they were being courtly. It took that long for me to realize they liked taking the stairs because the steep and narrow steps offered more thrilling rewards.

The architecture created a tight passage that forced bodies to squeeze tightly against one another as they passed. Grandfather especially enjoyed the stairs when younger women, going the opposite direction, pressed against him. It was only after I developed a more womanly figure that he insisted we begin taking the elevator.

The Club, a members' only restaurant, was open only for the duration of Rodeo. It served a limited menu of steaks, burgers, and the like, but alcohol was its main attraction. No other place on the Coliseum grounds sold mixed alcoholic beverages. While it may not have had the best food in town, compared to the hot dogs, turkey legs and cold beer sold at the concessions stands, the Club offered sit down dining with a full service bar.

The membership, which changed annually, depending upon who participated in the exhibits that year, was an amalgamation of big ranchers from around the state, farmers from local counties, sponsors like the brewery reps from the big beer companies, and the members of A.L.E.C. Politicos from around the state belonged, and of course all sorts of local and national beauty queens had access, one or two of whom was present in the Club at all times. Patrons could always meet and have a photo taken with Miss Rodeo, Miss Texas, Miss Texas USA, Little Miss Rodeo, Miss Real County, and Miss Bexar County, Miss Guadalupe County, or other titled guests.

The beauty queens somehow managed to look comfortable in tight fitting, brightly colored western clothes. Each wore an attention-grabbing color, coordinated from boot to hat, outfits' custom-made by tailors who understood the need for yokes, sequins, and embroidery. Stetson hats, dyed to match, finished their ensembles, making them as conspicuous as Easter Eggs on fresh mown grass. More conventionally dressed women look tired and uninteresting by comparison.

While the Club had a lenient dress code, it was suggested one wear western attire: yokes and piping; snap front and cuffs; Roper or Lucchese; Stetson, Hi-Brehm or Resistol. Some of the crowd complied good-naturedly, while others competed as if vying for a prize. Tooled silver embellishments were everywhere, either on collar tips, hatbands, bolo tie-slides, belt buckles, or more flashy squash blossom necklaces. Men and women both sported chunky turquoise jewelry.

Even the most conservative local banker added something to reflect a commitment to Rodeo Week, usually boots and hat, occasionally a bolo tie, to westernize their more traditional Brooks Brothers suits.

I blended in among them quite nicely and felt inconspicuous, until I was escorted to the table where Eloy and Graciella Grisham waited for me. There I joined the center of the Cowboy Club universe.

Eloy was wearing another of his Nudie Cohn suits, a lavender one with matching M. L. Leddy custom boots. He provided the only true competition for the beauty queens. I actually felt sorry for him as he tried to eat his lunch between 'Hellos' and handshakes. He seemed to love the attention and almost vibrated with importance.

Graciella was quite the contrast in her all-black broomstick skirt, ruffled blouse, boots, dyed lambskin vest, and the most gorgeous turquoise and silver squash blossom necklace I had ever seen. With her hair pulled up a high French twist, she bore an uncanny resemblance to our local celebrity, the Mexican singer and star of *Fiesta del Noche*, Rosita Fernandez. During lunch, one of the Hispanic busboys asked for her autograph and refused to believe she was not the celebrity. She had hurt his feelings by refusing his request, something the real Rosita would never do.

She leaned over to me and confided, "He thinks I am Rosita. Should I sign something anyway?"

"I don't think you should impersonate her. Someone will explain to him." We watched another of the employees pointing and shaking his head.

There were few opportunities to speak to Eloy, and my plan to present him with information was not working. Constant interruptions from people vying for Eloy's attention made it impossible for me to discuss anything.

Graciella noticed my attempts to gain her son's attention and said, "You have a purpose, do you not? You called to speak to Eloy?"

"Yes, but I don't think I'll be able to talk to him here. It's so noisy and he is the man of the hour," I admitted.

"More the man of the year." Her voice could not hide the pride she felt in her son's accomplishment. "This volunteer position is taking more time than running the stores ever did."

She told me again how she came out of her own retirement to fill in for him and admitted it felt good to do so, for many reasons. "Eloy is the first non-Anglo to chair this event."

That statement made me realize how significant his appointment was to her, and wondered if his accomplishment made her feel vindicated. I'm sure she wished her parents were still living so they could see her son in such a prominent, high-profile position. I hope it assuaged the hurt she endured following her marriage to Eloy's father. Her words also made me consider what being chairman of this show might mean to her and to Eloy. I felt slightly more compassion for him.

Graciella made me realize the role Eloy's combined heritage played in his position of responsibility and acclaim. An unkind part of me wondered if the committee would have asked Eloy to fill the high profile role if his last name had sounded more Mexican, like Martinez or Gonzales.

I could see he had another reason for not wanting to change the status quo during his tenure. He wanted to prove he could do the job as well or better than any previous Anglo chairman.

I always think about the book and movie *Giant* and its underlying theme of cultural prejudice and how those old time bigotries still exist in parts of the state. Some people in San Antonio were actually dreading the inevitable day that an Anglo/Hispanic population flip will take place. The old guard, still shocked by the election of our first Hispanic mayor, didn't believe he could achieve the prominence national newscasters predicted.

The line of people waiting to shake Eloy's hand, unaffected by this underlying political refrain, wanted his attention. They annoyed me because they kept taking up time I needed to talk about Paris and Charga.

I decided to tell Graciella everything about the girl's illness, prognosis, and her reason for wanting so desperately to save the steer. I hoped she would become an advocate and talk to Eloy about it when they were alone.

"Have you heard about the Nash girl?" I asked Graciella while Eloy spoke to one of the suited throng.

"Do you mean the girl who raised the Grand Champion?" Graciella asked. "The girl who fainted at the steer judging?"

"Yes, have you heard her story?" I hoped she had not.

She frowned. "No, what story do you mean?"

"She is quite ill. Still hospitalized." I said.

"I wondered what happened to her," Graciella admitted. "I have only seen one story on the news. There has been gossip." She wrinkled her nose. "It seems the family is keeping private anything about her." She leaned close to me and whispered with her hand covering her mouth, "I hate gossip, but some people are saying she might be in the family way."

"No, that isn't it. I wish it were something so ordinary. The truth is, the girl is dying, Graciella." I stopped talking hoping the impact of what I said would take hold.

The expression on her face softened and it was at that

moment that Eloy interrupted to speak to me, "Siobhan how is your mother? I hear she now lives in Maine?"

I risked stretching the truth, "Yes, she lives in Maine and she loves it there. She's painting and sells quite a lot. She loves having her work admired."

I'd repeated what Grandfather last told me about my mother, pretending she and I shared a closer relationship than we did, hoping the stretch would save me from having to explain our estrangement.

In a moment of respite, Eloy remembered his manners and inquired about me. "How are you, Siobhan?"

"Fine, thank you. I am working at KWNK. Field reporting." I smiled.

"The station of her grandfather," Graciella added, showing surprising pride in my accomplishment.

"Yes, I saw your story on the judging," Eloy said. "Nice work."

"Thank you. In fact, that is why I wanted to meet with you." I seized the moment, "I have a question about the Grand Champion Steer. I think you spoke with Mr. Nash, the father of the girl who showed him."

"Yes, we spoke. The man said his daughter wanted to remove her steer from the auction," he laughed. "That's impossible. It's much too late for that."

"How so?" I asked, hoping to use the question as an entry to talk about the publicity A.L.E.C. would get from helping Paris save Charga.

"Tradition and the rules state the Grand Champion Steer goes to auction and is immediately transported to a processing plant. It is the purpose of the show: raising the animal, the judging, everything that goes into producing quality beef. It is not possible to pull the animal on a whim. There are many thousands of dollars, not to mention the reputation of our show, at stake here. How would it look to pull the Grand Champion Steer because a girl changes her mind?" He straightened his bolo tie, "Rules are made for reasons and ..."

I interrupted, "A.L.E.C. being magnanimous in this instance would generate positive publicity."

Graciella gave support to my story. "Eloy, the girl is gravely ill."

He looked from her to me. I nodded and added, "This isn't a whim. She is dying, Eloy. I need to know if there is any avenue we can explore to find a way to..."

He interrupted me. "There is no way to do this by Friday. No, I'm sorry." He stood and gave a curt bow in my direction. "Mama," he said, bending to kiss his mother's cheek. He turned his back to me and shook hands with another man who had been waiting patiently during our exchange.

Graciella reached for my hand, held it, and said, "Some things are better left unspoken, Siobhan."

Her comment puzzled me, and I pondered it as we left the Cowboy Club together, walking down the stairs to the concourse and saying our goodbyes. I asked if she had advice to give me.

"You are a very capable woman," she answered. "You have handled your life and the disappointments of your life with great poise and determination. I have noticed. You need no advice from me, Siobhan. You will do the right thing."

I knew the next right thing I had to do. I searched for a pay phone in the concourse so I could call BZ at home.

Chapter Ten

I woke BZ from a deep sleep and immediately asked, "Can you meet me at the hospital? I need your help. I have a plan."

"Will it get me fired?" He sounded drowsy, sleepy.

"No, it won't. Either it is something that will convince Bud we need to be involved, or it won't. Eloy wouldn't listen to anything I had to say about Paris or Charga, so if we are going to help her, we will have to get Bud on our side and work around A.L.E.C."

"I'll meet you at the hospital. In the lobby, okay?" BZ sounded game to try.

"No, come to Paris's room, 285. And, BZ..."

"Yes," he answered warily.

"...bring your camera equipment. We are going film her."

My next call was to Paris. She answered and without asking if she was free to talk, I told her BZ and I were coming by to film her telling her story. I wanted to get her reasons on tape.

"You want to film me? For television?"

"No, I have a different motive today. I want to take the tape to my boss. Are you up for it?"

"Sure, I can be ready in an hour, okay? I need to get cute for that." She giggled, acting the way any typical teenager would at such a request, and hung up.

BZ and I arrived at the hospital parking lot at the same time and I was able to help him load his equipment on the folding cart he used to transport it. Over the years, BZ had bought the best professional equipment anyone could wish for, usually at pawnshops around town, and worked side jobs to earn extra money. He often spent his weekends doing videos of weddings, baptisms and other events. The extra income he earned went into a college fund for his girls. The equipment, and the expertise he brought, made it possible for him to create exceptional results.

We made our way to the second floor and found Paris sitting cross-legged, yoga-like, in the hospital bed. She looked like any teenage girl sitting on her bed in her room, with the exception of the saline IV drip and shunt in her arm, those stark reminders Paris would never again be a typical teenage girl.

"Hi," she smiled and dramatically put the back of her hand to her forehead. She turned to profile and did her best Gloria Swanson: "I'm ready for my close-up." She laughed at her joke. "I saw that movie on T.V. just the other day." She added, "You must be BZ."

I'd been watching BZ's face to see his response to Paris. He had two lovely little girls and I knew his first thoughts would go to them. His eyes watered, and he turned his head to his work so Paris would not see, but I saw, and I knew he could not refuse helping her again.

118

Charlie, who had been sitting on the edge of the bed holding Paris's hand, got up to help BZ set up the tripod and lights. As I watched him, I realized what a perfect match he and Paris were for one another, even though they were opposites: Charlie, taciturn; Paris, gregarious; Charlie, swarthy; Paris, ethereal; Charlie, guarded; Paris, eloquently open. They were perfect for one another, and at that moment, I felt more compassion for Charlie losing Paris than I did for her leaving us. She would die in the midst of their young love, but he would live on holding that love as a standard for all future relationships. Charlie, too, was doomed in a way.

A nurse came in to take Paris's temperature, blood pressure, and pulse. They had stopped the IV fluids, but encouraged her to drink fluids to help her with hydration.

Paris asked the nurse, "Do you want to stay and be in the video?"

The nurse said "No," in a tone that told us she did not approve of such foolishness in *her* hospital.

A polite tap on the door rescued us from the woman's antipathy, and Franklin and Cardiff sidled past BZ's equipment, into the small room, both pressed and combed, prepared to go on camera if we need them. Paris reached her arms out to them, "Oh, good, you're here. I told them to come," she told me.

BZ tapped me on the shoulder. "I'm ready when you are." He extended his hand and introduced himself to Franklin and Cardiff.

"Thank you for your help," Franklin said.

"My pleasure," BZ answered.

I took a deep breath and cleared my throat. "The reason I've called this meeting. . ." I laughed at myself, and everyone else joined in. "I asked to do this because," I became serious and went on, "we have to get the station behind our attempt to save Charga. I met with Eloy Grisham at lunch today." I shrugged and shook my head indicating my lack of success.

Franklin muttered to Cardiff, "The little bastard's too busy getting his glory than to think about anyone else."

"Not now, Franklin," Cardiff patted his chest to stem his anger.

"The only way to get the station to help us," I continued, "even if it's only the assurance BZ and I won't lose our jobs if we help with this, is to win Bud Johnson's support. He's the station manager and our boss, and we have to get him to give us his blessing before we can go on."

BZ smiled and gave me a thumbs-up.

"So, I want to get Paris on tape. Thank you, BZ," I saluted in his direction. "It will be easier and faster to get a tape to Bud than it will be to get Bud to Paris."

Another tap at the door and Dexter Hardwick stuck in his head. He glanced at the camera and other equipment, ducked out and back in again. "This isn't the right room. Shouldn't we be on the obstetrics ward?" We looked at him with blank faces.

He looked at each of us with his face blank and wide-eyed. "A star is born? Right?"

We all groaned.

Paris asked, "So, Dr. Doom, got some news? Did they find out the lab made a terrible mistake and I only have the flu?"

"Nope, not quite. We found you only have," he looked at his watch, "a minute left to live."

Franklin stiffened, not liking the game they played, and Cardiff's hand went to her mouth, her horrified expression giving her husband pause. He held her close and shook his head.

Charlie grinned at Paris and the doctor. He was used to their irreverent banter. However, BZ and I were not used to it. Neither of us spoke. It was their game and we were not invited to play along.

Paris used her acting skill, became somber, and in a weak barely audible voice said, "I buried the bank robbery loot in a coffee can under the oak tree next to the. . .aaagh, cough, aaaaah." She slumped to one side, lay still, forced her eyes to roll up and let her tongue loll to one side of her mouth.

Dr. Hardwick applauded. Charlie did, too. The Nashes shook their heads in disapproval. BZ and I smiled.

I grabbed the Styrofoam carafe from the bedside table and announced, "For Best Performance in a Drama, the Styrofoam carafe," I fumbled with my notebook, pretending to hold an envelope, "goes to. . ." BZ did a drum roll on the nightstand. . . "Dr. Dexter Hardwick."

"Hey," the recently deceased Paris sat up, voicing bitter objection over the decision, "I should have won. . .I had my speech all ready."

"No doubt," Charlie teased.

She pouted and pointed an accusing finger at Dr. Doom. "Okay. But it's only because he's been in the business a lot longer than I have."

The pragmatic Franklin suddenly wanted to participate in the game. "They don't put men and women in the same category, do they? You should win for the best acting for women."

Paris smiled at him. "Thank you, Daddy. I knew you'd be on my side."

I looked at my watch, a signal to everyone that we needed to get the tape to Bud before he left the station for the day.

BZ caught my gesture and said, "Let's get to work."

Dr. Hardwick told us he would come back later. "I've got to go polish my pitcher." He clutched the carafe and left the room.

We did not use a script to tape Paris, nor had I listed the questions I thought important. I simply asked Paris to tell us, in her own words, as she told me when I visited with her before, why she wanted to save Charga.

This time, as she spoke, she did not sob. Tears streamed down her cheeks and her voice sounded tight, but she managed to convey everything: every fact and every emotion and with a simplicity that mirrored honestly and truthfulness. I could not imagine anyone saying no to her, not even Eloy Grisham.

Her mother and father looked away from her and then to one another, their anguish tangible in the stark room. I wished we had been able to get that on film, too. When Paris finished speaking, her mother went to her, both for and to comfort.

Charlie helped BZ pack his equipment, and I went to Paris. I complimented her on the wonderful job she had done telling her story. She looked up at me, smiled, and surveyed the room. Her dad had retreated to a corner where he wiped his eyes on a handkerchief while Cardiff wept silently sitting on the bed next to Paris, holding her daughter's hand.

"Let's see Dr. Doom top that!" She challenged, making us laugh aloud.

BZ pointed to his watch, reminding me we needed to get going and we said our goodbyes. As we walked by the end of Paris's bed on our way out, BZ squeezed her foot. "See ya. Nice meeting you," he said.

I waved and blew a kiss. "I'll call as soon as I have news."

In the elevator, BZ handed the tape to me. On the ride down he said, "I'm sorry about all this talk about me needing to drop out, but Sylvia started me worrying about my job."

I nodded.

"I've got two little girls of my own, you know."

I nodded again and told him, "There's a reason for everything, and I bet what Paris did today will make you think about those two little girls in a whole different way."

His eyes watered. "Yeah, she already did."

"You are a good daddy," I reassured him. "I understand about your reluctance, but if Bud tells us it's okay with him for us to go on?"

"I'll be there. I'll do everything I can think of, but first I have to be sure my job isn't at stake."

"I'll do what I can," I promised, as the doors to the elevator opened on the ground floor. We went our separate ways, he home to his family and me off to the station where I hoped I would find Bud Johnson in an amiable mood, which was not always the case at the end of a long day.

I was surprised to find the Sunday traffic running heavy from downtown to the station. It usually flowed easily on weekends, but today, because I needed to be there in a hurry, it did not.

It seemed like the crazies were out to get me. Drivers either poked or darted, making me brake and accelerate as traffic determined. Two elderly drivers, in different colors of the same big Oldsmobile, drove side by side, well below the posted limit, making sure no one broke the speed maximum. It felt as if they had received an urgent broadcast from the universe to keep the woman in the old blue Mustang from reaching her destination and did their damnedest to comply.

All the way, I worried that Bud would leave before I could get there and didn't feel my body relax until I saw his black SUV parked in its usual front door parking space. I raced up the fire stairs, instead of taking the elevator. I bounded into the deserted newsroom; everyone except Bud had either left for the day or was in the studio participating in the six o'clock news broadcast.

I could see a halo of light emanating from around Bud's tall desk chair and knew he was watching our team's news report. I tapped on his door, he swung around, and as soon as he saw who it was, he motioned for me to step inside, put a finger to his lips and turned to give his undivided attention to Tracy delivering a story about a tiny kitten trapped in a sewer drain. She amazed me. Even when talking about a sewage-covered kitten, the woman smiled.

Tracy set up Larry Sweeten's weather report with an inane segue about rain to wash the kitten clean, and Bud turned his chair around to give me his full attention.

"What are you doing back here? I gave you time off."

"And, I thank you for the time off, but I really need to talk to you about something." I held up the cassette. "I need to ask for your help."

"What do you have for me?" He gestured to it.

"Well, Bud, this is something I feel very strongly about. I think I should give you some background before I show. . ."

"A good story speaks for itself," he gestured for me to hand him the tape.

"Well, Bud. . ." I stammered.

"Gimme," he said.

I shrugged, handed him the tape and hoped BZ had rewound it to start at the top before he took it out of his camera. Bud swiveled away from me and slid the VHS case into its slot in the player.

Chapter Eleven

The screen remained dark, but I heard my voice encouraging Paris to, "Just be you." Then the screen filled with light and Paris, sitting cross-legged on the white sheeted hospital bed looking small and lovely, her dark hair and blue eyes capturing the screen.

"Paris, in your own words would you please tell us your story," my voice directed.

She took a deep breath and squared her shoulders to the camera. She began to speak, "My name is Paris Nash, and I am dying." BZ zoomed on her beautiful young face. "I have advanced melanoma cancer and the doctors tell me I probably have about six months to live. I am fifteen years old and my steer Charga won Grand Champion at the Livestock Show. He will only live until this Friday unless you help me save him. You see, there are these rules. . ."

Paris mesmerized on camera. She had a natural delivery, even through tears, sounded clear, and poised, her soft-spoken words holding unquestionable meaning.

Bud did not move. I could not see his face, could not tell if he was reacting to her plea. She told about A.L.E.C. rules and explained how her father tried to change Eloy's position on the matter. She repeated Eloy's flip response about paying the hospital bills. Then she told about the day she went searching for a calf to raise and how she'd found Charga, why and how she had chosen his name, and about the promise she had made him.

". . . and, so you see, I promised Charga he would be the way for me to get an education. I told him I wanted to go to A&M and become a veterinarian. I believe he understood our agreement and that he knew he was going to make that sacrifice for me. I know this sounds crazy, but I think he was willing to die because he knew his life had a purpose, like I believed I had a purpose. . ."

Now tears were streaming down my face. Bud still had not moved. I had no idea what he was thinking about Paris.

". . .or at least I thought I did, but like my new friend Siobhan told me," she smiled to where I'd been standing off camera, "about a Jewish proverb that says 'Man plans, God laughs', and well, God must be having a real knee slapper about me." She forced a wan smile that tore at my heart. Bud still did not move.

"I need help to save Charga. The promise I made to him isn't good anymore because I can't keep my word. I won't be going to A&M." She smirked, referring to Eloy's flip remark, "and I don't want him to die for my hospital bills." She paused and after a moment looked into the camera. BZ zoomed in on her eyes again, her lashes wet with tears. "Please help me save Charga."

I dug for another tissue in my bag because tears were obscuring my vision. I looked up when I heard what

128

sounded like a garbled sob. Bud Johnson was sitting in his swivel chair, his arms folded on top of his desk, his face hidden in them. Bud sobbed, too.

I did not know what to do. I wanted to go to him, but I stayed where I sat. His tears confused me. I had not expected that kind of emotion from him. I knew why I was emotional. I had a friendship with Paris Nash, but Bud's reaction seemed out of proportion. This was our local Walter Cronkite, our Charlie Gibson. As I waited for the consummate professional to stop crying, I thought about the people who had told me how he had covered everything from JFK's assassination to the Challenger shuttle disaster without so much as a quaver in his voice. I wished they could see him now.

I did not understand why the tape had affected him like this. When I decided to bring the tape to him, I thought he would look at it as just another story. Bud never reacted emotionally to any story, always made decisions based upon what would be good TV news.

I sat silent and motionless. After a few minutes, he pulled a handkerchief from his pocket lifted his head, blew his nose, wiped his eyes and glared at me. "You pulled a damned dirty trick, Siobhan."

I did not know what to say. His reaction exceeded anything I had expected.

"Who told you?" He challenged me through tightly clenched jaws.

"Told me?" If my expression conveyed only half my confusion, he would understand I did not know what he meant. "Bud, no one told me anything. I brought this tape. . ."

The expression on his face made me stop speaking. His lips narrowed as his eyes filled with tears, he shook his head and looked away from me. "Pull the damn curtains."

I pulled the cord to close the last sheer drapery and mentally zipped my mouth tightly shut. I sat back across from Bud's desk and looked at him expectantly.

"I still want to know who told you," he squinted, calling me a liar.

He made me feel like an innocent person charged with murder in one of the film noirs I liked to watch. I stayed silent.

Bud paced behind his desk muttering, "No one here knows."

I heard him murmur those four words repeatedly as he paced. He stopped, closed his eyes as if trying to clear some vision from his mind, and sat behind his desk again.

After a few moments sitting silently, "Bud," I began softly, not wanting to disturb the quiet, "I don't know what happened here, but I am very sorry for whatever I did that upset you so much." I did not mention BZ; I used the royal *we.* "We wanted to ask for your help, and since we were moved by Paris telling us her story, we thought if she told you, then you might understand why we feel the way we do."

Bud reached inside his top desk drawer and took out a small dark blue, leather-bound case. He pushed a small latch on its side and as the case popped open, he turned it toward me. On one side, a much younger Bud Johnson held an infant; on the other, an older Bud, nose-to-nose with a child of about twelve, both their heads shaved white. "Alyssa Marie," he told me.

I fought new tears as I realized what I had done. I tried to apologize, "Bud, I'm so sorry. If I'd known..." There were no adequate words to express my sorrow.

I waited for him to speak. Several minutes later, he told me the story of his only child.

"She was a precious girl. She fought hard, but she died a year after they told us she had leukemia. She had chemotherapy at St. Jude's, but the treatments did not faze the kind of cancer she had. It took her life. She always wanted to be a teenager, but didn't make it to December. She died in August when she was still just twelve years old.

"What got me about this, Oshun," he pointed to the television screen where we had just watched Paris Nash, "is that Alyssa's last words to me were, 'Daddy, please take care of Baby Flea. She's going to miss me'. There is something about girls and their animals, isn't there?"

My throat tightened and we cried together. Bud for his precious Alyssa Marie, and me for Bud, the pain I had not meant to, but did, cause him, and for Paris Nash, and probably a little for myself.

"It's been over twelve years since Alyssa died," he told me, "and sometimes it comes back so full of force that it feels like it all happened just yesterday. After Alyssa, my wife and I joined a support group at church, and they warned us it would be like this, 'the horrible pain won't ever go away, but the times you feel it will get further and further apart.' I haven't cried like this in quite a while."

We spent several minutes talking about his daughter's life, about her death and the end of his marriage, "Which they also warned us about in support group. Most marriages don't survive the death of a child, and ours sure didn't." He stopped for a moment, then said, "Alyssa would be twenty-four years old if she'd lived. I'd maybe be getting ready to walk her down the aisle, or be a grandfather, probably still be married to Eleanor." He shrugged.

"After what would have been her twenty-fourth birthday, I thought I'd healed. When she had been gone longer than she lived, I thought it would be less painful, but time never heals this loss." He looked away from me.

I smoothed and refolded my damp tissue and thought about how easy it is to make assumptions about people when you do not know their story. I always thought he was aloof and distant, but I would never see him that way again.

When we got back to talking about Paris and the reason for the video that started it all, I told him about BZ and how we were both worried about our jobs. I explained that we did not necessarily expect the station to take any action on Paris's behalf, but we both needed assurance, that whatever we did regarding Paris on our own time, we would stay employed.

Bud smiled at me. "You won't get fired; neither will BZ. Short of killing Eloy Grisham, that is." His joke made me feel more at ease. "Okay?" He laughed and then was serious again. "Please don't say anything to anyone about my daughter. I've kept his secret very close to my heart, and I wouldn't have shared it with you if Paris hadn't reminded me so much of Alyssa."

I nodded and promised him I would not say a word to anyone.

"And you'd better not treat me any differently, young lady, because I'll go back to being the mean son-of-a-bitch I've come to be. Got it?"

I smiled and nodded at him, glad we were friendly again. "Bud, before I go can I ask one more question."

He looked at me and shrugged, "What?"

"What is a Baby Flea?"

He laughed. "Baby Flea was Alyssa's flea-bitten appaloosa mare that lived to be about twenty-nine years old. I spent more time and money on that horse than anything else before or since. Do you know how much it costs to bury a dead horse?" He smiled and looked upward. "But I kept my promise to you, sweetheart."

I could not stop myself. I gave him a long hug before I left his office. His revelation would forever change the way I saw him. I never told anyone about his daughter. I had promised him I would not. I always keep my promises.

Driving home, I could not stop thinking about him, Paris, Alyssa Marie, and about my own mother. I had never been able to understand how she could leave me the way she did. I'd watched Bud, a grown man whose daughter's death decimated his life, and about the Nashes, whose daughter's happiness means everything to them. I couldn't help but compare them to my mother, a drive-by parent at best, who couldn't even remember to send a birthday card. The contrasts saddened me and made me promise myself, if ever I had a child, I would not be the kind of mother mine had been to me.

Then, I had another thought. If it were I dying, who would grieve for me? I had no family. Grandfather was gone, and my mother would not miss me. I guessed Phyllis would be the only person I could count on to cry.

Chapter Twelve

I called BZ as soon as I dropped my keys on the front hall table. It was later than I thought because it took longer with Bud than I anticipated. I heard the anxiety in BZ's voice when he answered the phone.

Without giving him any of the details about Bud's daughter or his reaction to the tape, I told BZ, "Short of murdering Eloy Grisham, we have Bud's blessing. We can help Paris Nash."

He sounded relieved. "Listen, we have to meet at Tristan's first thing in the morning. I've been thinking. My cousin and I talked. I've got a plan."

"So now your cousin knows, too?"

He laughed at my concern, "I'll tell you all about everything tomorrow."

We confirmed the meeting time and I hung up the phone, sat on the edge of the bed and, thought about what I'd learned in Bud's office.

The phone rang, Phyllis calling to ask, "How'd it go with Eloy?"

"It's a long story. Everything turned out okay in the end. Nevertheless, Eloy wouldn't budge. You know, Phyl, this seems crazy, but he won't consider doing anything to jeopardize the status quo with A.L.E.C."

"Does he have a good reason?"

"He didn't give one, other than it's against the rules, but I think it's because he's the first Hispanic to hold the job. You know how unwilling the A.L.E.C. people are to do anything new or different. Appointing Eloy as chairman went halfway to breaching their history of maintaining Anglo dominance.

Phyllis said, "I didn't realize there never was a Hispanic chair before Eloy."

"Nope, never, and they've yet to have a woman, a black, an Asian or Native American. They've done everything the same way, year after year after year, tradition, tradition, tradition."

"What is *Fiddler on the Roof?*" she answered like a contestant on "Jeopardy." I loved my friend Phyllis. No matter how serious a situation we found ourselves in, she would come up with some non sequitur to make me laugh.

"It's obvious to me that Eloy's mother considers the appointment an honor, and I doubt he will do anything to break the established long-standing traditions. He won't risk making a mistake. The good part is BZ feels reassured and is back on-board. I showed Bud a video of Paris, and he gave us dispensation for anything other than murdering Eloy Grisham."

I didn't tell Phyllis what had happened in Bud's office, even though I wanted to share his story so badly. I'd always shared everything with Phyl. This was a first.

"I'm glad the station has your back," she said.

"We would love to have the newspapers involved, but I don't think we have enough time, and I don't have any contacts high up at either daily paper. If we get something in print, we might be able to generate a strong enough public outcry to force A.L.E.C. to pay serious attention to Paris's plea."

"Lannie White is my client," Phyl said quietly.

"Lannie White? The columnist for the *Light*?"

"I told you when you were here earlier. She is a new regular client of mine."

I had totally missed the connection. I was so preoccupied with trying to see Eloy that morning that I did not remember her saying anything about Lannie White.

"Yep, Lannie's had that front-page column forever. I'll give her a call and ask if she'd be interested in doing an exclusive story about Paris."

I thanked her, said good night, and drifted off to sleep, thinking I could not wait to tell BZ that my friend Phyllis had a connection to Lannie White. I would call him first thing in the morning to tell him. A soft haze enveloped me and I realized how relieved I was to have him committed to helping, again. BZ inspired confidence in me the way Phyllis did, and it occurred to me that he and Phyllis were the female and male versions of the same supportive personality. With them on my side, I believed I could accomplish anything.

The phone ringing woke me, and I looked at the clock with one eye open. It was not yet seven o'clock in the morning. I wanted to roll over and ignore it. Instead, I moaned, gave in, and mumbled, "Hello."

"Hey, you up?" BZ asked when I finally picked up the

receiver.

"Now I am."

"I'm going to be at Tristan's in about forty-five minutes. Get the lead out," he urged without sympathy. I could hear in his voice excitement about the plan he'd come up with.

"Hey, BZ," I interrupted, "Phyl is calling Lannie White for us. Bye." I hung up the phone. I felt smug satisfaction at giving him something to think about for a change.

As soon as I walked into Tristan's, BZ waved me over to the corner table where he waited.

"I already ordered your *Chilaquiles*," he told me as Tristan delivered a steaming plate to the table. BZ grinned at me. "The way to anybody's heart."

Tristan laughed, and out of pure orneriness, I dropped my purse onto the seat of an empty chair, scooted closer to the table, my chair leg screeching against the linoleum floor, and fixed my elbows on either side of the plate. I rested my chin on my palms, pretended I was not starving and that the steaming aromatic food could not buy my heart.

"Spill," I commanded BZ.

"Eat," he directed.

I did not need more encouragement. I put a fork full of egg and cheese sauce into my mouth and drifted into the caloric ecstasy of a heart won over with food.

Tristan pulled a spare chair over to our table, flipped it around, straddled it, and watched me eat. BZ waited until I took another bite before he said, "Tristan is going to help us steal the steer."

I tried to say, "What?" but made an incoherent sound instead. The look on my face must have completely confirmed my confusion over this latest development.

"Wait a minute, and listen to me before you get all

worried," BZ cautioned. "I know you're worried about getting too many people involved, but we need him. I've got it all figured out."

Tristan smiled at me, a new co-conspirator in the plan. Obviously, he already knew the plot.

BZ explained. "If Phyllis can get Lannie to write a column about Paris it will be a big plus for us. Did Phyllis get her to help?"

"She's hasn't called to tell me. It's only eight o'clock."

"Well, if she will write a column," BZ continued, "then when the steer is stolen, the story will be everywhere, on all channels, radio and television stations, and all over the paper, not in just one isolated column. If Lannie interviews Paris and publishes the whole story, the public will react. *Viola*, Charga will live."

I swallowed. "Go back to the *is stolen* part? Who is going to steal the Grand Champion Steer?"

His index finger circled the air. Then he stopped to butter a flour tortilla.

"Us? We are going to steal a steer?" I was incredulous. "That's cattle rustling, a crime, BZ. A felony and if I remember correctly," I used the loudest whisper I could manage, "hanging for cattle rustling is still on the books."

BZ, looking totally blasé, took a bite of the tortilla. The man was trying my patience.

I sounded sarcastic when I said, "You've figured out how we are going to successfully smuggle a twelve-hundred pound bovine from the pen in front of the Coliseum, in front of God and everybody?"

He grinned first at me, then at Tristan. "It's genius. Pure genius."

Tristan nodded enthusiastically.

"Past the security guards at the gate?" I added to my doubt.

Tristan stood up, flipped the chair back around and slid it under the table. As he walked away he mentioned, "But we have to do it tonight."

I had always done as I'd been taught as a child and chewed food with my mouth closed, but I think that particular moment qualified as a legitimate exception to rules of etiquette. Under these circumstances, anyone's jaw would have fallen open. "Tonight?"

"Yes, we have to do it while Paris is still in the hospital," BZ explained, "so she won't be suspected."

I stared at him, waiting for more information.

"Charlie needs to be there with Paris. And her parents need to be there too," he added. "It can't look like any of them have anything to do with taking Charga, or the A.L.E.C. bunch will file charges. That would make this a bigger nightmare than it already is."

"So *we* can do it and get arrested, instead? No big deal for us." I wondered if they had considered that little detail.

"We won't even be suspects," BZ assured me.

"I've got to hear this plan," I leaned toward him, "from the beginning."

BZ explained it in detail, and I could not believe his idea actually sounded feasible.

"How did you come up with all of this so fast? Yesterday you weren't even sure you were going to be involved at all. How did you get Tristan and the other's to agree to it? BZ, you mystify me."

He grinned. "Last night my cousin, Tristan, and I came up with it right here." He tapped the table. "You can't get a bunch of Mexicans thinking and not come up with genius," he bragged. "It's *una peligrosa aventura.*"

Tristan came back to our table. "What do you think of our dangerous adventure?"

I agreed with them. "It's pure genius." I thought to myself, *there are lot of ifs and buts, and if even one thing goes wrong, we are in deep shit, but it is genius.*

I started my part of the plan as soon as I left them. I went to the hospital and told Charlie and Paris that my friend had come up with a plan to get Charga home. I did not tell them how BZ's genius plan worked. I simply asked them to trust us; we did not want to give out details because it would be better for them if they were ignorant. Then I asked if I could have Charlie's FFA jacket, cap, and the key to Charga's pen.

"I won't tell my parents anything about what you are doing, Paris said. They left for Kingsland early this morning to talk to my sisters and brothers. They wanted to tell them about me before the press conference tomorrow morning. They're going to come back tonight and spend the night at a hotel so they won't be late for the press conference."

Charlie added, "They're taking Paris home right after the press conference tomorrow. Dr. Doom released her."

BZ was correct. We had to do it tonight. It was our last chance. We had to follow through before the family left for Kingsland. Tonight, they would have an alibi. As long as Paris remained in the hospital, she would not be a suspect.

After I got Charlie's blue FFA cap and jacket and the keys to the padlock on Charga's pen, I called Phyl from Paris's hospital room to tell her she had a part to play in the plan to steal the steer.

"Girl, you must be psychic. Lannie White called me back a few minutes ago. I told her a little bit about Paris, and she wants to do an interview with Paris. Tonight!"

I could not believe the way everything was falling

together. It was if we stepped onto the exactly right path, and the universe had decided to reward us in a mighty way. I hoped everything held together and did not come apart like seams on a cheap skirt.

Phyllis continued. "She wants to meet with you and the Nash family around eight tonight. I pretty much promised her you would be there. I told Lannie everything I knew about the aunt and what you've told me. I don't have the exact details. I told her you did, so she wants you to be there, too. Lannie can't wait to do the column. You know she loves punching holes in petty bureaucracies. Well, she can't wait to take on A.L.E.C."

"Phyl, you are wonderful. Will you call and tell her we will all be here at eight tonight. I'll meet her in the lobby."

I felt a tiny bit sorry for Eloy; I would hate to be in his shoes when Lannie finished with him and A.L.E.C.

"And Phyl, while I have you on the phone there is one other little thing we'd like you to do for us."

"Anything."

She possibly wished she had not answered that quickly after I told her what we wanted her to do.

Paris and Charlie were listening to my side of the conversation, and as soon as I hung up, I told them what Phyllis said about Lannie White wanting to schedule an interview at eight that night.

Paris was ecstatic. "For the first time I really believe Charga will be okay."

I asked her to get in touch with her parents to make certain they would be at the hospital before eight o'clock. I guessed Lannie wanted to meet with them, too. When I left, Paris was dialing her parents at home to tell them they had to hurry back to San Antonio.

Phyllis's part of our adventure was for her to take a bag of range cubes to Tristan's around six o'clock that night. I asked her to wait for me there. I thought I would be finished with Lannie's interview between nine and ten o'clock. I wanted her to ride with me when we took Charga out of town.

I had told her, "If you don't want to wait all that time at Tristan's place, come back around nine. He'll be closed, and the front door will be locked, so park your car around back and use the service door, okay?"

I returned to Tristan's for the second time that day to give BZ a run-down of the conversations I had with everyone. BZ was sitting at the same table where we had our breakfast, but this time a teenage boy who looked amazingly like Charlie Garza occupied the extra chair at the table.

BZ introduced me to Pepe, his cousin's teenage son. Earlier he had told me the boy was integral to the success of our plan, "Pepe is perfect for the job."

I had balked about how many people were getting involved but BZ argued me into submission. He had sworn, "The plan can't work without Pepe." It was obvious to me why.

I handed Pepe the jacket, cap, and key Charlie had given me. The jacket fit a little looser on him than it had on Charlie. Pepe was slightly leaner, but had the same jet-black hair and light olive skin. The shape of his face was Charlie's shape, and his eyes crinkled like Charlie's when he smiled. I could not wait to introduce the doppelgangers to each other.

BZ told Pepe, "Go out to my car and get the sweatshirt from the back seat. Wear it under the jacket."

Pepe grinned at Tristan and squared his shoulders. "I'll eat more today," he said.

BZ's enthusiasm about the plan flared my

imagination. The more he talked, the more comfortable I got with the idea of stealing the steer from the Coliseum. Either we were going to have one magnificent *una peligrosa aventura*, or we would all end up in jail.

Pepe left to get the sweatshirt, and I took the opportunity to tell BZ about Lannie White and the interview planned for eight o'clock that night. When I finished, BZ started bragging about his plan, "See. I told you everything would work out." He practically crowed he was so proud.

"You did no such thing," I contradicted.

"Yep, I did. I told you, 'If Bud gives us an okay, it's no holds barred'."

"Well, yes, but I didn't think you were speaking for the entire universe. Seriously, BZ, why are Tristan, Pepe and your cousin doing this? They don't even know Paris. Why are they risking so much? Don't they realize what we could be getting into?"

He smiled at me. "Its *la familia, Gringa*. Something you will never understand. We Hispanics place more value on family than most other cultures even think about. I only had to tell them I needed help and they were there."

Pepe returned, and BZ started bragging about Pepe's dad, Luis. "My cousin, his dad," he pointed at Pepe, "goes into these bars carrying beer kegs, one in each hand, right Pepe?" BZ fake-punched the boy's bicep and the youngster ducked and backed off like a boxer. "It's going to work, Oshun!" BZ was as guy-giddy as I had ever seen him.

I was still thinking about what he'd said about me never understanding about family. He was right on target. I did not understand how family worked because I had never known that kind of support. To me, family was the place I went when I had no other place to go. I had never experienced how normal families function.

My grandfather had tried his best to be both mother and father to me, him and his wives and girlfriends. However, the more time I spent with the Nash and Zuniga families, I knew my grandfather had failed. For the first time I was seeing what belonging to a family meant and began to understand how much I'd missed in my life because of my upbringing.

Somehow, I'd gravitated to these people, and they'd given me a sense of belonging, one I had never known before. I realized they were extending themselves to me, welcoming me. It felt good to know I was surrounding myself with people I could trust and depend upon.

BZ said, "I can't wait to read Lannie's column tomorrow!"

I gave Pepe the instructions I got from Charlie and told him he needed to follow Charlie's same routine. He had difficulty following my dialogue and after several attempts to explain, I decided we all needed a walk through.

"How about a field trip?" I asked.

Since we had a long afternoon to spend, we decided to go to the Coliseum grounds so we could show Pepe what he needed to do that night. We took separate cars, arriving simultaneously, pretending we did not know one another. When we got there, I went straight to Charga's enclosure and they followed a few minutes behind. We acted like strangers who simply happened to be in the same place.

I climbed up on the railing of Charga's pen and reached over to pet the big steer. He ignored me, even though I called out, "Charga, Charga, come here, boy."

He finally looked up when I said, "Paris misses you." He actually turned his head and looked at me. He lumbered over to where I was and let me scratch him on the wavy spot between his wide-set eyes. He ducked his head so I could scratch where the halter wrapped behind his ears. I kept saying, "Paris" and as long as I spoke her name, he stood still, but as soon as I stopped, he lumbered back to the hay. Pepe and Charlie watched my success and tried to call him over.

"Charga, boy. Come over here, Charga."

For a second I think Pepe's likeness to Charlie confused the poor steer, because he tilted his head and sniffed the air. He figured it out, because he didn't venture away from the hay he was eating.

I walked close by and said, "Say Paris to him."

Soon Charga ambled over and let Pepe scratch his head while BZ ran his hand on the animal's side. I could not help smiling as I listened to the two of them crooning, "Paris, Paris, Paris" to soothe the big red steer.

People started arriving in larger numbers around five o'clock. Alan Jackson was the headliner for the concert that night, and the grounds were filling with his fans arriving to beat the evening traffic jam. The rodeo started at seven and the concert let out around eleven. Then the standing-room only audience would flee from the Coliseum like ants from a twig-poked hill. At least we counted on that scenario being the case.

Charlie's routine was to feed Charga during the evening concert when fewer people were out. He told me he always exercised Charga by walking him around the grounds, to the cow wash for a bath; after bathing him, he would leave Charga in a temporary pen until he cleaned up the pen out front. He changed the water and put out fresh hay, and then after he finished the housekeeping, he'd lead Charga back to his fresh and tidy Grand Champion enclosure, which meant he kept Charga away from his pen for about an hour each evening. No one would be suspicious if the pen were empty for that amount of time.

The winning handler, even though technically no longer the owner of the steer, was still responsible for taking care of the animal until the auction. Normally, it would be Paris doing the routine every-day tasks. Her willing siblings all volunteered to take care of Charga, but that would have meant missing school, and besides, Charlie wanted to do it so he could stay in San Antonio with Paris. Paris liked the idea because she wanted him close, too, and insisted he be the one to fill in for her because "Charga knows Charlie. He won't balk with Charlie."

When I went to get Charlie's jacket that morning, he whispered his secret to me. "It is because Charlie keeps range cubes in his pockets at all times. That's why Charga likes me so much."

Phyllis had to buy range cubes, for Pepe to fill his pockets with them.

I walked away from the pen and stopped at one of the nearby concession stands, bought a cotton candy, and headed to the area where Charlie told me I would find the cow wash. Pepe and BZ bought two sodas at the same stand and, from a safe distance, followed me.

As we approached the cow wash, a girl was in the process of washing her Black Angus steer with a soft long-handled brush. A tall boy dodged to avoid an errant water spray: teenage flirting. Charlie told me the handlers used the cow wash as a meeting place: several were standing nearby waiting.

The loading ramp BZ remembered being near the cow wash was only sixty feet farther down the road. The dock was the loading place we'd use for Charga that night. Charlie assured me no one would be around because, "Every night the kids go inside to see the concert."

We walked back to the entrance and stopped at

Charga's pen on our way out. I reached inside to scratch the curly topknot on Charga's huge head. "You'll be seeing Paris real soon," I told him.

The huge steer looked at me, snorted, and I imagined him thinking, "You keep promising, but I haven't seen any action. I want results."

I had never seen Charga be anything but gentle. Nevertheless, as I stood appraising his size, I would not want him angry with me. A twelve-hundred pound animal could do serious damage by accidentally stepping on a foot. I could only imagine what an irate steer would be able to do with intent.

We left the Coliseum after Pepe felt assured he could do Charlie's routine. I had time to go home and change before I went to the hospital. I wanted to be presentable when I met Lannie White.

As I left Pepe and BZ, they yelled, "Break a leg." I walked away, pretending to be unconcerned, but my stomach was buzzing like a hive full of angry bees.

Chapter Thirteen

A middle-aged woman was waiting in the hospital foyer where I was supposed to meet Lannie White. She looked like an older version of Lannie's byline photo.

I extended my hand, "Siobhan O'Shaunessy."

"I recognize you from the news," she told me. "Lenore Landrieu White, but call me Lannie."

I read her column every day and had pictured her being a modelesque Amazon woman. I looked down on her from my lofty five foot four. She was not a large woman. She carried a pen and pad, toted a large Gucci handbag, wore a simple black suit and a look of serene volatility. I sensed the presence of power.

I guided her to the elevator bank that arrived closest to Paris's room and when we reached the second floor, led the way to Paris's door. I tapped and Franklin Nash greeted us.

"Come on in," Franklin invited.

I introduced Lannie to him, and he told her, "I've been

impressed by your column for years."

Cardiff smiled shyly and extended her hand. Charlie, sitting on the bed next to Paris, stood to meet Lannie, and Paris reached out her hand. "Thank you for doing this," Paris said.

Lannie White may have been the smallest person in the room; however, when she said, "Let's see what I do before I get the thank you," the Amazon was revealed.

Chairs scraped across the shiny-waxed floor as everyone gathered closer to Paris's bed. First Lannie interviewed from a list of questions she had prepared on her notepad. They covered the same information Paris had shared on tape. Next, Lannie asked Franklin about his meeting with Eloy.

"The little…"

"Now, Franklin," Cardiff interrupted, her hand on his arm.

"Sorry, Ma'am," Franklin nodded. "Eloy said nothing could be done. The rules were the rules. We should sell the steer and use the money to pay the hospital bills."

Lannie made brief notes, turned to me, "And, your meeting, Siobhan?"

"I think he's afraid to rock the Anglo boat," I encapsulated my experience with the Chairman.

Lannie laughed. "Well put. I get that."

"I've known his mother for years," I explained, "and she came to lunch with us. She is very proud they asked her son to chair this year's event. She was the one who helped me understand why Eloy does not want anything to go wrong during his tenure. I drew my own conclusion about it being because he's the first Hispanic to fill the role."

"I think you're right, Siobhan. He's over-compensating because of the Anglo-intimidation factor."

Lannie turned to Cardiff and asked if she had anything to add to the discussion about Eloy.

"This is my fault," Cardiff cried, breaking down completely for the first time. "If I'd taken Paris to Austin or brought her here to have that mole looked at, maybe..." Sobs racked the slight woman, and we knew it was the strain breaking her reserve.

"Mom," Paris swung her legs over the side of her bed and rushed to her mother. "I've already told you. Do not feel guilty. Don't. It's not your fault. It's not anyone's fault."

Cardiff wrapped her arms around her daughter and sobbed.

Lannie bowed her head as if in church and the rest of us were mice, frozen in place, the moment too private to interrupt. Charlie remained steadfast and calm. Franklin offered support by standing behind his wife and patting her shoulder.

When Cardiff's tears abated, Charlie helped Paris get back into bed, while Franklin knelt in front of his wife.

The mood had changed. Cardiff's tears were strong reminders that Paris's condition was terminal. The concerns about Charga made it easy for us to forget how ill she really was.

Lannie broke the silence when she asked Paris to explain what she wanted the public to know.

"I want them to know I want Charga to avoid the slaughterhouse. I want to take him home to Kingsland with me. You can say I'm going to die if it helps explains why."

Lannie clipped her pen to the spiral of her notebook. "I think I have my article. Thank you all for your time."

Paris added, "Dr. Doom came to tell me he is letting me go home tomorrow. He's going to hold a mini-press conference in the morning and we'll all be there to answer questions from the media, and then my Mom and Dad will drive me home."

Lannie said, "That's good with me. I have my exclusive article. It will run in the morning paper and everyone will have the whole story regardless of what happens at the press conference. I'm going back to the paper to work on it now. I've only got a couple of hours before the morning press run."

"Can we see the article before it's printed?" Franklin wanted to know.

"No, sorry, it's against all the rules," Lannie gave a rueful smile. "But I promise you, Franklin, you are going to like it."

Lannie left Paris's room, and most of the energy went with her. Tomorrow Paris would go home, and the realization hit me, again. She is going there to die.

In that moment, I knew all of the risks we were taking to save Charga were worth it. By saving him, we were giving Paris something she dearly wanted, something that would make her remaining life less burdened. The outcome of *una peligrosa aventura* was important. We were going to give Paris a victory.

Franklin tried to lighten the mood by telling Paris about a few surprises her brothers and sisters had in store back at the ranch.

"Rome is cooking. He's actually making chicken and dumplings for you. Can you imagine that, Paris? Rome in the kitchen? I wish I could be a fly on the wall to watch that."

"And," Cardiff was faking enthusiasm, "who do you think ironed every last thing out of your laundry bag?"

Paris's eyes widened. "Not India?"

"Yep, India." Franklin smiled.

"Everything?" Paris looked incredulous. "I think there were some things in the bottom from fifth grade that don't even fit me anymore."

"Yep, she found them. And they look real good on her," Cardiff chuckled, this time with a genuine mirthful expression. "They're just her size."

By the time, I left the hospital, the mood had gradually changed to eager anticipation of Paris's homecoming the next day. Franklin and Cardiff could not wait to take her home with them.

Paris and Charlie were not as enthusiastic. They knew tonight was going to end either in celebration or our arrest. They were reserving happiness until they heard the outcome about Charga.

I drove away from the hospital anticipating a full report about what happened in the first stage of *una peligrosa aventura.*

My mind did not find peace in the crisp winter night. Adrenaline had kicked in and my heart started beating faster and faster. As I drove, I looked at my reflection in the rear view mirror. My palms, damp with perspiration, slipped on the steering wheel and I wiped them on my skirt.

The rational part of my brain tried to ruin the adrenaline rush. A tiny voice kept intruding on my thoughts, asking me if I'd lost my sanity. I wondered what force had pulled me to Paris and allowed me to get this invested in her life?

When I was in college, for one of my classes, I did an interview with a psychic. He believed we continually meet people in this life from some past life. He said, "That is why we feel we've known someone forever on first meeting them."

That was how I felt about Paris. She was more than a

story with follow-up. There was a bigger purpose to it, but I had no idea what the bigger purpose could be. Was it to save a steer, or to make the last months of Paris's life more peaceful? I liked to think it was for the latter. On that drive, I became fully aware of the pain I would be experiencing in the not too distant future when Paris Nash died. The closer she and I became, the more difficult it was going to be for me.

My grandfather always told me, and made me believe, "All things happen for a reason." I wanted to know the reason I'd entangled myself in Paris Nash's life. I did not want to wait to discover the reason. I wanted to know at that very moment.

It had not come to me by the time I reached Tristan's. I did not see Phyllis's car right away, and that added to my angst. I'd looked forward to seeing her and hoped she would help me figure out an answer. I always depended upon her to make sense of my life.

She either would say the right thing or would lighten my mood by making me laugh. I relaxed when I saw her car parked farther behind the restaurant than I had expected. I headed to the back door of Tristan's restaurant expecting her to greet me when I entered.

However, when I stepped through the back door into the darkened restaurant and called her name, a male voice whispered, "She's not here."

"Tristan, you scared me to death," I whispered back at him. "Where is Phyl?"

"She went with them. I stayed behind," he explained.

I was stunned. "She what?"

"I wanted to go and let her wait here like we decided when BZ didn't get here in time," he tried to explain, still whispering.

154

"She went with them?" I interrupted my voice louder than his.

"I couldn't leave her with Romeo out there." He hissed this time, and pointed to figure lying in the front door entrance.

The streetlight, shining through the front window, illuminated enough for me to recognize the shape of a man curled up there.

"He comes for dinner a couple of time a week. He wouldn't leave until I fixed him something to eat."

"Why did she go with them?" I repeated my yet unanswered question.

"Because of BZ." Tristan told me in an emotionless voice.

"What about BZ? He was supposed to get Charga." My stomach churned.

"He didn't get here in time, and when I couldn't leave, your friend went instead," Tristan explained.

"Well, where the hell is BZ?" I could hear the alarm in my voice. "It's his brilliant idea, and he didn't even go?"

"He should be here any minute," Tristan said. "Just a slight change of plans, is all."

"I don't think so," I couldn't help worrying that Phyllis was in danger. "This is a huge change in the plan. Phyllis's job was only to bring the range cubes and then wait for me. Crap, if they've been arrested. . ."

The sentence hung in the darkened restaurant, eerie shadows formed across the unfamiliar disarray. Tristan had pushed all of the tables toward the front window and lined the chairs seat-toward-wall along the other side, making a clear space in the center of the dining room. Moonlight filtered through the back screen door where I came in and made a widening path into the room.

155

Tristan asked me, "Do you want something to eat or drink?"

"It's a shame you don't serve alcohol." I told him, "I need a bourbon and coke."

"I've got the very thing," he flickered his way to the kitchen on the beam of a small flashlight, reminding me of a gargantuan lightening bug. I blessed him when he returned with two tall glasses of bourbon and Coke.

"I can't turn the lights on," he explained pointing the flashlight beam toward the front door. "Romeo will want to come in and talk if he sees me in here."

I looked at the man, now sitting, leaning against the front door. Tristan sensed my concern about the stranger.

"He won't hurt anyone as long as he's on his meds. He has a mental problem, and he acts up when he goes off his pills. He's on them now; I can tell because he sleeps so much." He turned the light toward the front window, "During the day he wanders around over there."

I could see San Pedro Springs Park through the dimness. "I usually see him out there sleeping on a bench in the afternoon. He comes here for dinner a few times a week. The poor fellow makes stops at all the restaurants around here and everyone gives him something to eat. We know he eats well. He usually sleeps in front of my door because it has the recess and stays dry when it rains. I consider him cheap security," Tristan laughed.

"I'm not as worried about him being there as I am about him telling people what he might see in here," I explained.

Tristan said, "I don't think you have to worry. He doesn't have a lot of credibility on the street."

I changed the subject back to Phyllis. "I still can't believe Phyl decided to go with them."

Tristan rubbed the back of his neck, "If you ask me, she didn't want to just wait here, and she really didn't want to miss out on anything. When BZ couldn't get here in time, she volunteered and said she just *had* to go, we couldn't hold her back." He chuckled and it annoyed me.

"Sounds like her." I acquiesced and took off on B.Z. not being there. "And, what is so important that BZ couldn't get here in time?"

"He went to get a truck," Tristan answered.

"That was not the plan," I said.

Tristan shrugged and was quiet. The minutes did not flow like the sands through an hourglass; they fought kicking, fighting and screaming with every tick-tock of the Miller Beer Clock on the wall. I paced, and I tapped; I sat, and I stood. Finally, Tristan said, "You are making me nervous."

"Well, I'm not good at waiting," I explained.

"Then I'll never hire you," he said.

It took a minute for it to sink in, but I finally got his joke. I groaned aloud and realized he reminded me of Phyllis and her offbeat sense of humor.

"How long have you been in the restaurant business, Tristan?" I lapsed into reporter mode to distract myself from worry.

"I've been doing this since I got out of high school," he told me.

"Where? Here?" I asked. "This location?"

"Yep, here and there," he waved his arm as if gesturing to everywhere. "I went to high school at Harlandale. Do you know it?"

"Yes, on the west side, right?" I answered.

"Yep, that's it. One of my teachers, Mrs. Pena, got me interested in food. She used to make a Mexican feast when

157

everyone passed one of the big tests. She grew up in Mexico City, and her father owned a restaurant there. She earned her way through college by cooking."

"Is she still teaching?" I asked him in my interviewer mode.

"Yeah, she comes in occasionally, and I never let her pay for a meal. She changed my life."

"So, you went from high school to owning a restaurant?" I had underestimated this man.

"No. First, I joined the army, and I learned how not to cook." His laugh was one of those deep, rolling, did-you-get-my-joke-laughs. "When I got out, I went to visit Mrs. Pena and told her what I'd been doing. She's the one who suggested I work with her father in Mexico."

"Really? In Mexico City?"

He nodded.

"Did you go to chef school there?"

"Nope, I learned from the master himself, a grand old man. He's the one who told me that food makes the restaurant, not the décor. He encouraged me, 'Go back to the U.S., open a little place and watch it grow.' It has. I started with a taco stand."

"No wonder the food is so great. I could eat here three meals a day."

"Some people do," he laughed.

It was then that we heard a commotion out behind the restaurant. A Lite Beer draft truck pulled in next to the loading ramp at the back door. First Luis jumped out of the cab and then Pepe ran around from the opposite side.

"Where's Phyllis?" I panicked when she did not get out of the cab.

Pepe motioned to the back of the truck.

Luis opened one of the side bays and started off-loading empty beer kegs. After they removed three stacks, there stood Phyllis, her arms around Charga's neck, hay in her hair.

"We made it!" Her face flushed, her eyes flashed, and her grin could not have been more joyful. She spoke to Charga, "Didn't we big boy?" Then she told me, "We had a little change in plans."

"Where's BZ?" Pepe asked, "Isn't he here yet?"

"I haven't seen him." My voice grew panicky. "I thought he was going with you, until I got here and Tristan filled me in on the change in plans."

Phyllis explained on BZ's behalf, "He called Luis and told him he'd thought of a better way to get Charga out of town. He worried that the beer truck might be too conspicuous driving in from Comal County at midnight, so he borrowed a truck from his wife's uncle or something, so I decided I'd ride along with Charga."

Phyllis pulled on the gentle steer's harness and led him through the back door to the dining room inside Tristan's restaurant. Pepe got two buckets from the cab of the truck, filled one with water, the other with range cubes, and then tossed the empty Range Cube bag into the dumpster. He left the filled buckets by the back door.

I wish I'd had my camera. I would dearly love to have photos of this unlikely group of cattle rustlers standing around a lone steer in the middle of Tristan's eerily lit restaurant: Luis, Pepe, Phyllis, Tristan, me, and of course, the Grand Champion Steer of the Alamo City Livestock Exposition.

The three new arrivals talked about what had happened at the Coliseum, and I picked up snatches of their conversation. I overheard something about a guard, a cap and, one of the FFA youngsters almost ruining the whole escapade.

I waved my arms and said, "Wait, wait, wait. From the beginning!"

I wanted to hear the whole story from top to bottom. The piecemeal bits and pieces were making me feel even more nervous than I'd been all day.

Chapter Fourteen

Charga settled down after he backed his way around the restaurant a few times, making sure nothing dangerous lurked there. He must have decided he liked this new enclosure because he stopped right in the center of the room. Tristan went out to the loading dock and scooped range cubes onto a dinner plate, and then set it on the floor in front of Charga. The touch of whimsy added to the ludicrous scene before me. Phyllis stood petting the huge steer as if he was a large dog and started telling us about her part in the story.

"I got here a little after nine, right, Tristan?" She looked at him.

Tristan nodded.

"And, a few minutes later Luis and Pepe came for the range cubes."

They nodded.

"BZ called Luis and asked if they could manage without him, that he had to get a different truck to take

Charga out of town. Then he called me so I could tell you what was going on. He didn't want to call at the hospital and interrupt Lannie's interview."

"Which worked out best for me," Luis said. He endorsed BZ's decision to find another truck. "My boss wouldn't notice I had the truck out late. If he did, I'd tell him I stopped for breakfast or something, but if I got pulled over by police in Comal County, I wouldn't be able to explain that."

Luis wanted to tell his version of the story but quit when an ancient, squeaky, faded-blue truck inched by the front window. BZ leaned low and waved at us from inside the cab. Even though he could not see us inside the restaurant, he knew we would be watching for him.

He drove the truck around back and we crowded at the screen door, puzzlement registering on every face as the dilapidated truck came to a stop. I wondered if the darn thing would even make it out of town.

"That's the truck?" Phyllis was mistrustful.

BZ's voice was full of pride. "It's a 1950 stake bed hauler." He slapped the fender with satisfaction. "It belongs to Sylvia's Uncle Ignacio. Dependable for forty years."

"Why doesn't that make me feel better?" I asked.

The truck did not seem sturdy enough to hold a goat, much less a twelve-hundred-pound steer. Granted it looked bigger than most of the pick-up trucks I'd seen, but it did not have solid sides like most trucks. It had a fenced flatbed instead. It certainly did not befit transportation of a Grand Champion, especially not a stolen one. Anyone could look right through the fence slats and see what was inside.

"BZ," my voice dripped cynicism, "how can you sneak a stolen steer out of town in an open truck? They are going to notice he's missing and soon there will be an APB out looking for him."

"Not to worry," Phyllis announced, holding up a paper bag. "They'll never recognize him, when we get through."

Luis interrupted her, his impatience obvious. "Come on, guys. Help me clear the hay out of my truck. We have to get back to the warehouse. I have an alibi now."

"Charga left a little something extra in there, too," Phyl chuckled, crinkling her nose. She motioned me to follow her back inside the restaurant. "Come on Siobhan, I need your help." She shook the sack and grinned over her shoulder.

We went inside, and the two of us commenced to give Charga a complete makeover. While Tristan shined the flashlight so we could see what we were doing, we took off Charga's halter and Phyllis hacked at his curly white top knot with a pair of scissors she had brought in the sack. Then she chopped at the fluffy plume at the end of his tail with a barbers razor until it resembled a worn out string mop. Charga stood content to let us work as if he knew it was necessary to make this kind of fuss. He did not move when we got on our hands and knees and scuffed his shiny-black hooves with sandpaper nail sponges or while Phyllis dabbed JustforMen hair dye over the white part of his face or while I splotched the dark brown dye in random blotches all over his body, including the now chopped, previously white, tail plume. Poor Charga did not look like anything *but* ugly walking hamburger when we got through with him.

After we wiped off the dye with paper towels, we sponged and wiped with big car wash sponges until we were certain we had gotten the immediate evidence off him. Tristan hovered, collecting used paper toweling, bringing fresh bowls of water as we dabbed and wiped. At some point, he noticed Romeo, the homeless man, standing with his face pressed against the front window glass. Romeo made blinders with his hands so he could better see what was going on inside.

Tristan walked to the window and mirrored Romeo's actions, nose-to-nose, eye-to-eye, moving around the glass as Romeo did. Tristan blocked Romeo's line of sight, and finally, the homeless man must have tired of the game because he turned and walked off toward the park.

When we finished with Charga, Phyl, now Charga's new best friend, led him to the back door and into the open bed truck where BZ waited. He had moved the hay from the beer truck to the back of the hauler and then loaded the two buckets Pepe filled with water and range cubes onto it, too. Charga went right for the buckets. BZ had also fashioned an old cotton rope into a hackamore style halter for Charga. He slid it over the steer's head and square knotted the ends to u-hooks welded on each side of the truck cab.

As soon as BZ secured Charga in place, he climbed out of the bed and into the cab of the old truck. He waved at us as he drove away, a slightly nervous lone rustler in the night.

Phyl and I stayed behind to help Tristan clean up the mess in the restaurant. He would not hear of us waiting. He said he would take care of it himself and for us to go on.

We grabbed up Charga's halter and lead, promised Tristan we'd be back soon for *Chilaquiles,* sprinted to our separate cars, and spun gravel as we left the parking lot. I followed Phyllis to her house so she could drop off her car. We would take mine to catch up with BZ so I could open the gate for him.

I tuned my car radio to KJ97, the official station for the rodeo because they did live broadcasts from the Coliseum during the run of the event. Since their remote trailer sat near the front gates, and because the DJ.s did hourly updates on everything going on at the Coliseum, I figured they would be the first station to report the missing Grand Champion. Sure enough, at 11:45, Cowboy Cullen, the station's pre-eminent DJ, broke into the middle of a Reba McIntire song to announce in his gravelly voice, "Folks, it seems we've had some cattle rustling out here at the Livestock Show."

I sped up next to Phyllis's car and waved to get her attention. She looked over at me and waved back.

I pointed to my radio and mouthed the words, "It's on the news." Phyllis waved back at me. She bounced her head to the music on her radio, oblivious to what I had pantomimed.

I lowered my window, circled my fist to act out "roll down your window." She got the message, but she could not hear me over the car engines and road noise. I prayed for a red light, but we hit all green.

As soon as I stopped my car in front of her house, I jumped out and yelled. "Come on, come on, Phyl."

She trotted over to me and said, "What's going on? Why the hurry? I've gotta' pee."

"You've gotta' hold it; we don't have time to pee. It's on the news already. Cowboy Cullen announced that there were rustlers at the stock show."

I got back in the car. Phyllis slid into the passenger seat and her eyes grew wide. The door had barely closed when I peeled out of her driveway, and we both listened for the next update.

"Yes, ladies and gentlemen, I'm trying to get confirmation on this. They're tellin' me the Grand Champion Steer is missing. You think we have rustlers out here? Got a golden oldie that might get him back; here is Eddie Arnold's *Cattle Call*."

"It's me," Phyllis spoke, suddenly awed by the realization. "Me. I'm the rustler."

"Okay, Miss Rustler, tell me what happened."

"You aren't going to believe this." She waited for my full attention before launching into how *she* stole Charga.

I turned the radio volume down, leaving it loud enough to hear any breaking news bulletins, low enough to hear Phyllis tell me about her *aventura*.

"Are you ready?" she noted my interest in the volume dial. I split my attention between her, the highway, and my rear view mirror, fearing flashing lights coming after us.

"First of all, I got the phone call from BZ before I left the spa. He told me what you already told me when you called, to meet Luis and Pepe at Tristan's with the range cubes a little after six. Then he told me he didn't want to bother you with Lannie, but that he'd decided to get the open sided truck to take Charga out of town. He didn't know how long he'd be, but if he hadn't gotten back in time, for them to go on without him and he'd be there with the truck when they got back. He was worried about getting to Tristan's too late to get Charga out of town before they reported him stolen. That's when I got the idea about the make-over."

I smiled and shook my head, still not believing she actually participated in stealing Charga from the Coliseum.

"BZ thought I had a brilliant idea," she complimented herself. "When I got to Tristan's I waited for Pepe and Luis, and Tristan kept looking at his watch and pacing, hoping BZ would get there soon because I'd already told him I was going to go in BZ's place if he didn't get back in time. Tristan thought it would be too dangerous for me, but he didn't feel right leaving me at the restaurant alone with that homeless man out front. He didn't think Romeo would hurt me, but he didn't want to chance it. Luis and Pepe got there after all the customers were gone, and we could not wait any longer."

I shook my head. She had actually done it.

"Speaking of not waiting any longer...," she squirmed in her seat and gave me a pleading look.

"No way are we stopping." I told her, "Kegel!"

She crossed her legs and continued the story. "While we waited, Tristan warmed up some enchiladas for me. I hadn't eaten all day. Did you know he learned how to cook from a master chef in Mexico?"

"Yep," I answered, not wanting to distract her from telling me what happened at the Coliseum.

She went back to the story. "I went right out and met Luis and Pepe. I told them there had been a slight change in plans. We had to wait to see if BZ could get there in time. If he couldn't be there to ride with the steer, I would."

"Didn't they try to talk you out of it?" I could not believe they would let her get in the back of that truck with Charga.

She shook her head. I opened my mouth to speak, and she answered my question before I asked it.

"I have no idea what possessed me. There I sat in the back of a refrigerated keg truck with kegs full of beer stacked all around me, holding on to this two-way radio Luis gave me. Tristan is sweet." She smiled. "He worried about me being cold in that refrigerated truck and loaned me a blazer someone left at the restaurant a while ago.

"Anyway, from that point on, things started moving really fast. Luis told me, when he gave me the walkie-talkie, 'use it if there's an emergency.' They got that big bag of range cubes out of my trunk, and Luis shoved it into the corner where the cab meets the refrigerated part and told me to sit on it and to call him on the walkie-talkie if the load started shifting. That's when I realized I could be crushed by beer."

My mouth dropped open. I had not thought about that possibility.

"Luis drove very carefully, so nothing shifted," she reassured me. "He had tied the rows off with some kind of dirty, mesh divider-screen things. The whole truck smelled like sour...," her nose crinkled, "...puke. Anyway, we got to the entrance gate at the Coliseum; it took about thirty minutes or so to get there. Then we had to stop and let security check us in to the grounds. That dude made Luis open the bay doors so they could look inside the truck.

"Luis introduced Pepe to the guard and told him, 'My boy is my helper tonight.' Then they started talking about it being good for kids to learn to work instead of sitting on their butts watching TV all day, and things like that. Anyway, I guess the guard waved us through because they closed up the bay and we started moving again.

"Luis talked to me on the walkie-talkie radio, telling me the route he'd be driving to the big cooler where they store the beer out there. We stopped, and he and Pepe threw all the bays open, got hand trucks from the back and started off-loading the beer while I hid in the corner behind those rubber divider things.

"I could hear the receiving clerk talking to them; he's the one who counts the kegs when they deliver. I thought for sure he'd come inside the truck and look around, but he didn't. I sat like a statue on the range cube sack, barely breathing or blinking. At least those rubbery things weren't slapping at me anymore; they hung there like Spanish moss from an oak tree.

"Then, while Luis went inside to do the settling up, Pepe came into the truck, made me stand up, took a box cutter, and slit open the top of the range cube sack and filled Charlie's jacket pockets. He put the jacket on, pulled Charlie's FFA cap down low, and said, 'Wish me luck.' Then he took off on a run for the pen out front to get Charga.

"Luis closed the bay doors when he finished inside and told me to 'hold on,' while we drove to another building where they store empty kegs for pick-up."

"So you are in the back of an empty keg truck?" I asked.

"Yeah, me and the range cubes and those hanging, divider thingy's." She shuddered in a way that let me know it had not been pleasant.

She continued. "Luis talked to me on the radio, telling me, 'I'm going to pick up empties,' so we drove to where the beer companies take turns picking up empties from the Coliseum during rodeo week; it saves on expenses." She understood, ever the business woman. "Tonight was our turn."

I noticed the ownership she took in the adventure.

"Then Luis said, 'Hang tight,' and he made a sharp turn that nearly threw me off the bag onto the floor. We got to the pick-up area and luckily, didn't see anyone else around. I stretched my legs and inhaled fresh air while he loaded the empty kegs. That guy has some bi-ceps." She obviously appreciated his physique.

"He's married," I scolded her.

She laughed. "I'm only saying the man is strong."

I laughed back at her. "I think he might have been lucky you were in the *back* of the truck."

She slapped the air toward me. "Anyway," she drawled, "he made the rows of empties stack from the back to the front of the truck and pull the dividers tight across them to keep the kegs in place. He stacked to leave space up front where no one could see if he had to open the bays for security again. He double hung the dividers to reinforce the space where Charga and I had to hide. Boy, did I hope they'd hold."

I listened, nodding and thinking how none of her spa clients would ever believe she would even think about, much less do something like this. She glowed with excitement, a neon version of her normal self.

I checked the time. If nothing went wrong from here on, we would finish BZ's *una aventura peligroso* in less than twenty minutes. However, as Phyllis told me the details of the theft, I realized that we had broken the law. This was not some fraternity prank. Unlike the Aggies painting Bevo's horns maroon, we were stealing a steer.

"...So," Phyllis continued, "we drove over to the cow wash and Luis got out and used the hose to rinse his arms, like he'd gotten beer all over himself or something. A couple of those FFA kids were sneaking a cigarette across the way. They asked him if he had any free samples. They had a good laugh at that and I started sweating. Apparently, the kids left because the next thing I knew the bay door went up and Luis was throwing bales of hay inside. He clipped the wire around them, and I helped scatter hay over the floor of the truck. Then he backed the truck over to some kind of loading ramp. I stuck my head out and saw Pepe walking Charga toward us as if he did it every day. He walked the steer right up the ramp and into the truck.

"I kept holding range cubes in my hand, keeping my palm flat like they showed me." She demonstrated so I could see. "Then Charga started eating right out of my hand! Luis said, 'Remember to use the radio if there's an emergency,' and he pulled down the bay door. I stood there, shut up in the back of a keg truck with a twelve-hundred-pound animal, and I realized that would normally constitute an emergency." We both laughed at that thought.

"We drove away with me singing, *I love Paris in the Springtime.*"

An announcement on the radio got our attention and I turned up the volume so we could hear better, "This is Cowboy Cullen, live from the Stock Show and Radio, and folks, you aren't going to believe this. Apparently, the Grand Champion Steer, Charga, has disappeared. They've got security and cops and every Rodeo honcho they could muster out here runnin' round like ole Leon Coffee clownin' in the bull ring."

Phyl and I looked at one another and at the same time said, "Oh, shit!"

Cowboy Cullen introduced a George Strait song and said, "I'll be keeping you posted."

A red light stopped our progress and we sat quietly, letting the news soak in. We started moving forward again, and Phyllis kept talking as if she were telling me about a movie plot.

"Anyway, the guard stopped the truck at the security checkpoint and Luis got out of the truck. I kept holding out those cubes, I didn't want Charga to moo or something. Luis told the guard, 'I got you the cap you wanted,' and I could tell how happy he'd made him, even over the noise of the truck I could hear all of these, 'Thank you, man's,' and 'nothing a-tall's' and 'see ya on the flip flop's'. He didn't even ask to open a bay. Then we drove to Tristan's, and you know the rest."

She smiled like a proud Mama.

We were making good time driving out Highway 281, had left the last red light, and now nothing else could slow our progress. We only had a few miles to go until we reached the FM 1863 cutoff at Bulverde.

"I think it's brilliant that you are keeping Charga at the ranch, Siobhan. No one would think of looking for him there. Have you been out there much since your Grandfather died?"

We were about ten minutes from the property I'd inherited and almost sold. I was glad at I'd decided to keep it, even though the taxes would take a huge chunk out of my salary. It was the perfect place to hide Charga.

I asked, Phyllis, "Do you want to hear about Lannie and what happened at the hospital?"

She nodded, and I started bragging about how gently her friend had treated Paris and her family. I told her about Cardiff breaking down, how sad I felt to see her cry.

Phyllis said, "I can't wait to meet them. You've told me a lot, but other than seeing Paris on TV the day of the judging, I don't have a clue what they are like. I need faces," she said.

I mentioned that they were having a press conference in the morning. "It's supposed to be about Paris's going home, but I think everyone will be asking about Charga, instead." She agreed with me.

"Look, up there. I think we've caught them!" She could not contain her excitement as we caught up with BZ and Charga. We passed them at the Highway 46 crossroad when BZ pulled to the side of the road and motioned me to drive ahead. We turned left on 46, right at Hueco Springs Road, drove a couple of miles, made several turns until we reached the gate to the ranch my grandfather left me. It was Charga's new home.

Chapter Fifteen

Paris called me in the wee hours of the morning, trying until I got home from getting Charga settled in the old corral at the ranch. I couldn't call her because the hospital switchboard closed down at ten o'clock, so it had been up to her to call out. She'd tried about eight times before I walked in the door.

She'd asked in a code we'd made up, "How's the weather out there?"

I'd answered, "It's beautiful." Then I slept peacefully, knowing I'd kept my promise to her.

The next morning, when I smuggled Charlie's cap and jacket back to Paris's room in a Taco Cabana sack, I could see the tension in her face had eased. I told her everything had worked out, but did not give any detail. It would benefit everyone if she went to the press conference secure in the knowledge that Charga was safe, but without knowledge of how or who committed the act.

The fact that Paris desperately wanted to save her

steer only surfaced in the newspaper that morning. It had been the crux of Lannie's column. The additional news that Charga disappeared the night before, combined with the information in the column that morning, made everyone feel sure the Nash family had something to do with the apparent theft.

Our office betting pool added another category for wagering. In addition to, *Is Paris Nash Pregnant?* they added, *Did the Nashes steal the steer?*

Dr. Hardwick, Cardiff, and Franklin Nash were adamant Paris not speak to the media; the men decided they would be her spokespersons. I was not sure they could keep Paris quiet, but she promised them she would not say a word. "I'll sit in the wheelchair and look pathetic, okay?"

Charlie and I went down to the main floor meeting room ahead of their arrival. We stood in the back of the auditorium, inconspicuous among the curious who lined the back wall. Since Bud had given me a few days off, I was not present in a professional capacity. On the off chance someone recognized me and asked why I was not down front with the rest of the reporters, I planned on saying, "I'm on vacation, but I covered the steer selection and I am curious about the girl," but no one recognized me.

The meeting room was full. Print reporters and photographers arriving early claimed the front row seats; television reporters and their camera jockeys bunched as close to the front as they could get. The radio reporters clunked tape recorders on the podium and stood close by so each could hit the record button.

The media, summoned by the hospital public relations staff, were supposed to do a simple follow up to the public's curiosity about Paris Nash. What had happened to her was a much-discussed local mystery.

When Dr. Doom and the Nashes entered the room, flashes popped and necks craned hoping to get a look at the slight young girl in the hospital wheelchair. The agenda called for Dr. Dexter Hardwick to issue a statement about Paris's physical condition. Together, Dr. Hardwick and Franklin approached the microphone, and Dr. Hardwick read a statement: "Paris Nash has advanced melanoma cancer. Her prognosis is grim. It is her decision to go back to the family ranch in the Hill Country and live out her remaining days in the love and privacy afforded her there."

The pall that ensued did not last. Few people knew the extent of Paris's illness before that statement, and I had expected a few minutes of reserve while the information coalesced. The correspondents, surprised by the gravity of her situation, figured the most appropriate way to react. The agenda called for questions, and all the reporter's hands went up immediately. To their credit, they respected the magnitude of Paris's situation and began their questions by saying they would add her name to their prayers or some similar comment acknowledging her prognosis and their desire to see it change.

The first reporter, after wishing Paris well, asked Franklin, "Have you heard that the steer, Charga, is missing from the Coliseum grounds?"

Franklin Nash leaned into the microphone at the podium. "Yes," he responded, giving the one word nightmare response.

Tracy Brennan, KWNK's smiling star anchor, worded her question with an open-ended query, without a word to Paris. "Due to Lannie White's column in this morning's paper, Mr. Nash, you must be somewhat happy to know Charga disappeared from the Coliseum." Her smile confused Franklin.

175

He frowned as he attempted to avoid Tracy's web. If he said "No," it would mean he did not care about the steer living or dying, if he said "Yes" it would put more suspicion on the family. All eyes were on Franklin. His face revealed every thought darting across his mind.

I stepped up the main aisle and locked eyes with him, slowly shaking my head I attempted to give a hint. He came through and stymied Tracy. "Ma'am," he answered, "if we knew what happened to Charga, I might be happy. But as far as we know, the steer could have been stolen by a bunch of frat boys for some big bar-b-que down south."

I smiled when, as if on cue, Paris blew her nose and wiped at her eyes. Only Charlie and I knew she used the maneuver to hide a giggle.

The reporters continued asking every conceivable question about Charga's disappearance. The final insult came when one of our competitor station reps asked Franklin directly, "Do you know anything about Charga's abduction?"

Franklin, a forthright man, might have trouble answering direct questions requiring that he lie. That was why we decided not to tell him anything about our plan to steal the steer. I was sure he suspected all was well with Charga. He knew Paris would not be so calm if a random group had taken the steer. I cringed when Franklin opened his mouth.

"Son," he squinted and deepened his voice, sounding a lot like John Wayne, "as far as I know, it could have been some aliens from outer space."

His remark brought a chuckle from the assembled media, and I breathed a sigh of relief. Dr. Hardwick took the podium, and Franklin stepped back.

"Ladies and gentlemen," the handsome doctor said, "the Nash family thanks you for your concern and interest;

however, we need to relinquish this room for other hospital business."

He ignored several reporters who tried to slip in another question; however, he could not ignore the tall dark suited police detective who came in flipping his wallet open, showing his badge. I glanced at the shiny brass emblem as I filed out with the rest of the media. Tracy cornered the officer and Dr. Hardwick, and the KWNK camera light clicked on.

I glanced over my shoulder and gave Paris a pantomimed "Call me." Then I almost ran to my car to escape. I was sure Eloy would give my name to the police as a suspected individual because of my unsuccessful plea at lunch. Of course, I had an alibi for the time when Charga disappeared. I had five witnesses who could vouch that I had arrived at the hospital with Lannie White at the time the steer disappeared and that I did not leave until she had finished the interview with the Nash family, far too late for me to be involved in the steer's abduction.

Immediately following the press conference, the Nashes took Paris back home to Kingsland. I was upset that I did not get to say goodbye to her and felt much better when Cardiff called that evening and invited me to come for lunch at the ranch the next day.

On the drive out Highway 281, I realized I'd never driven the route before. On other trips to the chain of lakes, I had always been a passenger, traveling with a group to water ski on either Lake Marble Falls or Lake L.B.J. It seemed strange for me to be driving the winding highway alone.

From the north side of San Antonio, the trip normally took ninety minutes, but since I stopped at the Basketry to pick up gourmet cookies for the Nashes and then detoured to

New Braunfels to check on Charga, it took an hour longer.

I shed my leather jacket after I checked on Charga and refilled his manger with hay, added more range cubes in his feed bucket, and flipped the pump switch so the water trough would fill.

I drove down to the river toward the mobile home I rented to Melvyn and Marla Gerfers in exchange for his help around the place. She was a student, finishing her degree at Southwest Texas State in San Marcos, and he didn't make enough working for a local homebuilder to live on otherwise. He made sure vandals or squatters did not take over the property, made sure the fences stayed up and that sort of thing. I asked Melvyn if he would, on his next trip into New Braunfels, pick up a couple of bags of feed for a heifer I was keeping for a friend of mine.

We spent a few minutes talking about the weather when Marla came out, still in pajamas, and asked if I would like a cup of coffee.

"Next time. I don't have time today," I told her as I walked back to my car.

A George Strait marathon played on KJ that day. He was a local celebrity and the headliner for the concert at the Rodeo that night. I listened to his songs lauding Texas and wondered if the early settlers saw this country the same way contemporary songwriters did. I tried to imagine what it would have been like to put all of my belongings in the back of a wagon and take off across an unknown wilderness to start anew, and then I wondered what caused them to settle in south central Texas.

My grandfather's theory was that they must have come in the early spring when the winter grass waved tall and green and the wildflowers colored the land like rainbows on the ground. He said *Who in their right mind could leave that."*

I wished I had been alive to see Texas the way it looked then when dense prairie grassland flowed, a sea of green down through the center of the entire continent, with herds of bison and antelope roaming from Canada to Mexico.

Now asphalt highways slice the land, fence posts puncture it, wire and plank fences divide and isolate it into parcels governed by man, though still nourished by nature.

The highway I drove connects the coastal plains to the Hill Country. It is different down along the coast, flat, barren of large trees. It changes north of San Antonio when the highway climbs and finds itself lined with scrub brush and tangled masses of vine beneath Live Oak Trees. The thorny vines, nature's razor wire, intertwined dark grey coils, shelter for everything from fragile birds to tough-skinned armadillos.

The fences divide small ranches, though there are few big ones like the Classen Ranch had been. They are smaller now, like the Steubing at Spring Branch and Licata near Bulverde. It made me sad to know the era had passed when the sweat and muscle of hard-working people could make fortunes from the land.

Franklin Nash was one of that dying breed. Authentically Texan, he did not wear fringe, fancy shirts, or polished boots. Instead, he chose heavy twill pants and long-sleeve khaki shirts, rough-out boots, and, depending on the season, picked either a tight woven straw or well-worn felt hat to cover his head.

My grandfather had not been like Franklin. My grandfather had been one of the wealthy men who bought land but did not work it, hiring men to manage and maintain his little property on the Guadalupe River. Grandfather bought it because he got it for a steal and planned to use it as a weekend getaway, not as a means of survival.

I think he left the ranch to me because he knew how much I loved going there with him when I was young, and that the solitude of it had saved my sanity after my divorce.

When I reached the sign for Johnson City, hometown of Lyndon Johnson, I stopped at the Dairy Queen and used the ladies' room. I bought a hot chocolate, and went to sit in my car so I could study the directions Cardiff gave me when she called. According to her, I only had to drive another thirty minutes to reach their ranch.

When I crossed the Llano River, I remembered Cardiff saying, "You can't miss the gate." She was right, because as soon as I turned on the county road, I saw a huge one dominating the landscape. Two fifteen foot pink Texas granite pillars supported a span of ironwork that proclaimed in four-foot tall letters, Nash Ranch.

I stopped my car, waited for the white caliche dust to settle before I got out, and opened the cross-timber gate hanging on enormous black hinges. It was a very humble looking gate, especially because of its grand supports. I fought an impulse to ride the gate across the road, and followed the cardinal rule of gate opening and stopped to close it immediately behind my car so no livestock could escape.

The Nash ranch was a complete contrast to my little place. This ranch showed years of care had tamed the rugged land. Clusters of oak trees stood on open ground, branches formed leafy umbrellas where cattle sought shelter. A herd grazed in the distance near a large stock tank, the scene so peaceful I felt I had stumbled upon a private park.

A white caliche lane led me away from the road and I drove for several miles, wondering how far "a little ways" would be. Soon barns and implement sheds came to view, and I laughed at the request someone, Cardiff I supposed, had tacked onto a cedar post beside the road asking visitors to "Please drive slowly I have to dust this place, you know!"

One turn more and I could see the house, exactly as I imagined it would be, Victorian, built from Texas limestone, two tall stories of stability. A porch wrapped the lower floor, making a balcony above. Pens and corrals ringed outbuildings, whitewashed lumber housing horses, and a coop of Rhode Island Red chickens with a very proud rooster strutting by. A herd of Mouflon sheep scattered as I got out of my car.

A welcoming shriek distracted me, and I watched Paris bound down the front steps of the house, running toward me, her arms out-stretched, looking anything but ill.

Chapter Sixteen

Paris hugged me and pulled me up the steps into the house, yelling, "She's here, she's here!"

My eyes adjusted to the darkness and I followed her through a sitting room, around a formal dining table in an even darker alcove to a bright and sunny kitchen with a glassed sun porch beyond.

Cardiff smiled and we touch-hugged, her hands covered with flour, and Franklin stood extending his hand for me to shake, reconsidered, and pulled me into a hug. He offered me his chair, but Paris stopped me from sitting.

"No, wait, I want her to meet everybody first." She pulled me to the long sun porch where the kids were playing a hot and heavy game of monopoly. She told me, "They got to play hooky because this is my first day home." Then she told them, "Everyone, this is Siobhan."

I tried my best to connect each name and face as she introduced her brothers and sisters to me. "This is my brother, Rome. He made me chicken and dumplings last night," she beamed. Rome stood taller than Paris did, though younger by a year and he probably looked like his daddy had at his same age.

"You're the one who stole Charga, right?" He definitely had Franklin's rough-edged directness.

I did not know how to respond so I looked from Paris to Cardiff and Franklin. Cardiff rescued me with a word.

"Rome," her tone was a stopper in a bottle.

Rome dropped his head and flopped back in his seat. He threw dice and moved the top hat seven spaces, proceeding on to jail.

"This is India." Paris tugged her sister's ponytail. "She's the one who ironed all of my clothes for me."

"I'm so pleased to know you," India said and smiled. I could tell she represented the proper child in the family, the one who always tried her best not to cause a problem, especially now that her older sister had become so ill.

Ireland, the youngest sister, charmed like a pixie. She grabbed my hand and leaned against me, looked up through long eyelashes, and said, "Hi, I'm Ireland." She could not have been more than five years old. Little London, the youngest of them all, would not be outdone. He grabbed my other hand and mimicked his sister. "I'm London," he told me. I could not resist reaching down to tousle his curls. He ducked and frowned at me.

I could see the family resemblance among them, noticeable, not obvious. Every child's hair color differed in its shade of brown, from Paris's darkest, almost black, to London's lightest golden. Their unmistakable smiles, genuine and quick, were the common denominator. Even Rome, after his mother's warning word, had broken into a broad apologetic grin.

Cardiff offered me lemonade, and Paris said, "Bring it

with you. I want to show you around."

The rest of the kids wanted to go, too, but Paris said, "Maybe later we can play another game or something. I need to talk to Siobhan first."

There were grumbles, but I distracted them by holding up my car keys and asking, "Who'd like to go out to my car and get the basket of goodies I brought?" Rome grabbed my keys and headed to the front door with London right behind.

We could hear Rome say, "Who locks a car on a ranch?"

Cardiff said, "Rome."

Paris looked to her dad, "Truck?"

He tossed her two keys on a ring and she caught them with one hand.

"We won't be long," she said and led me toward the door to the yard out back.

"Lunch will be ready in about thirty minutes," Cardiff warned as Paris skipped down the back steps, stopping to scratch the ears of an orange tabby cat that ran to meet her. "That's Marmalade," she told me.

I gave the cat a pat and caught up with Paris at the gate. "Be sure it's closed good and tight," she said, motioning to the small herd of goats heading toward us.

Once we were in the truck she said, "Tell me all about Charga and what happened."

I did, repeating every detail and ended by telling her, "Charga is a guest at my ranch on the Guadalupe River outside of New Braunfels."

"I can't wait to see him, and I can't wait to meet Phyllis! She sounds like my kind of friend."

"I'll book a day for us to go to her spa, not that you need it. Paris, you look wonderful. I did not expect this. I thought you looked good when you were in the hospital, but you look even better now. I've been wasting my time worrying about you."

"They gave me transfusions, fluids, and vitamins. I'm still taking vitamins by the bucket," she smiled at me. "They said I'm anemic."

"And," I coached.

"And, Dr. Doom said he isn't predicting anything about the other. He said, 'Go! Live!' and that is what I'm going to do. I made everyone promise not to treat me differently. I still catch a look every once in a while, and it reminds me. However, I am not going to be one of those poor-me people who milk being sick. I am going to live everyday like it's one of a million ahead of me."

"Okay, I'm with you." I marveled at her bravery.

"I'm not going to go back to school, though; there's no use," she said. Then she turned down the truck down another caliche path and asked, "When can I go see Charga?"

"You can follow me to the ranch this afternoon, and I'll give you a gate key so you can see him anytime you want."

She smiled and took my hand. "Thank you so much for everything, Siobhan. I can never thank you enough. How can I ever repay those people who did it? I don't even know them. How do I thank them for what they did?"

"Be happy. We all did it so you would be happy."

"I should have a party here." She pointed through the windshield, and I could see a glade of winter grass standing boot-top high. An ancient gazebo stood in the center of the clearing. "This is my happy place," she told me.

We walked toward it, and I could see tables, benches, and chairs inside. Behind it, the lake shimmered silver in the winter daylight. I wanted to stay there forever.

"In the summer Mother brings out the cushions and curtains and we hang hammocks. I spend as much time down here as I can. It's cool here by the water."

We walked to the water's edge and saw tiny minnows, tranquil as they swam beneath the softly rippling surface, fleeing as our shadows disturbed the calm. Paris pointed to a rope tethered to the thick limb of a huge cypress tree.

"We swing out on this, as far as we can, and then we let go and hit the water. We actually fight to be next in line."

"Sounds like fun. I'd love to try it sometime."

"Come out when it gets warm enough. Charlie loves to swing way out, farther than anybody else," she told me.

"Speaking of Charlie, where is he? I thought you two were inseparable."

"He's coming for lunch. He had to go to school today. He's way behind, stuff he missed while I was in the h-o-s-p-i-t-a-l."

When we got back to the house, Charlie was waiting for us. I hugged him, and Paris took him out on the front porch to tell him about Charga. They asked Franklin if it would be okay for them to drive to my ranch when Charlie got out of school that afternoon.

We ate pot roast, potatoes, squash, beets, green beans, biscuits, and lemon meringue pie.

"Mom's a really good cook," India told me when I commented on how good everything tasted. I offered to help clear the table, but Cardiff told me to go sit down and relax.

Little Ireland asked me to play a game of Battle with her. We both lay on our stomachs in the middle of the sunroom floor. I'd almost lost to her when the telephone rang, and Franklin answered it. His side of the conversation went "Hmm," pause, "Yeah," pause, "I'll be damned," pause, and "Yep, she came out for lunch. You want to talk to her?"

The notion that anyone knew I had come out here perplexed me. Franklin handed me the receiver, and Lannie White spoke, "I've been looking for you all over. I took a chance the Nashes would know where you were," Lannie explained.

"What's going on? What do you need?" I asked.

"The most incredible thing is happening," Lannie said. "My story about Paris and Charga, it's taken on a life of its own. Kids all over the city are taking up collections to help get him back for Paris. They think the steer has been steer-napped."

"They're what?" I could not comprehend what she meant.

"They are going door to door collecting money, having bake sales, car washes, and lemonade stands. Three hundred and seventy-five dollars in small bills and change has been brought in to the paper since noon."

"I'm speechless." Obviously, I was not.

"Television news crews are covering the kids, and the radio stations are asking people to donate money. What are we going to do? It's not like we've gotten a ransom note or anything like that, right?"

"Right. Oh, boy. This is an interesting dilemma. Have you any suggestions about how to handle it?"

"Nope, I hoped you had something." I heard her sigh.

"Let me get back to town and make a few calls." My mind tried to grasp the ramifications of what she told me.

When I hung up the phone, I turned to see everyone looking at me. I held center-stage, and I felt like the actor in a big stage play who had forgotten all her lines. I did not know what to do. I had nothing.

I could not explain in detail about the conversation because we were still keeping information from the Nash family to protect them. I simply told them about the rally of support from children in the city. Franklin and Cardiff passed worried glances back and forth, and Charlie tried to get out of going back to class.

Franklin convinced him to go, and I promised we'd sit right where we were until he got back. Charlie knew better and laughed at that idea.

After he left for class, Paris and I drove out to explore more of the ranch. She showed me other cattle they raised here, mostly quarter–three-quarter cross Angus-Hereford. We explored the little house where her grandparents lived long before they built the big house where the family lived now.

After Charlie returned from his last class a little before four, we left with him following my car in his Jeep so he could drive Paris back home after she had a visit with Charga. On the hour drive to my place outside of New Braunfels, she and I talked openly about Lannie's news.

"If we don't do anything," Paris said, "then those kids who have been out raising money will be disappointed. I don't think that's right, do you?"

"No, I don't think it is right. But, if we tell the truth and everyone finds out what we did and how we did it, all of us could be in serious trouble."

Paris nodded, "What if we get Charga back to the Coliseum before the auction?"

"Then we're back where we started aren't we?"

Paris's eyes filled with tears. "Well, I didn't mean like that. We'd have to get someone to talk to A.L.E.C. and get them to make the exception we asked for in the first place, or we could get Phyllis to sneak him back in!" She laughed.

"I don't think our little caper can be reversed," I admonished. "And, besides, I'm sure security has been tightened since Charga disappeared, for everyone coming or going."

"What if Charga shows up somewhere else, maybe with a note pinned to his halter?" The idea excited her. "It could say, 'We are returning the steer for the children' or something like that." She looked for my reaction.

"Well, yeah, except remember Charga doesn't look like Charga anymore," I reminded her about his makeover. "They'll think someone substituted a different steer."

She deflated like an unknotted balloon. "Can we get him a wig or something?"

Both of us got the giggles picturing Charga in a curly wig, my eyes filled with tears until the road blurred. Poor Charlie, following us, missed the joke.

When we reached the gate to my place, Paris took the key from me, jumped out, unlocked the padlock on the gate, and pushed it open. I pulled two car lengths up, and she waved me on, indicating she would ride the rest of the way with Charlie.

My winding road was not at all like the smooth caliche passage at the Nash Ranch. No one had driven in this gate on a regular basis in over five years. The center mound between the wheel ruts had overgrown with grass and cactus. Limestone slabs, honeycombed and smooth, jutted up to roughen our ride.

We bounced along to the little house where I'd lived out my divorce, walked through to the back porch toward the corral, and had not set foot off the porch steps when Charga came loping out of the barn. He trotted to the gate and stood, shifting his weight from side to side, raising his head, sniffing the air, his eyes on Paris all the while. He made a bawling sound. He knew Paris had come to him.

She called in a soft singsong voice, Charga baby, stay

Charga." She climbed over the wooden fence, and dropped inside the corral, put her arms around the big steer's neck and gave him a fierce hug. Charga rubbed his neck up and down Paris's torso, circling her, making her stand in place. He would not allow her to leave.

Charlie, who had not heard the story of our makeover, did not believe the steer was Charga. He told me later, "I kept waiting for Charga to come out. I thought maybe that one was a crazy one of yours."

"Poor, poor Charga," Paris crooned. "Just look at you."

Charlie went to the Jeep and got a small duffle bag out of the cab, brought it to the corral and hung the handles of it over a fence post. He told Paris, "I brought his grooming stuff."

We let Paris brush Charga while I showed Charlie where I kept things around the house and explained how Melvyn and Marla Gerfers helped. "They keep an eye on the place for me. Mel will be happy to feed Charga for us. That way we won't have to be here every day.

"I don't think you need to do that," Charlie said. He pointed to the corral. "She won't stay away."

He did not say it, but we both knew she would come as long as she could. It did not seem possible that the vibrant young Paris we were watching had such a short time left to live.

After an hour or so, I said goodbye to them. Charlie walked me to my car and I gave him the spare set of keys to the house. He promised to lock everything up before they left, and I departed for San Antonio feeling pleased with my friends and with myself. I drove out the gate and beeped my horn three times, something Grandfather and I had always used as our corny way of saying "I Love You."

Chapter Seventeen

I heard the phone ringing while I tried to unlock my door, ran inside, tripping over the front hall rug, and just as I reached the phone, heard the answering machine pick up. I put my purse, coat, and sweaters on the bed and listened for a voice but only heard a loud click. The red light on the answering machine blinked and I pushed the play button to see who had left messages. The LED indicated I'd gotten twenty-six calls since I'd left that morning. I listened while I started a pot of coffee. Eight of the messages were from BZ, ten from Phyllis, four from Lannie White, three from Bud Johnson and one from Dexter Hardwick, a.k.a. Dr. Doom.

All of them, except the one from Dexter, asked some version of, "Where the hell are you?" The first few explained about the kids and the radio stations being involved. The rest were panicky demands to call back as soon as I got home.

Since I'd already spoken to Lannie, I skipped calling her until after I talked withBZ and Phyl. First, though, I called Bud.

"Hi, Bud, it's me," I put a smile in my voice.

"Well, hello," he answered, his voice soft as lambs ear. "Have you got a paddle?"

"A paddle? To spank me with," I asked, confused.

"No, it looks to me like you're up shit creek and I hope you have a paddle, cause without one your canoe is on the rocks."

"Am I fired?" I couldn't stop the words from coming out of my mouth.

"No, I told you I wouldn't fire you unless you killed Eloy Grisham. You haven't, have you?" He laughed; I laughed. He continued, "I am slightly curious about the direction this has taken. I'm only guessing, in light of our earlier conversation, that you might know something about the disappearance of the champion steer?"

"You don't want to know, do you?" I'd read enough Ann Rule true crime stories to know criminals never tell loved ones about their crimes. "You could get in trouble if I tell you. I'm trying to keep you from being involved, Bud. I don't want you to be an accessory."

"And I appreciate your concern, but please, tell me you've got a plan for this...the kids and everything?"

"Oh sure, Bud. We've got it under control," I lied.

"Good to know," Bud said. "Are you coming back to work tomorrow?"

"Uh, sure, yeah. I'll be there."

As I hung up the phone, my doorbell rang. Through the peephole, I could see Phyllis trying so hard to look inconspicuous that she looked conspicuous. I opened the door and she slid in.

"Are you wearing a wig?" I asked. I could see dark hair under the floppy brimmed hat she wore.

"Hi," she took off the hat. "How do you like me as a brunette?"

She looked marvelous, "You look like Pat Benatar."

Phyllis liked the comparison, went to the front hall mirror to admire her image, and fluffed her dark bangs, turning from side to side.

I watched her and then I casually mentioned, "I went to see Paris today."

"I wondered where you were; I called a few times." She still primped in front of the mirror.

"Ten times," I corrected. "I had twenty-six messages when I got home. I already called Bud back. I talked with Lannie from the ranch. I still have to call BZ. They were calling about the kids. There was one from Dexter Hardwick."

Phyllis frowned at the mirror, still getting used to her image. She shook her head, "What kids?"

"It's on TV and should be in the paper, too." I reached for the remote and turned on the evening news. Tracy smiled as she tossed to a field reporter, "Tell me Jimmy, what's happening out there?"

Jimmy Anderson said, "It's the darnedest thing. Kids from across the city are collecting money to pay ransom on the Grand Champion Steer stolen from the Coliseum. As far as we know, no one has sent a ransom note. One of the DJ's mentioned cow napping and the kids took him at his word. Now the children across the city are trying to raise money to help get the steer back for Paris Nash. I'm here with Jodi Collins," the camera switched to a girl who looked to be about nine years old. "Jodi, tell me what you've been doing?"

Blond pony-tailed Jodi said, "I emptied my piggy-bank

and I've been collecting money. I made a big sign and I've been on the corner holding my boot asking for donations." She showed a scuffed red western boot.

"How much have you got?" Jimmy asked.

"Fourteen dollars and seventy-eight cents," she looked at the camera with a shy smile.

"Back to you, Tracy," Jimmy closed the report

Tracy ginned at the camera, "Thanks for that, Jimmy. Tell me did you put any money in her boot?"

The live shot went back to show Jimmy emptying his pocket change into the girl's palm.

I turned the TV off and Phyllis said, "Oh, my. I had no idea."

"Yeah, I was shocked, too, when Lannie called to tell me."

"Did you say you got a call from Paris's gorgeous Dr. Doom? The one you knew from Lubbock."

I nodded and her voice sounded like a tease. "And what does he want?"

"Probably to ask about how we plan handling the money the kids are raising," I guessed.

The phone rang and I answered. It was BZ's voice. He said, "I have a plan."

"Thank God," I answered.

"You sound a little desperate," BZ said.

I told BZ, "My day started out perfectly. I drove to Kingsland…"

He interrupted. "I thought that's where you were."

I continued, "…and met Paris's brothers and sisters, who by the way are as special as she is. Then Lannie White called to tell me about the kids and the money they are raising. When I got home, I had twenty-six messages about the kids and the money. I already talked to Bud." I told BZ about our conversation. "You'd better have a great idea!"

I didn't mean it as a threat, but BZ said, "Yes, ma'am, sir!" He made me laugh and I felt better. "Meet me at Tristan's in an hour?"

"Can Phyllis come, too?" I nodded at her. She was in the kitchen pouring coffee for us.

"The more the merrier," he said.

I looked at the clock. "Phyllis, we are going to Tristan's."

She saluted. I laughed. I told BZ we'd see him in an hour.

Phyllis said, "Why don't you call Dr. Doom back before we leave? Call him and find out what he wanted."

I dialed the number he'd left, expecting it to be his service. He surprised me when he answered the phone himself.

"Hi, Dr. Hardwick, it's Siobhan O'Shaunessy. You left a message."

"Hi, Siobhan. Thanks for returning my call," he said. "I have a question for you."

"Shoot," I answered.

"Do you have plans Friday night?"

His question took me by surprise. I think giddy is the only way to explain my reaction. Phyllis, standing next to me, went into panicky pantomime as she noticed the change in my demeanor. Her eyes were exaggerated wide open, her shoulders met her earlobes and her lips, whispered, "What, what, what?" She looked like a bowl-trapped goldfish. I shared the receiver.

"No," I answered, being coy, I hated being coy, but it seemed the thing to do. "Why?"

He started by explaining, "There's a new restaurant down on the Riverwalk, and this buddy of mine and I decided we want to try it out."

My jaw dropped, my chin doubled, my eyes popped. I couldn't believe he wanted to take me out. I fought to keep myself from bouncing. Phyllis had overheard and started dancing a tribal gyration.

"That sounds like fun," I tried to be calm.

"He's a very nice guy, a doctor. A podiatrist. I told Jeb I'd found the perfect date for him."

My emotional pendulum slammed to its zenith, and now slid to its mid-point and hung like wet laundry. Phyllis's expression said it all. She mouthed, "Oh, shit."

I felt trapped by my coyness. If I declined, he'd know I thought he wanted to ask me to go out with him and on the other hand, if I acted too enthusiastic, he'd figure I was pretending and know I'd been disappointed that he *wasn't* asking me out. I said nothing.

He went on, "You know my date, though. That might make the evening more fun."

"Oh, really?" I tried to sound interested and wondered which nurse from the hospital he dated.

"When I suggested to Tracy that you and Jeb might hit it off, she said 'Maybe, it's worth a shot'."

"Tracy?"

"Yeah, Tracy Brennan from your station," he explained.

"Oh yeah, Tracy." I said. Tracy the smiling gargoyle. The insult-to-injury cliché couldn't fit any better. I had no easy out so I lied. "I'd love to meet your friend Jeb."

Phyllis paced while I finished talking to him. We agreed to meet Friday evening at Boudro's on the river. I kept my hand on the receiver after I'd replaced it on the phone as if waiting for another ring and a do-over where I'd say, "Sorry Dexter. I have plans."

Phyllis' pacing fired her up. "You are coming to the Spa on Friday, before you meet them, and I'm picking out your outfit." She pulled me toward my bedroom closet.

After insulting my taste in clothing and footwear, she finally agreed to let me wear a simple black sheath and black pumps.

"I'll accessorize?" She made it sound like a question, so she'd seem less pushy. She meant, "I'll accessorize!"

We made plans for me to go to the spa on top of the plan for the Friday night dinner, and I felt my life leaping further out of my control.

The phone rang again; it was BZ.

I didn't give him a chance to speak. "I told you I got all of those messages?"

BZ said, "Yeah?"

"There was one from Dexter," I told him.

"Who?" BZ asked.

"Dexter, Dr. Doom, Paris's doctor," I reminded him.

"Yeah?" There was caution in his voice.

"I called him back. I thought he was asking me out, but he called to set me up on a blind date, instead. Did you know he's dating Tracy Brennan?" I didn't wait for him to answer. "Then Phyllis totally creamed my wardrobe with rude criticisms about my taste in clothing. I apparently have nothing worth wearing in my entire closet." I paused and took a deep breath.

"First of all," BZ took the opportunity to speak, "I didn't know he was dating Tracy. Second, Lannie's meeting us at Tristan's, too."

"Okay, I'll see you." I hung up.

On the way to Tristan's, Phyllis admitted, "I think it's wonderful the way the kids are rallying around Paris and Charga." She un-wrapped a piece of gum and offered a stick to me. I declined it, and she popped it into her mouth. "Isn't Paris touched by that?"

"She's touched and concerned about the children. She doesn't want to disappoint them. She wants to return Charga…"

"Oh boy, another adventure!" Phyllis was primed as a pump. "Can we do the same thing in reverse?"

I shook my head and rolled my eyes. "I think security is a little tougher now."

I told her about how Charga reacted when he heard Paris's voice. By the way, she wasn't all that upset with our makeover. She said she'd get him looking good again. Poor Charlie though. He thought we'd replaced Charga with an imposter steer. And, Paris wants to meet you so she can thank you. I told her we'd stop by the spa."

Phyllis decided she wanted to give Paris a complete spa day the next time she came to town.

"Do you think Paris would look cute in a short bob?"

I nodded and let her plan the makeover she wanted to do. When she finished I asked her, "Do you realize how much I admire you? You are such a generous person. You give freely of your time and are generous with your business. I know how often you contribute to fundraisers. I see your silent auction packages at charity events. You are a very special woman, Phyllis. I'm lucky to have you for my friend."

As we drove, I realized how fortunate I was to have surrounded myself with a whole group of happy, creative, hardworking, enthusiastic people who actually seemed to care about me. The realization surprised me. I wondered if I deserved them.

Chapter Eighteen

The most interesting thing that happened at Tristan's was Tristan himself. He couldn't take his eyes off Phyllis. The poor guy kept saying, "Are you sure you're the same person who rode in the beer truck with the steer? You look so different!"

Phyllis blushed and seemed strangely subdued.

BZ, oblivious, hadn't noticed Phyllis's changed hair color. He said, "Hi Phyllis; you look different."

"Different? Not better?"

Tristan jumped to her defense. "Better, definitely better."

I wanted to say, "and, Tristan, *you're acting* different. Are you sure *you're* the same person I waited with when we stole Charga," but I didn't. BZ appeared to be the only person in the room who didn't notice the electricity coursing between them.

BZ said, "Let's go sit," and he pointed to our usual table.

Tristan rushed around to hold a chair for Phyllis. She sat and looked up at him and smiled, "Thank you."

Phyllis acting demure? Crazy, crisp, business-as-usual Phyllis basked in the attention Tristan gave her. It even made me consider changing *my* hair color before Friday night!

Before I had time to take my jacket off, BZ started talking. He had a plan. It was pretty much what Paris had suggested on the way to see Charga. However, it wasn't until I called Paris to tell her what BZ said, that I was convinced it was the perfect plan.

Paris said, "I love it. The children will believe they made it happen!" Her enthusiasm reached me. "We can take care of our end."

When I got to work the next morning I found a large brown envelope on my desk, FRAGILE stamped on its front. As soon as I opened it, I knew I needed to interrupt Bud's meeting with the sales staff to show it to him. I walked into his office holding the sheet of orange construction paper to my chest. I went behind his desk and held it in front of him so only he could see it. He glanced and nodded. I didn't say a word. I turned on my heel and left their meeting clutching the ransom note.

When he asked, and I knew he would ask me eventually, I'd say, "I had no idea how the envelope got on my desk, wink-wink."

I had to get in touch with Eloy to start negotiations. I dialed *Comida Y Mas* and left a message on the answering machine.

"This is Siobhan O'Shaunessy, and I have received a ransom note concerning the Grand Champion Steer." I recorded.

It was true. I *had* received a note. Not exactly, a

ransom note, though. The orange construction paper had cutouts from magazines pasted on it, much like the ones I'd seen in kidnap movies and it said,

WE HAVE SAVED THE STEER
STEER MUST LIVE AND GO HOME WITH GIRL!
No $$$$
WILL WATCH NEWS FOR AGREEMENT

The auction, less than two days away, would not feature a Grand Champion Steer for the first time in its history. We believed Eloy would jump at the chance to let Charga return under any circumstance, and would be happy to let Paris withdraw him so the bidder money would spread out among the other steers at the auction.

While I waited for Eloy to return my call, I checked the assignment board to see where I was going that day. I'd be covering a City Council meeting from eleven to conclusion, a boring day of proclamations and ongoing citizen complaints about attempts to fluoridate the city water.

I sat formulating ideas for my script when a shadow crossed my desk. I looked up to discover why Eloy hadn't called me back. He'd come to the station and stood in front of me.

"You have a note? From the thieves?" Eloy asked.

The way he said it made me doubtful about the success of our plan. "I think fraternity guys did it as a prank. It wasn't true thievery," I chattered, trying to soften the accusation. "See, it's on Texas Longhorn orange paper."

"You don't think it has anything to do with the Nash girl?" He sneered. "I do. I think those people would do anything to save the damn steer."

He wasn't following our plan. He was not being

grateful and forgiving.

Before I knew what was happening, Bud Johnson was standing at my desk, too.

"Can I help you, sir? I'm Bud Johnson and I run this place," he said to the smaller man.

"Eloy Grisham." He extended his hand toward Bud.

Bud's face registered recognition. "Come in to my office, Mr. Grisham." He ushered Eloy by the elbow toward his glassed aquarium office. He turned to me and instructed, "Siobhan, call Maxine. Tell her to cancel security."

I watched them walk away, and, BZ, who started toward my desk, saw the short man and did a U-turn. He sat down at the sports desk, his back to me. My phone rang.

"What is going on?" BZ demanded.

"I left a message, and then he showed up here," I tried to explain using verbal shorthand.

"What's Bud doing?" BZ's voice sounded panicky.

"I have no idea. He didn't invite me in." I got defensive.

BZ's sigh blew exasperation. Mine matched his. We each sat holding a receiver to our ear and didn't say a word. We waited.

When their meeting ended, I can tell you, I loved Bud Johnson. He and Eloy came out, Bud's arm resting on Eloy's shoulders, and they were laughing like the best of friends. Bud motioned me over, and we stood at the elevator, waiting for the doors to open.

"Why don't you show Eloy the way out, Siobhan?" Bud directed me.

Neither BZ nor I had any idea what had happened. I stepped onto the elevator with Eloy, and as the elevator doors slid shut, I had to stifle a laugh. I caught a glimpse of BZ. His stare was as blank as a sheet of copy paper and his face as white as one, too.

On the elevator ride, Eloy told me to come to the Coliseum in an hour with my cameraman. He would make a statement. I handed him the ransom note. He looked at it and laughed aloud. I didn't get off the elevator when we reached the lobby. I watched Eloy, laughing as he went toward the glass front doors. I held the door open button until Eloy was out of the building. I let the doors slide shut and leaned back against the handrail so lost in thought that when the doors slid open, I started to step off. I didn't realize the elevator hadn't moved off the lobby floor.

One of the KWNK salesmen stepped in. He asked, "Floor please."

"Newsroom," I answered, standing facing the doors, my head up, watching the numbers change. I held my shoulders back, bluffed my way, faked my confidence as usual, smiling all the while. However, I could feel something changing inside me.

I wasn't sure what it was that I felt, but suddenly I felt myself developing authentic confidence, feeling rounder, as if an invisible file had rasped my rough edges away and then used the ground off bits to fill in the empty spaces I hadn't even known were there. I'd suddenly become more solid and certain of who I was. I felt good about my life for the first time in a very long time.

When I reached the newsroom floor, I told myself not to get too cocky; after all, at any minute, I might be charged as an accessory to cattle rustling.

When the doors slid open, BZ nearly leapt across the newsroom to me before I could step out.

"What's going on?" He demanded.

I shrugged. "I haven't the slightest. Let's go ask Bud."

Bud, sitting in his big leather chair, looked more self-satisfied than I'd ever seen him, like a child who'd mastered tying a shoe; he had his hands clasped behind his head and leaned backward, tilting his chair away. We didn't say a word, went to the twin chairs that faced his desk, and sat down. I propped my elbows on the edge of his desk and stared innocently at him; BZ stretched his legs out in front and leaned into the back of his chair as if we'd just dropped in for a friendly visit. No one spoke. Bud looked at us, waiting, smiling and, we looked back at him, waiting, and smiling too. No one said we were playing a game of chicken, but all knew we were. The three of us, as committed as teenagers racing toward a cliff, were determined not to be the one to break. Who would waver first?

Of course, it was me. Bud rolled forward. BZ leaned over the desk. Then two of them slapped palms as I opened my mouth to utter my first word.

"So, what did you say to Eloy?" I asked over their victory.

"I said," Bud began, "'Eloy, you must be some kind of genius. No one in the history of the Stock Show has generated so much publicity. Everyone in town is talking about it. I called Lannie White this morning to tell her some kids dropped off over eight hundred dollars at the studio. Tell me, Eloy, did you pay someone to take the damn steer?'"

BZ and I had a moment of peripheral eye contact, thinking, but not saying, "Bud's a freaking genius."

"He denied being involved in any way," Bud told us.

We shrugged. We already knew he wasn't involved.

Bud continued. "I said, 'How can we make this work to the best advantage for you, Eloy'." Dragging out the explanation, he paused and took a drink of coffee from his World's Greatest Boss mug. "I told him that getting the kids involved was a great touch."

He took a long pause. We could wait.

We finally grew tired of waiting. "And..." We asked in unison.

"He said he didn't have anything to do with getting the kids involved. Of course, we knew that, didn't we?"

We nodded.

Bud added, "We tossed around a few ideas. He's going to choose the one he likes best, and you. . .," he waggled his finger back and forth between the two of us, ". . .are going to take the remote truck and do a live interview out at the grounds. Eloy will lay out his position. I'll get Jimmy to cover City Council."

"What is Eloy going to do?" BZ and I both asked at the same time, again. "Jinx, coke," we said together.

Bud laughed. "I'm starting to worry about you two. There's such a thing as too much togetherness." He continued, "I have no idea what Eloy's going to do. We will all be surprised. Nevertheless, don't talk about this, we don't want the competition to get wind of it."

"We should call Paris shouldn't we?"

"Okay, let Paris know," he said, "But, no one else. I want this to be our exclusive story." He looked serious.

We left Bud's office and noticed the rest of the staff react as if they'd gone from pause to play. Everyone knew something was happening, and we knew there would be a siege of questions we were sworn not to answer.

"*Que pasa?*" Javier Soto, the sports guy got to BZ first. He locked step hoping to find out what was happening.

I slipped back to my desk and telephoned Paris. The line was busy so I left a cryptic message on Phyllis's answering machine, "It's going to work out; please call Paris, and ask her to watch the five o'clock broadcast and for her to call Eloy immediately afterward. Tell her to be completely grateful, surprised, and humbled. Tell her to thank Eloy and the committee. Go overboard." I ended the message with an invitation: "Can you meet us at Tristan's at six tonight.?"

Chapter Nineteen

BZ signaled me after he'd gotten together with Troy Hammond, our remote truck engineer. Troy had to go to set up the live feed. When Troy signaled he was set, we headed to the Coliseum.

On the drive, BZ and I tried to figure out which tactic A.L.E.C. would use. He suggested, "They might offer a big reward for the steer's return."

"Yeah, but then from now on they'd have to beef up security on every animal out there."

"Mm hmm, you're right. Maybe they don't want to give them anything." BZ answered.

"Uh, BZ, lest you forget, *them* are us," I whispered so Troy couldn't hear.

"Right." He grimaced.

"Do you think they'll want to meet with the 'people' who did it," I suggested.

"No, he won't. He won't want to give them any publicity, and they won't want to get arrested." BZ seemed sure.

Troy had to stop to fill the tank with gas and while he was at the pump, I teased BZ, "When did you make the note? In fifth grade?"

"Wait, don't give me any crap." He glared at me. "What do you expect when you have to use your kid's round nose safety scissors and a half dried paste stick and cut words from *Highlights* and *Good Housekeeping*?"

After we reached the Coliseum, BZ and I went inside to find Eloy. Then we followed the Chairman to Charga's empty Grand Champion pen.

For the television interview, Eloy changed back into this rodeo finery and the man was puffed up so big with importance that I thought if I stuck him with a pin, he would take rapid, jagged flight and end up deflated somewhere on the Coliseum grounds.

Troy established the connection with the station, and I stood holding the microphone. Eloy and I waited for the three-finger count down and the interview began with Tracy introducing during the evening news report.

I said, "Thank you, Tracy. I am here at the Livestock Show and Rodeo with A.L.E.C. Chairman Eloy Grisham." I turned to him. "Chairman Grisham, with the auction only two days away, I'm sure you are concerned about the location of Grand Champion Steer, Charga."

Eloy puffed up even bigger and said, "Siobhan, we've received a ransom note of sorts. Whoever took Charga is willing to return him, but only if we agree to allow Paris Nash to take her steer home with her. The A.L.E.C. committee isn't willing to do that. Instead, A.L.E.C. decided to allow the high bidder, the winner at the auction, to determine the fate of the steer."

"Isn't this against the rules set out by A.L.E.C.?" I

asked, surprised by what he'd said.

"That's right, Siobhan. The rules state the entrant must agree to give control of the animal to the committee after the judging and take care of the animal until the auction, when the animal will be purchased and designated for immediate slaughter. However, the circumstances surrounding Miss Nash are such that the A.L.E.C. decided to allow a one-time exception to that hard and fast rule. The steer will survive if the high bidder wants to return it to Miss Nash. For this one occasion, the organization will exempt the steer from the termination rule. We will not file charges against the thieves. We have prepared a statement, and Lannie White is going to incorporate it into her column in tomorrow's *San Antonio Light*."

"Thank you, Mr. Grisham. Back to you, Tracy."

BZ and I packed up our equipment and helped Troy load the cable in the truck. While he drove us back to the studio, we sat like speechless-mouth-breathers. They hadn't complied with the demand in the note.

Back at the studio, as we walked to the newsroom, I asked, "Okay, BZ. How much money can you throw into the pot?"

"That's nothing to joke about, Siobhan." He sounded like a preacher. "This is serious."

"We need to call Lannie White. She's read the entire document and might have an idea."

I called her while BZ perched on the edge of my desk so he could listen in. She agreed to meet us at Tristan's at six and said she would bring the document and "Put her thinking cap on" in the meantime.

BZ looked at his watch. "We better get going if we're meeting at Tristan's by six." He left to get his car and I gathered my belongings. The phone rang as I pulled my jacket from the back of my chair.

"Hello," I answered, half-expecting it to be Phyllis.

"Siobhan," the voice said.

The soft velvetiness of it washed over me. My heart lurched and all the joy in my life recoiled to a hidden place where I hoped it would be safe.

"Mother," I finally answered. "How are you?"

We hadn't spoken since Grandfather died when she called to say she wouldn't be able to make it to his funeral. The last time I'd seen her face to face was when she showed up at the surprise party my grandfather gave me for my twenty-first birthday. I couldn't understand what prompted her to call me now.

As if she read my mind, she said, "Graciella Grisham called me." She said it in the dangerous marshmallow tone I'd learned to distrust.

"Oh," I wiped my damp palm on my pant leg.

"She told me I should be proud of you, that you are quite a lovely young woman." Her tone did not change.

I didn't respond. Should I say, "Tell Graciella Grisham, thank you for me," or should I tell her, "How nice of you to call and tell me that."

"Do you need my help?" she asked me.

"With...?" I left the question open.

"Money?" she volunteered.

"How kind of you to offer, Mother, but what for?" I was stymied by her offer.

"To purchase the steer," she said.

I had nothing to say. After not seeing her for years, she suddenly calls to offer me money. She couldn't have surprised me more if she'd dropped out of the sky like Glinda the Good Witch from *The Wizard of Oz* and hit me with her magic wand. Of course, since I'd watched the movie about twenty times, I felt I knew Glinda better than I knew her.

"Thank you, Mother," I said.

"You are welcome," she answered.

"Your call has taken me by surprise, and I feel badly about having to tell you this, but I'm on my way to a meeting. Can I call you later tonight?"

"That's fine, Siobhan." She sounded weary.

"I. . ." I fumbled through my purse trying to find a pen. "I need your phone number." She gave it to me, and I said, "I'll call tomorrow."

On the way to Tristan's, I repeatedly replayed our brief conversation in my head and made the decision not to tell my friends about the call or about her offer. I needed to work this out for myself before I started talking about it.

Phyllis got there a little late. Tristan didn't take his eyes off the door, waiting for her to arrive. He had prepared a wonderful Mexican food smorgasbord for us instead of having us order off the menu. I thought he might have prepared it so he could show off his culinary skills to Phyllis. If she didn't arrive soon, there wouldn't be anything left to impress her.

Lannie loved the food and told Tristan she planned to mention the restaurant in her column someday soon. He had shared the story about his relationship with his old high school teacher and about learning from the teacher's father in Mexico.

Lannie told him, "You know, Tristan, you have a great story. People would enjoy reading about your entrepreneurial spirit. You are an example to anyone who wants to start out or who is afraid to take a chance on his own. Knowing there are true 'rags-to-riches' stories like yours might help someone make a change."

"You could do one about Phyllis, too," Tristan

suggested. "She has a wonderful spa."

Lannie nodded, "I know. That's how I got involved with all of you." She laughed.

BZ's head popped up from behind the sports page. He looked back and forth between Lannie and Tristan, then at me. I smiled at him. He smiled back and went back to reading about the Spurs on their Rodeo road trip so the coliseum would be available for the week. Poor BZ couldn't have been clueless.

My enthusiasm was at low ebb after my unexpected phone call, but I tried to keep up with the conversations at the table. My mind didn't cooperate and often went back to the call from my mother. There had been hundreds of times in my life when her call would have meant everything to me, but she didn't call then. Why now?

Phyllis arrived, rushed to the table, apologizing about a client who kept her late. She hugged BZ, then Lannie, Tristan and me. Tristan rushed off to the kitchen and came back with a platter heaped with samples of the food he'd already served us. He had made up a special plate for Phyllis and had kept it under the warmer. She oohed over every bite and Tristan told her how he'd made each recipe. She listened raptly to every word he said.

Lannie looked at me, raised her eyebrows, and then looked back and forth between the two of them. I shrugged. Yep, Lannie got it.

After Phyllis finished eating, Tristan suggested we move to another table while one of his waiters cleaned up the residue of our feast. As soon as we were all seated, Lannie told us about meeting with Eloy.

"I believe," she told us, "Eloy has come to terms with the publicity value of the steer's disappearance. He understands he can be the good guy and come out of this all right. However, when he met with the committee, none of them wanted to change the rules for the entrants. They wanted to keep the terminal show provision in place. Therefore, they compromised.

"They think Paris will be able to find a company that will want to buy the steer and return the steer to her. That way a great deal of money goes to A.L.E.C. scholarships, Paris will have Charga, and Eloy will be admired by all."

"But" BZ interjected, "what if the winning bidder doesn't want to return Charga to Paris? What then?"

"Then he will be the Grinch who stole Charga and be hated by everyone in town," Phyllis answered.

Lannie said, "The die-hard A.L.E.C. members don't like the idea of changing the rules at all. Not only are they capable of buying the steer, they are also capable of standing by the rules and not giving a damn about whether or not anyone likes them. It's the *principle* for them. I'm grateful that enough of them were willing to give Charga a small chance."

"So, we need to find a sure-fire buyer." BZ, being the most pragmatic, leapt to the obvious conclusion.

We all agreed.

"Any suggestions?" Tristan asked.

"I think," Lannie, suggested, "The only way we can be sure to win Charga is to form our own consortium."

I got my notebook out of my bag and started making notes.

"How much money do we have from the kids' collections?" Phyllis asked.

"Right now," Lannie pulled a small tablet from her purse and flipped it open "Forty-five hundred fifty-eight dollars and fifty-two cents."

"Does that include the money the kids dropped off at

the station?" I asked her.

"Yep, I talked to Bud earlier today and he gave me the total. Its forty-five hundred fifty-eight dollars and fifty-two cents, total."

I liked the sound of fifty-two cents. It reminded me that children broke their piggy banks and foraged under sofa cushions to find money to donate for Charga's survival.

"How much more do we need?" Tristan asked.

"Last year's Grand Champion steer sold for. . ." she flipped through her notebook, but she couldn't find the entry, ". . .somewhere close to eighty-five thousand dollars if I remember correctly," Lannie guessed.

Tristan whistled a long shrill sound.

Phyllis understated, "So we only need to get commitments for eighty thousand dollars more."

BZ said, "Yeah, but with all the publicity surrounding the Grand Champion this year, I bet the bidding will be even higher than last year. We'll need to raise more than that."

"What do you think, Siobhan?" Phyllis asked.

I hadn't been paying total attention. My thoughts kept going back to my mother up in Maine and her offer to give me money to buy the steer. She said she'd heard from Graciella, so I assumed that she and Graciella must have remained friends over the years. Graciella probably told her the details of the A.L.E.C. decision.

I agreed with BZ.

"I think I can get some money from the paper," Lannie guessed. "We have a budget for charitable donations, and A.L.E.C. qualifies as a non-profit organization. After the article appears in tomorrow's edition about their decision to change the rules, I might get a few calls from potential bidders. Maybe even my brother-in-law will go in with our group. Let's talk again tomorrow evening after I have a chance to make some calls."

We agreed and this time decided we'd meet at The Spa That Loves Me. Phyllis said she'd order pizza for us from Capparelli's.

I was rarely the first to leave our meetings, but as soon as we'd taken care of business, I stood to go. BZ was jotting figures on the back of a napkin and didn't notice. Lannie stood at the same time and walked out with me. Phyllis looked up in time to give me a quizzical look. I waved goodbye and she mouthed, "Call me."

As Lannie and I stepped outside, she told me, "I finally made the connection. You're Gordon O'Shaunessy's granddaughter, aren't you?"

"Guilty," I admitted.

"I knew more *about* him than actually knew him," she said.

"He was a good man," I told her.

"No doubt about that, and he was generous too. We wouldn't be worried about raising money for the auction if he were still alive. I'm on a couple of non-profit boards, and I can tell you, several of those organizations wouldn't exist today if it hadn't been for your Grandfather's 'anonymous' donations. I think it was admirable that he never wanted publicity for making them, either."

"Thank you." I tried to make it to my car before I started crying, but my eyes filled with tears as we stood in Tristan's parking lot.

Lannie's eyes widened and she gave me an awkward hug. "I'm sorry. I didn't mean to make you sad."

She pulled away and I wiped at my face with my hand. "It's been an emotional day for me."

"Is there anything I can do?" She offered.

"No, I have to work through a few things for myself."

I smiled and she gave me a less awkward hug.

I drove home thinking about what she'd said about my Grandfather. I doubted she knew he'd been my only family. Most people didn't know. Grandfather avoided saying he was raising me, I think because that always led to the follow up question, "What happened to her mother? Her father?"

It was easy answering the father question. A drunk driver killed him when I was four. The mother question was more difficult. I never learned to explain that.

Phyllis told me to say, "She went off the deep end and is still falling." I couldn't though, it hurt too much to be flippant. Growing up without my mother damaged me.

When I was at the hospital, telling Charlie and Paris about my life, I hadn't been totally honest about her abandonment of me. Years of counseling made me aware that it had been much more staggering than I remembered or could admit.

I don't know what would have happened to me if my grandfather hadn't scooped me up and made me believe life was going to be a wonderful exciting adventure. He was not a nurturer and didn't understand the importance of it. He'd taught me I could survive, thrive, even without coddling.

When my marriage failed, Grandfather hadn't babied or cocooned me. Nor did he belittle me or say, "What did you expect?" He's the one that suggest I go to the ranch, to think and regroup. He was also the one who told me, after four years of thinking and regrouping, that I'd had plenty of time and I might want to get on with life.

If it hadn't been for him encouraging me to finish my degree so I could take over the station for him someday, I'd probably stayed on the ranch, never gone to Tech, never gotten my degree in RTF.

When he died so soon after marrying his manipulative sixth wife, everything crashed down again. I'd wanted to go back to the ranch to hide again.

That is why I hated my mother's phone call. Contact with her made me think of unpleasant feelings, memories, and insecurities. Once they started swirling, I couldn't stop them from making me feel small and vulnerable again, as fearful as the six-year-old girl who cried herself to sleep so many nights she couldn't count them all, the little girl who didn't know what she'd done to make her mother go away.

Chapter Twenty

I went to sleep thinking about the call and had nightmares all night. I woke worrying about what I would say when I called her back, and I had to call her back because I promised her I would. I decided to get it over with before going in to work. I got my notebook, glanced at the clock, and dialed her number, feeling slightly foolish about worrying if I were calling too early.

Actually, I didn't care if I did wake her. In fact, the little child within me rather hoped I would wake her from a sound delicious sleep.

"Siobhan?" She answered the phone with my name.

That set me back, "Yes, it's me."

"I've been waiting for your call."

I envisioned her not having moved from the place where she'd been sitting when she called yesterday, an ashtray full of cigarette butts, cold coffee in a cup. I didn't know what to say, so I said nothing. She initiated the contact, so she could do the talking. I didn't have anything to say to her, except maybe to ask what had been so important that she hadn't been able to come to her father's funeral. I waited.

The ticking of the Big Ben alarm clock on my nightstand broke the silence, I started counting the ticks as the circular metronome spent time. After twenty tics, I thought we'd been disconnected, but I heard her cough one of those deep smoker's coughs. I waited for her to speak. I'd made a promise to myself the last time that I would never reach out to her again. This time she'd have to do all the work.

"Graciella," she said, beginning in a voice hoarse from coughing, pausing as if choosing her words, or lighting a cigarette. "Graciella told me she had lunch with you. She told me you are working at KWNK. How did that come about?"

"I interviewed and got the job," I answered as succinctly as possible. I didn't tell her Bud Johnson almost fell out of his chair during the interview when I admitted I was Gordon O'Shaunessy's granddaughter. Or, that Bud promised he wouldn't tell anyone lest they think he'd hired me for that reason.

"Good for you, Siobhan." She cleared her throat. I couldn't tell if she was being sincere or was reverting to her cynical self.

I didn't respond to her. I sat, holding the phone to my ear, bobbing my crossed leg in time to the rhythm of my ticking Ben. I realized I could not picture her or see her surroundings as I could talking with Phyllis. I hadn't seen her in eleven years, had never been to her home.

"Are you doing all right, Siobhan? I mean, do you have enough money?"

Money. I knew she'd get around to that. She certainly had enough of it. She inherited everything when my father died and won a small fortune from the lawsuit against the other driver. None of her husbands had been poor men and Grandfather's trust fund was generous. She'd claimed that when she turned forty-five. She had plenty of money.

I answered her in a flat voice, "Well, I think money is relative, don't you agree?"

"I mean," she sounded wounded. "I know you have the trust fund…"

I interrupted, "And you know I won't have access to it until I'm forty-five, so funds are a little tight." I tried not to be so harsh.

"But you are living in my condo rent free?" Her reminder made me harden, again.

"Yes, your attorney made it quite clear," I replied. She had been generous about that. Her attorney's call had surprised me, and I'd taken the offer. I could have lived at the ranch and commuted back and forth two hours each day, but I hadn't wanted to spend that much time on the road.

"Yes, thank you, again, for letting me live here," I said. "Your attorney didn't tell me how long the offer lasted. Are you calling to tell me I have to start paying rent now that I'm employed?"

"Good grief, no." Her words were matter-of-fact, and slight annoyance edged her tone. "In fact, I'll sign the whole thing over to you completely right now, if you want."

"Thank you, but I can't afford to pay the taxes on it. I already have taxes on the ranch this year now that I'm employed."

This wasn't going well. I didn't like the mean way I was speaking to her. I was letting her get to me after all the years I'd concentrated my energy on becoming a better person than she had been. I was acting just like her.

She said, "Let me tell you why I called you yesterday."

She took control, Chairman of the Board calling the meeting to order.

"That sounds like a great idea." I replied in a voice flat as a pond.

"Graciella told me about the girl. She said you were determined to help get her steer back?"

I stayed silent.

She continued. "She told me you'd failed because they wouldn't relax the traditional rules. Then she called me yesterday and told me the rules had been modified and that now the buyer at the auction will decide if the steer lives or dies." She sounded breathless.

I waited.

"Siobhan, I have money. Do you want me to help you?"

"Help me how? Give me a loan? I'll be able to pay you back in twelve years when I get my trust fund," I answered.

"However you want to do it. It is your money in the end. I'm holding it for you until…" she didn't finish.

I wanted to shout, *until what, mother. Until you die…when? Next week? Next month? Or, perhaps the day after I die when I won't need it anyway?* I let her unfinished sentence hang in the air.

"Let me know what you need and when you need it," her voice sounded tired. "You know I have regrets, Siobhan."

"Yes, Mother. I do, too, lots of them. I have to hang up now. I have to get ready for work. I'll call you later." I hung up the phone before she could respond.

My feelings were a whirlpool sucking me under again. I ignored them as best I could. I couldn't, or didn't, want to sort right then.

As soon as I got to the station, BZ took one look at me

and asked, "Are you okay?"

I shook my head and lied, "I'm okay."

"And I'm Miss America," he posed with his hand behind his head.

"Really?" I smiled weakly.

"When you want to talk, I'm here." BZ gave me a slow wink.

"Thanks." I forced a smile.

Bud came out of his glass enclosure and motioned for us to come in. BZ pointed a finger at his chest, and Bud motioned both of us.

"Okay," Bud said as we settled into the chairs across from him. "Tell me what's going on now."

For a minute, I thought he knew about my mother. I couldn't figure out how he knew. I realized he was asking where we were with Charga and Paris.

I motioned to BZ and said, "You tell him."

BZ shared the plan he'd come up with to get Charga back to the auction. "Tristan," BZ began reciting the plan, "is very close to one of his high-school teachers, and a former student of that teacher is the Facilities Director for the school district. He is going to leave the gate to Alamo Stadium unlocked tonight. And sometime in the middle of the night Charga is going to turn up there." BZ's voice thinly veiled his enthusiasm.

Bud cocked an eyebrow, "And?" he asked.

"The police and all the news hotlines are going to get anonymous calls saying there's a cow on the football field. The *kidnappers*, he made quotation marks in the air with his fingers, "will have written a letter and put it in Charga's harness to explain. It will have instructions to call Eloy Grisham."

"Sounds like a photo-op to me," Bud said, rubbing his

palms together.

"Yeah, but we have to wait for the hot-line call. We can't show up too soon. It's going to take a while for Phyllis and Tristan to call Eloy, the police, us, and the other news stations." BZ said.

"But, nothing says we can't already have a crew in the neighborhood," Bud smiled.

"BZ and I aren't going to be involved in the discovery." I added. "At least, not when Charga is discovered in the stadium. That would raise too many red flags with Eloy."

Bud looked more closely at me. "Are you all right, Oshun?"

I tried an unsuccessful smile. "Paris has a seven a.m. appointment at the hospital tomorrow," I continued. "So she will be coming in to town really early for a legitimate purpose. She'll say she heard about the cow on the news while she was driving in and will show up at the stadium when the news cameras arrive. They'll catch her reuniting with Charga and then she'll have to convince everyone the steer really is Charga," I explained.

BZ told Bud, "Yeah. Charga needed to have a kind of reverse makeover, so he's not as pretty as he used to be." He wrinkled his nose, "Not cute at all."

I smiled, remembering what Phyllis and I did to the poor animal.

Bud raised his hand, a cop stopping traffic and said, "I don't need to know anymore."

"No, you really do," I interrupted. "You know that Eloy and A.L.E.C. agreed to let the high bidder at the auction decide what happens to Charga?"

"I saw the interview, Siobhan." He glanced at me over the top of his glasses.

"Well, how do we know the high bidder will let

Charga go back to live with Paris?" I asked.

Bud pursed his lips, "Hmmm."

"Yeah, hmmm," I mimicked, wishing I wore glasses so I could look over them.

BZ took over. "We need to get the bid. We need to form a group with enough people joining in so we can win Charga and make sure he lives."

Bud looked down and away from us. He chewed on his lower lip. We all searched for solutions to the problem we were facing.

Finally, Bud stood up. "Let me work on it."

We left him and went back to our daily routine after checking the assignment board to see where we were going for the day. Bud had assigned me to cover a Lite Beer celebrity who'd come to town to advertise the beer during rodeo. I'd read the press release when it came into the station the week before and hoped I'd be assigned to cover it. The public relations woman at the local distributorship did a good job coming up with a hook for the story.

Jim Shoulders, eight times Professional All-Around Cowboy, brought his brahma bull Buford T with him to advertise the beer and they were *both* staying at a five-star downtown hotel. No one before had let a bull stay in a hotel; it would be a fun story to cover.

Bud didn't assign BZ to go with me. He wanted him to stay at the station to cover breaking news. He either would be rushing to cover a fire, or might be cleaning camera equipment all day.

I had to admit I was glad BZ wasn't coming with me. He already knew something was bothering me, and I'd be dodging his questions all day.

Gregory Schumacher, the camera operator assigned to work with me on the Jim Shoulders story, started at the station even more recently than me. I knew his new status worked in our favor because we'd both be trying our best to prove our worth. I knew he'd go the extra mile to do a well-presented story, even though this wasn't going to be a big feature like the steer judging had been. This was more filler news, but it did give me more face time, a plus for me. That thought perked me up.

When we got to the hotel, the local distributor's P.R. woman met us. She ushered us into the courtyard of the highly rated hotel, where we found a temporary stock pen positioned on lush green grass near an ornate Spanish fountain. Jim Shoulders leaned against the railing in jeans, boots, and a fringed blue satin western shirt that had a huge Lite Beer logo embroidered on it. His tan Stetson shaded his grey-blue eyes, and he grinned as he reached his hand out for me to shake.

"Howdy."

"And howdy to you to, Mr. Shoulders. I'm Siobhan O'Shaunessy with KWNK News, and this is Gregory Schumacher, my cameraman."

"Call me Jim, and this here is Buford," he motioned proudly to the enormous bull that stood on the other side of the railing. "He only drinks Lite Beer from Miller!" He gestured to a champagne bucket in the corner of the pen. It held a brown quart-sized bottle of Lite beer.

During our interview, I asked, "Aren't Brahmas one of the meaner, more aggressive breeds of cattle?"

"Any bull will be ornery if you mistreat it, but this one," he patted the grey mottled bull, "I hand raised. He is as gentle as a kitten."

He's like Charga that way, I thought, and as if to prove the point, Buford T licked the side of Jim's face with a huge pink tongue.

"See what I'm tellin' ya?" Shoulder's bright blue eyes sparkled.

I loved doing the interview, though maybe I took a little too much time. It ended with me atop the bull, leaning down into the camera saying, "Buford T will be signing autographs out at the rodeo tonight." Then I sat up straight and looked back over my shoulder to Gregory, who stayed behind filming me as I rode Buford T, led by Jim, of course, into the hotel lobby. I ducked my head as we went through the door and gave a thumbs-up. Having a bull roaming through the lobby of a five-star hotel would definitely qualify as newsworthy.

Bud aired the piece on the five and 10 o'clock news, and it ran in its entirety. My little story became the topic of conversation when we met at Phyllis' spa that night.

Tristan arrived freshly showered and shaved, wearing tan slacks, a white shirt, and a dark suede jacket. Phyllis went to greet him as BZ wolf-whistled. Tristan blushed. He wasn't as comfortable being the center of attention here as he was in his restaurant. I realized I'd never seen him without an apron around his waist.

The article about A.L.E.C. and Charga ran under Lannie's byline in the paper that day. She had emphasized Eloy's decision to allow the winning bidder to decide whether Charga lived. She had equated the winner with Nero. *Thumbs up, thumbs down. "Which will it be?"* she'd written.

She asked BZ and Tristan to help get something from her car, and it took them two trips to bring in the trays filled with letters.

"These were delivered to the paper," Lannie said. "The stamped ones are from the original story we ran on Monday. I suppose we'll get more tomorrow after today's story."

We were all enjoying the pizza, when BZ wiped his

mouth with a paper napkin and asked, "Phyllis, why'd you named this place *The Spa That Loves Me*?"

I laughed and Phyllis frowned. "If I had a dollar for every time someone asked me that!"

I whispered to Lannie, "That's a sore spot."

"I swear, I thought people would pick up on it much faster than they do. Did you notice the address? Seven-zero-zero-seven? Do you remember my last name?"

"No," BZ answered looking as innocent as a newborn.

"It's Bond, B-O-N-D!" Phyllis' head bobbed with each letter spelled.

"Oh, I get it," BZ smiled as the light came on. "Like James Bond, shaken not stirred." He laughed.

Lannie asked, "Have you and Phyllis been friends for a long time, Siobhan?"

"Since fifth grade." I smiled across the room at my friend.

"We went to St. Mary's Hall," Phyllis added.

BZ raised his eyebrow. "Uptown girls," he said.

"I was a day student," Phyllis said. "Siobhan boarded." She touched me with her finger and then jerked it back as if I'd burned her with my hotness. "Everyone knows boarding students are extremely hot."

"Which is better than being extremely unwanted," BZ countered, not realizing the nerve he'd struck.

Everyone else chuckled, and I reached for an envelope, "Can I open some of these?"

Tristan reached into the crate, grabbed a handful, and handed a couple to Phyllis. The one I opened had uneven printing on lined tablet paper that said, "I'll never eat meat again!" I waved the note and a five dollar bill in the air.

Tristan said, "I've got one with a thousand-dollar check! It says I never wanted to let my steer go to slaughter when I raised it for FFA, but I didn't have a good reason like Paris to fight for it. This is for Paris's courage, even if Charga is never found."

"Ah's," chorused.

Phyllis acted as bookkeeper and started writing down the amounts we called out. She tallied the sums and by the end of the evening, added to the money from the day before, we totaled twenty-two thousand, eight dollars and sixty-four cents. We were all amazed by the generosity, especially the children's donations.

"I'll donate a thousand from the Spa," Phyllis said, and everyone cheered. Then Tristan told us he would add another thousand from his restaurant. Phyllis kissed him on the cheek.

BZ suddenly remembered something in his pocket and pulled out wadded bills. "My girls robbed their piggy banks and want me to add this. It's their birthday money." Their contribution totaled thirty-two dollars.

"Okay," Phyllis said after she added the sums. Tristan did a drum-roll on the glass top. "We have twenty-four thousand and forty dollars and sixty-four cents."

Lannie cleared her throat, "Well, I can't confirm it yet, but my sister is married to the Miller Beer distributor in town and..."

The rest of us darted eyes each to the other wondering if she'd found out how we'd gotten Charga off the Coliseum grounds.

Lannie didn't notice our nervous gestures and continued telling us, "...they were going to bid on the Grand Champion anyway, before any of this came up, but they are going to join up with us in the consortium if they can be the main sponsor name and do the bidding. In the beer business, benevolence only goes so far."

BZ said, "I don't think having kids associated with beer is such a great idea."

Lannie said, "Well, they bid on the steer every year. It's not like they were giving away free beer to the kids." Then she added, "And, I think I could get maybe ten thousand from my paper?" She shrugged and grimaced as if she might have over- estimated.

Without revealing anything about the conversation I had with my mother, I said, "I think I have a source for quite a bit." All eyes spun to me. "I'd rather not say more until I can guarantee it." I fake coughed. "And I'd rather not use my source if I don't have to."

There were frowns all around. BZ's gaze held mine the longest. I knew there would be questions the next day.

Chapter Twenty-One

The next morning the newsroom hotline received an anonymous call from a person who reported seeing a cow roaming around the football field at Alamo Stadium. The person suggested the cow might have been the victim of a prank by one of the local high schools. The radio stations had the bulletin on the air as soon as the first call came in. Their on-air personalities joked about the school district's new way to save money on fertilizer.

Paris showed up as planned. She said she heard the story on the radio and stopped by to see, if by the remotest chance, the cow was her steer, Charga. The news spread quickly! The missing steer has been found. The story led the news on every media source; radio used it every fifteen minutes, television teased viewers to watch the news at noon or as the day progressed, and at five for details. The front page of the noon and evening editions of the paper carried pictures of Paris hugging an almost unrecognizable Charga in the middle of the football field at Alamo Stadium. Bud sent Tracy to do the live interview, and she got there while Paris attempted to make Charga look better.

Paris brushed him while bewailing the poor steer's appearance. "Poor, poor Charga," she crooned turning to the camera. She appeared to be angry about how those horrible steer-nappers had ruined Charga's topknot and tail. "It's been chopped off. His tail had at least a ten inch plume," she said, holding up a stringy chopped up tassel. "And his top-knot is gone." She spread her thumb and index finger to show how many inches were missing. "Poor, poor Charga," she purred and hugged the steer's massive head while looking into the camera.

She seemed genuinely sad that he'd been so terribly mistreated. "He doesn't even have a white face anymore! They must have dyed him. Crazy people." She shook her head in disdain.

Tracy, always the pessimist, ended the segment saying, in a way that belittled Paris's concerns about Charga, "Whether or not Charga is having a bad hair day is not as important as whether or not he survives after the auction tomorrow. Remember the high bidder may or may not give the steer a total reprieve. How does it look out there, Siobhan?"

She threw to me at the Livestock Show, where I stood in the middle of the still-empty Grand Champion pen next to a smug-looking Eloy Grisham. I'd called him and scheduled the interview as soon as word came in about Charga's discovery at the stadium.

"Tracy, all we can do is hope someone cares enough about Charga to bid high and save him." I turned to Eloy. "Mr. Grisham, it looks as if the people who stole Charga have a heart after all. Are you pleased to have the Grand Champion back for the auction tomorrow?" I smiled my brightest smile.

"I had no doubt that the people who stole the steer had hearts," he glared at me. "I think they were trying to keep the steer alive for the girl. They must have known about her dire health. That's never been a question as far as I am concerned."

I struggled to maintain my passivity, though I remembered a different version of this story.

Eloy continued. "Now we have to see if the winning bidder has a heart." He looked directly into BZ's camera, challenging the public.

I could tell that Bud had created a media-savvy monster when he'd convinced Eloy to forgive the thieves and take advantage of the publicity. Bud had assured Eloy that he and A.L.E.C. would get great publicity if they didn't make too big a fuss about the missing steer. Eloy had taken him at his word.

Eloy said, "All is forgiven. We will not press charges against the perpetrators since the steer is returned." Then, almost as an afterthought, he added, "We have moved the auction time to three o'clock tomorrow afternoon inside the Coliseum in the Rodeo Arena, instead of in the auction barn, so more people can watch." Eloy smiled into the camera.

I was glad about the time change. It worked in our favor and gave our consortium more time to get money together. Unless things changed, it looked as if I'd need to ask my mother for a blank check.

After the interview, BZ and I left for the station. I got my green notebook out of my bag and looked at the totals for the money we'd counted the night before.

BZ said, "You know, because of all the publicity there will be a bunch more bidders than usual."

I nodded.

"Are you ready to tell me who you can get the big bucks from for us?" He asked.

"My mother," I answered unenthusiastically.

"I didn't know you had a mother," BZ laughed. "I mean, I knew you had a mother. I thought your mother died or something."

"It's the *or something.*" My expression betrayed no sadness. "My dreadful life story is that she and I are estranged. My grandfather raised me."

"Then the rumors are true?" BZ asked.

"What rumors?"

"The rumors about you being Gordon O'Shaunessy's granddaughter." He spoke without expression.

"Guilty. I am." I confessed. "I never tried to make it a big secret. But when Bud hired me, he told me it would be best if I didn't talk about it."

"I get that," BZ said.

"Insecure paranoia runs loose around here," I added. "Did Maxine tell?" I asked.

"No, Tracy's been talking.

"So is she telling about my divorce, too?"

"You were married?" BZ asked aghast. He'd gotten another surprise.

"Yeah, but that's pretty common knowledge."

"Not too common, I didn't know."

"You don't pay attention," I countered.

"Sheesh." BZ shrugged his shoulders. "You think you know a person..."

"You do know me," I said. "You don't have my backstory, that's all.

He waited for me to fill him in.

I gave him the brutal details on our way back to the parking lot. We were getting into the van when I ended my monologue. "Maxine watched me grow up."

"Well, Maxine hasn't been talking," BZ said, defending our mutual friend. "Tracy said it the other day when I stayed at the station."

"How did she find out about it?" I thought for a moment. "Hmm, I think I know. Dr. Doom probably told her."

"Oh, yeah," BZ said, "I forgot. She's dating him. Isn't tomorrow night the famous 'I want you to go out with my friend, not me' double date?"

"Yep, and if Phyllis is going to get me gorgeous, she's going to have to start early tomorrow because I'm not going to leave the auction until Charga is safe with Paris!"

As soon as I got to my desk, I dialed Phyllis at the spa.

"The Spa That Loves Me," her perky voice answered.

"Hey Phyl," I said. "We have to change our plans for tomorrow. They moved the auction to three in the afternoon and there is no way I'll be able to keep my five o'clock with you."

"Come in at noon. I can work magic on your lunch hour. Have I found the perfect dress for you to wear? Forget the boring black sheath; I found a purple knit. Do you still have those eggplant suede heels?"

"I think so," I answered.

"Bring them, and some black ones for back up. I think they are the exact same color as the dress. I have some amethyst jewelry you can wear with it. You will be hot, hot, hot."

My enthusiasm was not near the level of hers. In fact, I'd been thinking about canceling the date completely. I had a great excuse since the auction time moved to three.

"Phyllis, what do you think about me cancelling the date?"

"What? Cancel? Are you serious?" She could not believe I'd even think about it.

"Well, I have a good reason now," I defended.

"Call Dr. Doom. See if you can move it to a little later." She added, "But don't cancel. You could be meeting your Prince Charming. Remember, it's Valentine's Day."

Her enthusiasm made me make up my mind. So what if I wasn't excited about the date?

I said, "Okay, Phyl. "I'll see you at noon tomorrow."

Just then, the elevator doors slid open. Paris and Charlie stepped out, both grinning.

"Paris!" I hung up the receiver and rushed over to hug her.

BZ came to shake hands with Charlie, to hug Paris.

Bud saw and came out to meet them. He extended his hand first to Paris then to Charlie. "I'm Bud Johnson," he smiled.

"Siobhan has told me how much you've helped. Thank you so much, Mr. Johnson," Paris smiled up at him. "I know you are the main reason A.L.E.C. changed the rules for Charga."

She made Bud blush. He said, "Well, I tried."

"You succeeded," BZ said. "None of us were able to do it."

"By the way," Bud said to me," I have something for you." He reached into his shirt pocket and took out a folded piece of green paper. "I got this from corporate this morning."

He handed me a check for thirty-five thousand dollars. I loved that man!

I showed the check to Paris, and she squealed and hugged Bud.

The phone rang. I ran to my desk to answer. It was

238

Lannie White. I told her, "Bud asked our corporate owners for a donation and I have a check for, are you ready for this?" I paused for effect.

"How much? How much?" I could hear excitement in Lannie's voice.

"Thirty-five thousand dollars!" I exclaimed.

"Wow. That's great. And with the money we counted last night, that's almost sixty-thousand dollars."

"Did you get an answer from the paper?" I counted on the paper for another ten thousand.

"They are only in for eight." I could hear the disappointment.

"That's terrific; they didn't have to give anything."

"But, they promised to run advertisements for our consortium as an incentive to get more businesses to join us," she added. "That will sweeten the pot. Phyllis, Tristan, Lite Beer, and KWNK can get free ads for six months. So will anyone else who joins. It's easier to give away space in the paper than cash," she explained and sighed, "I'll be glad when this is all over."

"Aren't we all? Paris is here at the station now. She's very confident about taking Charga home. I'll tell her about the paper's donation."

I hung up the phone and turned back to see Bud ushering Charlie and Paris into his office. BZ came out of the break room carrying cans of soft drinks, and he motioned me to join him as he stepped into Bud's office.

"Here she is," Paris said, smiling at me from the chair in front of Bud's desk when I walked in.

Bud said, "Paris has been telling me what a wonderful friend you've been to her."

"She's like my big sister," Paris added. "It feels good having a big sister; I've never had one older than me."

"I think it feels pretty good to have one at all." I laughed. "I never had even one."

"And, what about me?" BZ interrupted, feigning hurt feelings.

Charlie saved the moment, saying, "You are like a big brother to me, man!"

All of us felt calm. We should. We had accomplished almost everything we set out to do. Charga was meandering around the pen in the front of the Coliseum again, our consortium had most of the money we'd need to bid, and, it seemed to us, by tomorrow evening, we'd be able to send Charga home with Paris forever.

Later that afternoon Lannie called back. "Here's the deal," she said. "The beer company will match KWNK's thirty-five thousand but, they want to be the bidder at the auction."

"We don't care who does the bidding," I said. "That sounds great to me. I'll check with Bud and see if corporate cares. And I'll tell BZ, Phyl, and Tristan about it too."

Lannie said, "All together, with the potential thirty-five thousand from Lite Beer, we have ninety-four thousand, forty dollars and sixty-four cents. I think that should do it."

She came by to see Paris and Charlie, collected all of the money and checks, and opened a special account at Alamo National Bank.

I slept well that night. I went to work as usual, then to the spa for my lunch hour which turned into my lunch two hours. Phyllis did a wonderful job of making me look glamorous. The purple dress matched my shoes perfectly; the jewelry she loaned me looked classy. She put highlights in my hair, then backcombed and tousled it into a fun, looser look.

I liked it. I felt pretty. I left Phyllis, and when I got

back to the office, I wished she'd been there to see the reaction I got. Bud came out of his office to see what had garnered the wolf whistles and added one of his own.

"So, I don't look this good every day?" I asked.

BZ said, "You always look nice. It's only that today you look especially good. I like your hair that way. Sylvia would look good like that, don't you think?"

I agreed.

"So you have a date tonight."

I poked him with my elbow. "Hush," I said.

Bud appeared at his doorway. Motioning at us, he said, "You two, come on in my office."

BZ and I looked at one another and frowned.

Bud closed the door behind us and explained, "We've got some competition."

BZ and I waited to hear what he had to say.

"I just found out that Eloy has helped put a consortium together for the conservative bunch."

"So, are they serious competition or are they in it for the publicity?" I asked.

They've got a car dealership, a grocery chain, and a farm and ranch store," Bud said. "They all have deep pockets. What's the total we have now?" Bud wanted to know.

"So far we have ninety-four thousand and a little," I answered.

"I hope it's enough," Bud seemed doubtful.

I knew what I had to do. "Bud, can I use your office for a few minutes? I have to make a private call."

I doubt anyone had ever asked Bud to leave his office. He stammered, "Well, uh, yeah, sure, why not?"

"I've got to get the number. I'll be right back." I went to my desk and got the green notebook where I'd written my mother's phone number.

BZ went to his desk, and when he passed me he said, "Good luck."

I headed back to Bud's glass office, and he met me at the door. He'd pulled all of the drapery closed so I'd have complete privacy.

"I won't be long," I promised him.

"Take as long as you need," he told me as he closed the door.

I went behind the desk, sat in his swivel chair, and turned my back to the door. I didn't want distractions from anything while I spoke to my mother. I called Maxine so she could place the long-distance call for me.

I gave her the number.

After Maxine got over the surprise of hearing my voice coming from Bud's phone, she said, "Calling your mother, Siobhan?"

"How did you know my mother's number?" I was curious.

"She spoke to me the other day when she called you. Are you okay?"

I couldn't fake my bravado with Maxine. She knew the true story.

"I think I'll be all right, Maxine. It's something I have to do."

I listened as she dialed the number. Before the first ring, she told me, "You can do it," and then left the line as the ringing began.

It took seven rings before my mother answered the phone. I'd begun to panic and thought it would be my luck if she'd left for the day. Finally, she answered.

"Mother," I began, trying my best to sound officious. "I need to take you up on your offer."

"I've got everything in place," she told me. "I wanted

to be ready if you needed me."

"Thank you," I answered. I felt humbled and saddened. I'd never wanted to take anything from her and had planned my life trying to avoid asking her for anything. Even during the days after Grandfather died, when I didn't know if I were going to survive, I wouldn't ask her for help. In this instance, I justified. I wasn't asking for myself. I was asking for Paris, and I would do anything for her.

"All you have to do is call Jack Mason at Alamo National Bank. He has a letter of unlimited credit for you. Show it to the cashier when you win the bid." She acted as if we were transacting a business deal.

"I'll leave to pick it up right now."

"Good," she said.

"Thank you, Mother." I hung up the phone and immediately broke into tears. I thought I'd succeeded in pulling myself together, but when I opened Bud's office door to let him back in, I broke down again.

He took one look at me, put his hands on my shoulders, and gently backed me toward a chair. "Why don't you sit down for a minute?" He handed me a pressed white handkerchief from his pocket. "And, you might want to check your eye stuff, before you leave."

"My mascara?" I laughed and let his remark transport me from sadness.

"Yeah, you have black under your eyes." He gestured under his own.

I wet his handkerchief with my tongue and dabbed beneath my eye. It came away dark and sooty. All of Phyllis' hard work was showing up on Bud's handkerchief.

"Oshun, are you sure you're all right?" Bud's bumbling concern touched me.

"Bud, I am, really. Thank you." I didn't want to tell

him anything more. I could tell Bud cared that I was upset. "I have to go pick up a letter of credit from Alamo National Bank before I head out to the Coliseum."

"Then go." He flicked his fingers as if brushing lint away. "Go," he encouraged. "You look fine now. No more black stuff." He bent down and looked from one of eye to the other to make sure.

"Can BZ drive me? That way I can get out and run in without having to park. He really wants to be at the auction," I explained.

"Tracy is covering the auction. BZ's got camera. I'll tell her BZ will meet her out there. Be sure he takes the van. She can drive herself."

I thanked Bud and went to find BZ. I explained to him what we were going to do and he could barely contain his excitement.

"I'll go start the van," he dashed to get the keys.

When he left the room, I called the bank and spoke to Jack Mason. He promised he wouldn't leave the bank until I got there to pick up the letter of credit.

As I walked to the back door of the station, I couldn't believe it had been on only seven days since I'd gone to cover the steer judging.

Since then I'd faced some of my worst fears and hadn't failed. My story was a huge success. I'd covered other features since then and gotten more positive recognition from Bud. I'd stolen a grand champion steer and helped the young girl I swore I'd known in a previous life.

I'd reconnected with Dexter Hardwick and Graciella Grisham, made friends with Lannie and Tristan and Cardiff and Franklin. I'd heard from my mother, took money from her, even, which I swore I'd never do, and I had survived. Now, for my last challenge of the week I had to win the bid for Charga. It had been quite a lot for the little six-year-old girl who was doing her best to grow up.

The pride I felt in myself was new. After all the years wishing I could become someone I liked to spend time with, I'd done it. I liked myself. For the first time in my life, I was proud, not of my grandfather or my mother's artistic abilities or our address or our heritage. For the first time in my life, I was proud of me.

Chapter Twenty-Two

I helped BZ carry his equipment into the Coliseum. The arena at the auction barn where the bidding usually took place would never have held this huge crowd. The Coliseum arena seated nine thousand, and it looked as though a third of the seats were filled. When we got inside, we could tell we'd come in the wrong way. The action would be taking place in the middle of the arena floor on the portable stage the performers used for their concerts each night.

"Oh, oh," I said to BZ when we saw the setup. "We need to get down there."

BZ turned back to the concourse and said, "We have to go back this way."

I followed him around to the north end of the building past the corrals where the animals for the rodeo events were housed.

BZ sauntered down between the pens, past the chutes, his camera hoisted on his shoulder. I lagged behind struggling to keep up in my purple suede high heels. When we reached the arena proper, I knew I should have worn boots or loafers at least. My high heels sunk into the arena loam even as I walked on tiptoe. I felt dirt invade my shoes, could feel grit between my toes as my feet squirmed. I couldn't help but think about all the things tilled into the rodeo soil.

We made our way to the white folding chairs that had been set up in front of the stage on uneven Plyboard sheets. I rushed toward the stable surface. At least I wouldn't be sitting in dirt. We reached the media area, and all the reporters from our competitor stations acknowledged BZ. And this time, a couple of them said, "Hello, Siobhan" to me.

"Hi, Randy" I smiled back, recognizing the KTEX anchor.

"Hi, BZ. Hi, Siobhan," I heard from one of the radio voices I recognized.

I saw Lannie already sitting in the bidder section. She waved to me.

"Goodbye, BZ," I said. "I'm going to sit with Lannie."

"Good luck," he told me.

A few minutes later Bud came in and sat next to me.

"I didn't know you were coming," I told him, pleased and surprised.

"I wouldn't miss this for the world." He looked around the building. "We're going to have quite a crowd."

I wondered where the beer company people were. I'd never spoken to them and had a fear they would drop out at the last minute. I tapped Lannie's shoulder, "Where are your sister and her husband?"

"They're making an entrance."

I frowned, not understanding what kind of entrance they could possibly be making. After almost everyone had settled into their seats, I heard applause from the spectators and turned to see Jim Shoulders and his brahma bull, Buford T, entering the arena.

"There she is," Lannie said wryly, pointing to a tiny woman sitting atop the massive bull. "There's Linda. Steven," she pointed to the man on the other side of the bull, "is walking." He held onto the halter where tooling spelled out Lite Beer.

"Well, they'll definitely get on the news with that entrance," I laughed. BZ and the other camera operators jockeyed for the best position to capture the colorful entrance.

Jim led his bull beside the section where we were sitting, moved a folding chair out of its row to use as a stepping stool, and then gave Buford T a command to bow. Steven helped his wife climb down from atop the bull. She curtsied, and the crowd went wild. Jim took off his grey hat, waved it in the air, and ushered the couple to seats, then stood next to Buford T and we waited for the auction to begin.

Lannie introduced me to Steven and Linda Gallagher, and I took the opportunity to thank them for joining our consortium. "And, thanks for bringing Jim," I said.

"Hey, there little lady," Jim Shoulders called out to me, noticing me for the first time. "Nice seeing you again." He tipped his hat.

Steven leaned over to me. "You did a nice job on the hotel story,"

"Thank you, Steven. Jim is a real gentleman."

"If it's okay with you, we'll let Jim do the bidding."

I smiled. "I think he will be perfect. It's a great idea," The similarities in the temperament between Buford T and Charga helped reinforce our position that Charga was worth saving.

We received a request for photos from the Rodeo's P.R. guy, and I really hoped he recognized me. I wanted him to know that the late arriving woman, who'd gotten the brunt of his rudeness the day of the judging, was now a buyer at the Grand Champion auction.

We posed for photos in front of Buford T, who Jim made bow again. Lannie, Steven, Bud, Jim Shoulders, and I all smiled.

BZ moved closer and shot footage for our news. Bud put one arm around my waist and the other around Lannie. Phyllis and Tristan hadn't gotten here yet and were missing the attention we were getting.

Jim stood behind me, leaned over, and whispered, "I understand we are supposed to win this?"

"Yes," I said.

"No matter what the cost?" He made sure he understood the rules.

"Yes." I patted my handbag where I'd put the letter my mother ordered from the bank.

"I'm going to wait and let the other bigwigs have their time in high cotton," he said. "Then I'll start bidding and put 'em back in the mesquite."

We sat down again, and one of the employees from the beer company offered us cups of Miller Lite. Steven handed them down the row, making sure we each held one. Bud and I clicked plastic, and I looked over and tilted mine to BZ. He frowned at me and then scrunched his face in a begging expression.

I pantomimed, "Sorry, you can't drink; you are working." He scowled at me. I shrugged and looked away to the stands where the spectator numbers were growing by the minute.

In one section, a uniformed high school band played a

rendition of *La Bamba,* until a signal from some invisible source gave them the cue to play *Texas Our Texas.* Everyone remained standing through the state anthem and continued standing while the band played the *Star Spangled Banner.*

Eloy waited on the stage with a conventional looking man I didn't recognize. He went to the microphone and said, "Ladies and gentlemen, the Pledge, if you please," and the colors were presented in silence. Afterward everyone recited the Pledge of Allegiance, holding hands or hats over heart.

I'd been scanning the crowd trying to find Charlie, Cardiff, Franklin and the kids and finally saw them coming down a ramp looking for a place to sit.

They looked like a Norman Rockwell painting as they waited. I waved to get their attention, and Charlie saw me first. He waved his hat and pointed us out to Franklin and Cardiff. They all waved back.

The trumpeters in the band played a medieval fanfare, signaling the beginning of the auction. Eloy introduced the man on stage with him as the auctioneer. "Mike Morris," he said, "Is a high school principal in the North East School District, and he will be our auctioneer today."

Negative murmurs permeated the bidders, and I heard some of the people who had more experience at auctions than I did say, "Why didn't they bring Andy Green back? This guy ain't a real auctioneer."

"I've never heard of this guy," another man grumbled in a loud voice.

"What's the deal?" One disappointed bidder complained to the man next to him.

Mike Morris approached the microphone and said, "In case you folks don't know how this works, we always begin the auction with bidding for the Grand Champion Steer."

As if on cue, Paris led Charga into the arena from one

of the Bronc riding chutes, and cheers erupted from the crowd. Paris looked adorable. I could see Phyllis's magic had worked. She'd invited Paris to stop in at the spa, and I could tell she'd cut Paris's dark locks into a long layered flip with soft bangs framing her sweet face that made her blue eyes stand out. She wore jeans, boots, and a denim western shirt that matched Charga's new halter.

"You may remember," the auctioneer said, "that this here steer got stolen and disguised, so he's not as purty as when he won this contest last week."

I swear I could hear English teachers from his district cringing at his grammar. He was doing a great job putting on a show, playing his country boy role perfectly up on the stage.

"No matter how he looks," the auctioneer pointed to Charga, "he's still prime beef."

I thought Charga looked very handsome, at least compared to the way he looked right after Phyllis and I finished with him. Some of the dye had faded.

Mike Morris explained the reason the Grand Champion Steer was auctioned first, why the Reserve Grand Champion would be next, before the breed champions. He explained that the entries that didn't place in the competition were auctioned last.

Having the bidding set up that way allowed the participants who dropped out of the bidding for the Grand Champion when the price got too high, to use their money to purchase the Reserve Grand Champion. If that bidding got too high, they could bid on the Best of Breeds, and finally they could bid and win one of the other entrants. There was plenty of beef for everyone.

Most of the bidders came with a specific amount of money to part with for the honor of buying one of the animals. If the bidding went much higher than their budget, they would quit and be satisfied that the name of their business received mentioned in the company of the high rollers.

I'd learned in preceding years, twenty or more businesses had banded together toward the end of the bidding to form informal consortiums. The auctioneer had difficulty announcing all of the odd bedfellows who wanted to share the spotlight. For instance, a beer distributor, an office supply company, a funeral home, a bakery, an insurance company, and more might join as a last-minute consortium. So many names took too much time and slowed the action.

Everyone knew the group with the deepest pockets always wins the Grand Champion, the publicity, and the beef, but everyone enjoys the show that goes along with the bidding. The fist waving, posturing, and group huddling added to the performance, meant to create tension and bring more attention to themselves and their company name. The A.L.E.C. Scholarship Fund benefited from the lively display.

This year A.L.E.C. changed the rules, deciding not to allow last minute groupings. All consortiums had to register as a unit before the bidding started and, could not pick up stragglers as the auction progressed. The reason, Eloy announced in explanation, was to keep more bidders in the pool to compete for the remaining steers. I thought the purpose might be a little more diabolical. I think they were keeping our group from picking up additional support in order to build our operating fund.

The winning bidder this year wouldn't get publicity because he won the steer. The publicity would be for what the winning bidder chose to do with Charga. That decision would make him either hero or scoundrel. The front page wouldn't be about their support of the long-standing event or the generosity of the company; it would be about the decision to return, or not return, the Grand Champion Steer to the dying girl.

I wasn't about to let any other group win the bid. I hadn't any idea what it would cost because I didn't know how much of a war chest Eloy had managed to put together. I had a letter of credit from my mother that I would use if I had to.

When Paris reached the area in front of the stage, the audience erupted into renewed applause. Paris smiled, blushed, waved, and followed instructions to walk Charga back and forth below the stage.

Mike Morris waited for the applause to die. He said, "I know there is a lot riding on this auction, and I want everyone to understand how it's going to work." He turned toward the spectators and said, "These folks," he pointed to those of us sitting below, "are the people who have signed in as official bidders. None of you," he gestured to the crowd, "can bid. If you want to bid, you've got to go get registered right now."

No one in the spectator seats appeared to make a move toward signing up to become a bidder.

"Your competition in the bidding," he motioned across the group seated in front of the stage, "are the folks from Lite Beer. Now just how did I know that, Steven Gallagher?" Morris scratched his head.

Steven Gallagher shrugged, looking as innocent as a cherub on high.

"We have Jim Shoulders, eight time Professional All-Around Cowboy. I say that in case you hadn't noticed," he added, tongue in cheek. Everyone laughed.

Jim brought Buford T to a bow, and Mike Morris said,

"Oh, yes, excuse me. And, Buford T. We've got Lannie White representing the *Light Newspaper.* Get the connection, Lite and *Light?*" Everyone groaned.

"They are joined by Bud Johnson, General Manager of KWNK television, and Siobhan O'Shaunessy, grand-daughter of KWNK's founder, Gordon O'Shaughnessy; The Spa That Loves Me. . ., I might need to go there when this is all over" he quipped. "Tristan's Mexican Food Restaurant, where I put on some of these pounds," he patted his belly, "And, last but not least, the children of our fair city who raised a lot of money to contribute toward helping save Paris's Nash's Grand Champion Steer, Charga."

A huge cheer erupted from the crowd, and I wished Phyllis and Tristan had been here in time to hear their names. They would have loved the comments Mike Morris made about their businesses.

"Now, that's what we call a consortium," the auctioneer continued. "They signed up as one bidder, and the person who is doing the bidding is...?"

"This ol' man, right here." Jim Shoulders waved his grey Stetson, revealing his silver hair.

"Okay, now we've got about thirty-three single bidders and another consortium. Some of these will bid on the Grand Champion, and some will bid on the other entries...but they can all bid on whichever they want. I'll name the single bidders as they bid, and right now I'll introduce the other consortium."

He cleared his throat and looked down at his notes. "We've got Eloy Grisham, Chairman of the current Alamo City Livestock Exposition, Frederick Barnstable representing United Grocers, and Ollie Marckwardt from Farm and Ranch Unlimited. Their bidder will be..." he looked to the group.

Eloy stood up and waved at the crowd. The spectators

applauded respectfully.

"Now, we have one other piece of business. I'm going to introduce my flagmen. These gentlemen will be out to make sure we don't miss a bid. If they don't see you, you make sure they see you!" He looked fiercely at the bidders.

The five young men wore crisp white snap-front western shirts, stiff-starched Wrangler jeans and black Stetson hats. They carried magazine sized Texas flags they would wave to get the auctioneer's attention when they identified a higher bid in the crowd.

All the time Mike Morris was explaining the procedures, Paris was walking Charga back and forth in front of the bidders, Charga lumbering, never balking. When she finally stopped, Charga stopped too and waited for her to position him the way she wanted him to stand.

Mike Morris said, "Let's start the bidding at fifty-thousand dollars. Do I hear fifty-thousand?"

The first part of the bidding started slowly. The auctioneer interrupted to introduce each bidder. Everyone got his moment in the sun. Either the individual or the business associated with the number on the bid paddle received mention to the crowd.

"I have fifty-thousand dollars from Lipscomb Motors," the auctioneer enunciated clearly for all to hear. "Do I hear fifty-five?"

One of the flagmen raised his flag and dropped it like the starter at the Indy 500. Mike Morris began his auctioneers chant, "fifty, I have fifty, do I hear fifty-five?"

Another flagman got his attention, and shouted the name of the participant's business. The auctioneer repeated it. The local flour mill was recognized.

The chant began again, "Fifty-five, I have fifty-five, do I hear sixty?"

"Sixty," the youngest flagger shouted from behind me.

I turned to see who had made the bid and saw Phyllis and Tristan standing at the back of the rows of seats on the arena floor. I waved at her to indicate they should come down front to join us, and Mike Morris said, "Miss O'Shaunessy, do I need to go back over the procedure?"

Everyone laughed, and I blushed. Mike Morris won support from among the previously grumbling bidders. He knew exactly what I'd been doing and called me out for the laugh. I laughed along with everyone else, and my color slowly returned to normal.

We squeezed together to make room for Phyllis. Tristan stood next to Buford T.

Phyllis said, "Sorry," in a soft whisper as she sat down next to me.

Paris caught our attention and rolled her eyes, acknowledging the auctioneer's disruption. She made a funny face, and those who saw her chuckled. The next time I paid attention to what the auctioneer said. The bid stood at ninety thousand dollars. My gulp must have been audible because Phyllis grabbed my arm.

"Ninety, I have ninety, do I hear ninety-five?" Mike Morris looked across the group. No one uttered a word. Jim waited for Eloy to start; Eloy waited for Jim. The car dealer yelled, "Ninety-five," and a shout went up.

Mike Morris said, "Ladies and gentlemen, we have a new record for the Grand Champion Steer Auction."

Steven Gallagher leaned over to me, "He's milking it. He knows we're determined to win. The little twerp would be really shocked if we let him have it."

"No, no," I answered, thinking he might mean he was actually considering letting Eloy win the bid.

The auctioneer's triple chant echoed. "Ninety-five, I

257

have ninety-five, who'll give me ninety-six?" The bidding continued in thousand dollar increments until everyone had dropped out except our group and Eloy's. "Ninety-six, now seven, now seven, will ya give me eight? Eight, eight shut the gate. I need nine, ninety-nine. How about one hundred, one hundred-thousand?"

Jim Shoulders shouted, "One hundred thousand," in a challenging way, which I'd wished he hadn't. I didn't want our group to goad Eloy's group into a pissing contest.

I lost track of where the bid stood; everything moved at such a rapid pace and, we were already well into my mother's letter of credit. I had no idea how much higher Eloy was willing to go.

Mike Morris said, "I have one hundred thousand dollars bid by Jim Shoulders representing the group made up of..."

Evidently, a hundred-thousand-dollar bid earned further mention. BZ aimed his camera at the KWNK group and ducked his head from behind the eyepiece wearing an expression akin to, 'Holyshit that's a lot of money.'

The auctioneer began again. "One hundred, I have one hundred. Do I hear, one-o-one? One hundred thousand going once..."

"Is it over?" Phyllis asked me.

Eloy announced, "One hundred one thousand." He looked my way with a smirk on his face.

The auctioneer called the names of the members of their consortium.

"I jinxed it," Phyllis apologized.

"No, you didn't," I reassured her. "Eloy is getting even."

"How high will it go?" Her eyes were wide.

Paris stroked Charga's muzzle, and he rubbed his neck

against her little body. She had to push against him to keep from toppling over.

"One-o-one. I have one-o-one, do I hear two?" Jim didn't wait, he waved his Stetson in the air.

Morris didn't skip a beat "I have two? Two? Two? I got it! Now three, three, I need three," the auctioneer droned. "I got three! How about four? Four? One hundred four thousand? I need four. I've got four, now five. How about five? Five? Five? I got four, I need five!"

Phyllis asked, "Who's has it?"

I said, "We do, I think." I wasn't sure.

Mike Morris said the entire figure of the bid as it currently stood. Pointing at Eloy's group he shouted, "Going once, going..."

Eloy shouted, "One hundred five thousand."

Before the auctioneer could fully turn to face our group, Jim shouted, "Six."

Eloy countered, "Seven."

Jim yelled, "Eight."

Mike Morris looked over at the spectators and said, "Y'all don't need me, now. Do ya?"

Everyone laughed. When the laughter subsided, he restated the obvious. "We are down to these two bidders, ladies and gentlemen. Our two consortiums. Nevertheless, gentlemen, I'm being paid to do a job here today, and you two bantam roosters are taking it over. Let me do my job, if you don't mind."

Properly chastised, the two men tipped their hats first to each other and then to the auctioneer who said, "I believe Mr. Shoulders has the bid at one hundred eight thousand dollars. Now that figure is way over any previous price paid for a Grand Champion Steer here at the Livestock Show. I think your granddaddy would be proud, Miss

O'Shaughnessy."

I had to admit Grandfather would have been in his element. He'd have been telling Jim, "Higher, higher."

Eloy said, "One hundred nine."

We were off again. After a couple more rounds, Jim finally said, "One hundred twenty-five thousand dollars," jumping the previous bid by five thousand.

The crowd cheered. Eloy took off his hat and bowed at Jim. Then he smirked at me as if to say, "You got the steer, but I got a record, so when push comes to shove, we got a tie."

Paris started crying and buried her head against Charga's neck. The steer sensed Paris being upset and moved in front of her. She looked up toward the roof, smiled through her tears and waited as the flash bulbs from the print media cameras popped.

Mike Morris said, "Okay, now, you guys have had your moment. Head on back and get your picture took for the papers."

A woman came with purple and red bandanas and put one on each member of the consortium. I pointed her to BZ and he got one, too, the only member of the working media group to get a winner's bandana that day. I figured, since I put in the most money, I could be generous with the bandanas.

Phyllis said, "They matched the bandana to the color of your dress."

I laughed and hugged her as we all walked back to have our picture taken with Paris and Charga. Tracy and BZ came to do an interview with Bud and included me in the story.

Tracy interviewed Paris, too, and the courageous girl managed to pull it together long enough to voice her appreciation. She said, "I want to especially thank all of the children who collected money for Charga. If it hadn't been for each of you caring what happened to my steer, this wouldn't have been possible. Thank you, thank you, thank you."

Cardiff, Franklin, Ireland, Rome, London, and India joined for a family photo taken with Paris and Charga. Franklin made me happy when he said, "Charlie, get on in here, son." Then they took one with BZ and me, and Paris asked for one with just the two of us.

While we gathered for our consortium photo Tristan said, "Okay everyone, dinner at my place."

I remembered my double date, and Tristan read the look on my face, "You all come, too."

Everyone hugged Paris, but Bud held her for a longer moment. I knew he must have been thinking about his daughter, Alyssa Marie.

Paris couldn't stop saying "Thank you, thank you."

When I reached out my arms for my hug, she said, "I love you," and I knew she meant it because I loved her, too.

Chapter Twenty-Three

Before BZ and I made our way back around the concourse, we stopped so I could empty the arena dirt out of my shoes. I held onto his shoulder, and took off one shoe, balanced on the other leg while he tapped the heel of the first shoe against the tiled concourse wall to loosen the dirt. It would take more than gentle tapping to get my shoes clean. My feet would require washing before I would be able to get off the grit that had sifted through my nylons.

"The perils of being a high-roller," BZ joked.

"I doubt Ivana Trump ever had this problem," I countered.

On the drive back to the studio to get my car, BZ and I talked about the past week. We both said seeing Paris smile and cry made everything we'd gone through worthwhile.

Lannie headed back to the newspaper so she could write her column for the evening edition. We couldn't wait to read her article. She was thrilled about our win.

BZ said, "I can't believe how high the bidding went.

Do you think your mother is going to be all right with that?"

"She told me it didn't matter." I didn't want a reminder of what she'd done.

"She's trying to reach out, you know." BZ took his eyes off the road and glanced over at me.

"Watch where you're going." I sent his attention back to the highway and away from me. Nevertheless, he forced me to think about my mother, and I wondered if she were reaching out to me or if she was trying to impress her friend Graciella.

In typical BZ fashion, he wouldn't let me avoid the topic.

"I said," he repeated, "She's trying to reach out." He emphasized the word *trying*.

"And, what do you suggest I do, BZ? It's a little difficult since she won't come here. She hates Texas. I don't want to go to Maine."

"Are you sure she wouldn't come here? Have you asked her? This time she might come." He remained adamant about staying on the subject. He even gave the steering wheel a slap to make his point.

"BZ, I love you like a brother, but you don't understand what she's done to me. I'll think about it." I was petulant as a child. Then I started to feel guilty about my attitude. I didn't like feeling that way. For most of my life, I'd felt guilty because I believed her leaving me had been *my* fault, and believed her staying away had been my fault, too.

"I'll remind you again in a day or so," he said as we pulled into the KWNK parking lot.

"Thank you, BZ," I acquiesced. "I know you think you're being helpful."

I went upstairs to call Dr. Doom and tell him about Tristan's invitation. He'd already heard from Tracy.

"Tracy told me. It's a great idea. I'm looking forward to seeing the Nash family." In the background, I heard the hospital loudspeaker paging him.

"I'll meet you there then?" I said.

I sat at my desk and thought about what BZ said about my mother reaching out. I called Maxine and asked her to place a call to Maine for me. After seven rings the answering machine came on. I listened to her voice instructing me to leave a message. After the beep, I said, "Thank you for helping make it possible for us to win the auction. Paris got Charga back." That was all I said. I planned to write a letter later.

When I got to Tristan's I read the sign he'd posted on the front door, *Private party.* I went in and could tell why he and Phyllis were late getting to the auction. There was no doubt she was in charge of the decorating. Drapery covered one wall, and the neon beer signs glowed: washed and no longer dusty.

Each table had been covered with red bandana material, and authentic multicolored bandanas were pulled through leather-stenciled napkin rings. In the middle of each table she'd put a small tin bucket full of grain with a single red candle pushed deep inside with purple hearts on green florist pegs sticking out. Purple and hot-pink ribbon curled out of the bucket, too, and flowed across the tabletop.

Two margarita machines sat in the space usually reserved for the cash register, and I noticed almost everyone held a stemmed margarita glass. Even Paris's little sister, Ireland, had one. She came to me as soon as I walked in the door, sipping the opaque green liquid from the salted stem. I looked down at her, doing my best to appear as shocked as I possibly could.

"Ireland, aren't you too young for margaritas?" I

asked.

She confessed, "Mine is made special," she said, licking at the salt. "None of that tickle-ya stuff."

I giggled and had to look shocked all over again when little London came up holding his stemmed glass, too.

BZ arrived with Sylvia and his girls, the older one wanted to meet Paris. It was definitely her night, a combination of senior prom and graduation. Everyone at the party realized this might be her last chance to be this happy.

Tristan and BZ talked together while Sylvia, Phyllis, and I went to the margarita machine to refill our glasses. When we rejoined the men, BZ looked at Phyllis and said, "When are you going back to your natural hair color?"

She touched her dark hair, "You mean you like me better blond?"

"Yeah, your natural color." BZ said.

Tristan interrupted, he put his arm around Phyllis and said, "This is her natural color."

BZ said, "So the carpet is matching the drapes, huh?"

He laughed at his joke. Everyone chuckled at Phyllis's red-faced reaction to the thinly veiled innuendo. BZ grinned as Sylvia took his drink out of his hand and said, "I think you've had enough already."

I'd had already consumed my second drink, the non-special kind with tequila, when Tracy, Dr. Doom, and Dr. Jeb came up behind me. They'd just arrived when Paris saw them and dashed across the restaurant with her arms outstretched. Dexter had to extricate himself from Tracy's tight grasp to hug his favorite patient.

I turned in time to see Tracy grimace, a smile I'd seen before when she hadn't gotten her way. It wasn't her most attractive look.

"Jeb," Tracy grabbed my dates arm and pulled him

toward me, "This is your date, Siobhan." Her voice sounded flat and unenthusiastic.

"Hello," smiled the fastidious man with his nails clipped, cleaned, filed, and buffed, looking nicer than my own. His shoes, polished to high gloss, made my heels look even dirtier than they were.

"Hi," I said and we shook hands. His were soft and felt smarmy.

I didn't like his primness. I wanted to muss his hair or scuff his loafers, especially when I caught him looking at my muddy arena-ruined shoes and dirty feet.

Dr. Doom put his arm around my shoulder and said, "You did it. You pulled it off, Siobhan." He spun me around. Tracy's eyes spit ice-cold shards while her mouth remained a Cupid's bow smile.

Paris put her arm around my waist and said, "She's wonderful. She's my new big sister, you know."

"And she's my date this evening," Jeb pulled me away from Dexter.

"There's Bud." I found an excuse to leave the group. Paris came with me to greet him.

"Hey, Champ." He gave Paris a fake jab to the chin.

She grinned up at him, "Thanks to you."

"No," Bud disagreed. "Thanks to her." He pointed at me.

"Not me," I realized. "My mother. She's the one who really made it possible."

Paris shook her head, "No you. She wouldn't have cared if you weren't involved."

"Oh, all right," I dramatized. "It was me…all me."

Bud and Paris gave me a spontaneous thumbs-down, and we laughed. No one really cared who did what that night; we were happy we saved Charga from slaughter and that Paris's wish had come true.

We celebrated for the rest of the evening. Tracy did a little too much partying, and it did my envious heart good to watch her hang on every man who came near her.

She started slurring words as her eyelids got heavier and heavier, and her voice lost its modulation. She started a sentence, softly and then, as if someone else were in control of her volume dial, spoke louder and louder until the words trailed off to a barely audible whisper. Then she'd smile extra big, as if she'd just gotten a joke.

Bud went to her and said, "Tracy, you've had a long day. Don't you think you ought to go home and get some rest?"

"Is that an invitation, boss man," she purred at him.

Bud turned fifteen shades of red and appeared relieved when Dexter came to his rescue. "That's my cue," Dexter said. "Let's go, Tracy."

I got Tracy's purse off the table and looped it over Dexter's shoulder as he led her toward the door. Jeb came over to me and said, "There goes my ride. How about a lift home later?"

"Sure," I said. I felt obligated.

We stayed for about an hour more and, Jeb wouldn't leave my side. After I said goodbye to everyone, I drove him home, listening to him talk all the way, telling me he was a resident at the University Health Science Center, had done his undergrad work at Tulane, went to high school in a small town in Oklahoma, graduated valedictorian of his class and played saxophone in the band.

He asked absolutely nothing about my life or me.

268

Chapter Twenty-Four

When I went back to work Monday everything seemed too normal. After the nonstop excitement of the past week, I was suffering a letdown. The morning co-hosts were bantering back and forth, talking about Paris and Charga, probably for the last time. Every person I saw made some comment about Lannie's front-page story in the Sunday paper. No one at KWNK treated me differently, even though now everyone knew my grandfather was the station's founder. I'd spent too much time and energy worrying about that issue.

Bud was sitting in his fish-tank office, conducting the Monday morning sales meeting, back to his professional attitude.

Being at Tristan's had been a huge exception to his self-imposed non-fraternization policy. Bud, usually all business, had pretty much closed himself off from socializing with employees.

The next months were uneventful for me. I covered

City Council and a few traffic accidents, but no other story generated the excitement Charga had. Rodeo Week had been so fully fueled that once spent, the energy could not be reclaimed. I kept looking for something else to grab my interest in the same way.

April came, and the sports reporters were excited to have the Spurs lead the division. They were sure our team would get home court advantage for the play offs. Fiesta approached and San Antonio got ready for the conservative-man's version of Mardi Gras. Vesta Muniz's noon show calendar was full of things related to that big event. She planned to show how to make *cascarones*, and Fiesta flowered door wreaths. She scheduled a show about Fiesta medal collecting, calling them an obsession and planned to show how to wear them without wrecking clothes. She also scheduled a story about the Night in Old San Antonio rain rock -- does it really work?

Not even the excitement of the parades and other activities surrounding the ten-day extravaganza grabbed me.

Tracy still dated Dr. Doom, even though I thought for sure he would drop her after the spectacle she made of herself at the after auction party. Jeb, the prim and proper podiatrist, had called, and we'd gone out to dinner a couple of times, but after he talked about nothing but himself hour after hour, I got bored with him.

Cardiff and Franklin gave a big party for Paris's sixteenth birthday. All her new friends were there, plus a few old ones from high school.

On another of my visits to the ranch, we figured out that my age sat equal distance from Paris's and her mother's. I guess that was the reason they kept asking me to mediate their disagreements. I usually took Paris's side because I thought Cardiff was becoming overly protective of her daughter. She wanted to keep Paris close to home, wanted her to eat the right foods, and to not get overheated that sort of thing. I couldn't blame Cardiff, but I also knew Paris wanted to experience as much of life as she could while she still felt healthy.

In one disagreement, I'd overheard Paris say, "Mother, do you remember Grampy telling us, 'Do what you can, while you can'?"

She used that to challenge her mother's argument more than one time.

"Grampy wasn't talking about this kind of situation, dear," Cardiff always countered.

Toward the end of April, I got a phone call from Paris telling me she had an appointment with Dexter the next day. She wanted to know if she could spend the night at my place. Her mother said it was okay, so Paris drove in to San Antonio by herself. Her new driver's license was another milestone of her independence.

I got home early and freshened up the linens in my tiny guest room. I shouldn't have gone to the trouble because she ended up spending the night in my bed where we stayed up talking for far too long into the night.

I had almost dozed off when I asked, "You are only going in for a checkup, right?"

"That and I have a few questions for him," she yawned. "I've stopped having periods, and I wonder if it fits with the disease."

I lay there for several minutes before I asked, "Paris, is there a chance you might be pregnant?"

"No, I don't think so. I don't think I could get pregnant with this sickness. Why, do you think I could?" She rose up on one elbow and faced me.

"Have you and Charlie. . ." I knew she understood my

question without me having to complete it.

"Well, yes. We have. I wanted to know what the big deal was all about. I'd always planned to wait until I was older, maybe in college or something. But, I'm not going to be older, you know. So, we did." She wasn't embarrassed.

"Once?" I asked.

"Well, more than once," she confessed.

"Do you want me to come with you to see the doctor? I can take the time off." I wanted to go with her, and I hoped she would let me.

"Sure, come with me. Hey, don't lose sleep over that idea. I'm pretty sure I'm not."

I lost a full night's sleep. My mind kept going to the *ifs.* *What if* she was pregnant? It wouldn't be too bad actually. *What if* she wasn't? That might be worse because it might mean her cancer had begun to spread. That *what if* scared me. I'd never wondered whether a person in her precarious situation could carry a child full term. We didn't even know if she would live out the year, much less live though a pregnancy. What if she miscarried? What if she died before the baby could be born? I started worrying about Charlie. Could he take care of a baby?

What would Cardiff and Franklin do? Certainly, they'd make the best of the situation. I tried to put myself in their position and thought a part of them would relish the idea of having Paris's child with them after she died. It would be like having Paris back again, in a way, I thought. I'd never had a child and hadn't any idea what parents felt. My own mother obviously didn't care about me, her child, much less a grandchild.

I thought Charlie would want to raise his child. But, how could he? His father couldn't support him financially on a ranchhand's pay, much less give the emotional support he'd need. How would he ever be able to be a father without help? Cardiff and Franklin would be the better parents, but I didn't think Charlie would let that happen.

I looked at the clock and tried to doze off again. This puzzle was far too complicated for me to figure out. I closed my eyes, drifted off, and felt as though the alarm sounded with my next breath.

Paris woke up in a good humor. "I dreamed I had a baby," she announced after she got out of the shower and was dressing. "I guess because of our conversation last night. I had a darling little girl who looked like Charlie, but she had my blue eyes. She was tiny, itty bitty, but could she wail. She wouldn't be quiet until I let you hold her."

"Oh, I'm in the dream, too?" I felt flattered in a crazy way.

"Yes, I have those jumbled, everyone-is-in-it dreams. Lots of stuff happens. Even Charga was in it. He bawled whenever the baby cried. I laughed in my dream." She laughed as she told me, remembering.

"What time is your appointment?" I changed the subject as I searched under the bed for my shoes.

"Eleven," she answered. She lifted up the dust ruffle on the opposite side of the bed and looked across the floor at me. "Here's your other shoe." She slid it across the floor to me. "Dust bunnies down here," she commented.

"Want to come to the station with me first, before the appointment?" I thought she'd like to visit with Bud and BZ. She hadn't seen them since her birthday.

We stopped at Taco Cabana, and I brought in breakfast tacos for the staff. On the way, she chattered about her brothers and sisters, her mom and dad, Charlie and Charga. When we got to the office, my exhaustion showed itself. I continued worrying and couldn't wait for her appointment so I could stop.

Everyone greeted Paris with happy smiles. Bud came out and took her back into his office and everyone who wanted to see her took turns going in to say hello. BZ rated a big hug. Everyone asked how Charga was enjoying his freedom.

While many people would have dramatized their illness, Paris made it easy for people to forget her sickness.

I checked in with Bud and told him I needed to take Paris for a checkup, and we left for Dr. Doom's office a little after ten. Dexter, always amazing with Paris, outdid himself. The first thing he did after she told him about not having periods anymore was have her pee in a cup. He sent the specimen to the lab.

"We should know something soon, depending on how busy they are. I asked for the result right away." He smiled at Paris, "So you've done the deed, huh?"

Paris blushed.

"I planned to give you the birds-and-bees lecture," he admitted ruefully. "I will anyway. This might be a false alarm."

Paris held onto the arms of her chair and squirmed. I reached over and put my hand on top of hers.

"Okay," she said, "but I think I already know this stuff."

"Well, I'm going to talk about birth control, and I'm guessing you may not have enough information in *that* area."

Paris blushed again.

Dexter continued, "I won't prescribe birth control pills for you. I don't know what they might do to the cancer. I'd be afraid the estrogen might speed up the progression. Condoms are not one hundred per cent, neither are diaphragms, but together they can increase the protection level."

And remove the spontaneity, I thought.

As if reading my mind, the doctor said, "You will have to prepare for intercourse; you won't be able to be spontaneous."

Paris wrinkled her nose and stage-whispered to me, "I think I might rather be pregnant."

We all laughed nervously.

"If you are pregnant," Dexter answered, "there is a chance your body might put you into a remission to protect the fetus."

We looked at one another, trying to get the implication of what he said.

"And the baby," Paris asked, "will the baby be," she swallowed, "normal?"

"No reason the baby wouldn't be as normal as any other. There is always a chance, but research shows many women with advanced melanoma give birth to perfectly healthy babies. Granted, there isn't a huge amount of material available, but I'll do some more checking, and if I find anything to the contrary, I'll let you know."

As he finished telling us about the research, an orderly tapped on the door and stepped inside. He handed Dexter a clipboard.

"Thank you, Joseph," Dexter said. He looked up at Paris and said, "Well, young lady, I'm going to recommend you see my associate, Ursula Becker. She's an ob-gyn. You, my dear, are going to be a mother."

To say we drove back to the office in silence was an understatement. If I remember correctly, I didn't hear the motor start, the air conditioner fan blow, or any other traffic noise on the roadway. Paris didn't say a word until we got back to the station. I turned off the key, and as I reached in the back seat to retrieve my purse, she touched my arm.

"You know," she said with the calm of a breezeless ocean, "I believe I understand everything right now."

I arched an eyebrow and waited for her explanation. I was slightly doubtful she could have come up with total understanding during the ride from the hospital to the station, all of thirty minutes.

"When I was very little," she began, "my grandfather told me I was a gift. He lived with us before he died, and I talked with him every day after school. Most days he wanted to talk about when he was growing up on the ranch, but one time he looked at me and said, 'You know I'm dying, don't you Paris?' I tried to tell him it wasn't true, and he would get well. He said, 'No, I'm dying, but do you know why I'm not sad?' Of course, I asked why."

I saw a grim maturity overtaking Paris. Sitting in the car in the parking lot, I watched a transformation. She evolved right in front of my eyes, the child into a woman with an awareness of purpose and a concentration I could only define as being powerful.

"He told me," she continued, "'You and the other children are me. Each of you is me, my mother, father, my grandmother, grandfather, and so on back to when we all began. I won't die because I live on through you. Do great things for me, Paris.' "

Tears welled in my eyes as I listened, and tears flowed from her eyes as she spoke. She didn't sob or shudder. If I hadn't seen her tears, if I'd been listening to her talk on the telephone, I'd never have known she cried.

"No one understood," she continued, "why I didn't want to do the chemotherapy. I had my own reasons then. Now, I know why I didn't. I think somewhere deep inside of me I knew I would be having a baby. Am I rationalizing this, Siobhan?"

Her question took me by surprise. I shook my head.

"I think I felt as though I was letting my grandfather down if I died without having a child, like I'd be hurting all of those people who saw me as them living forever. Does this make any sense?"

I nodded. In a strange way, it did make sense.

"If I'd taken the chemo, I couldn't have carried a child. Now, do you know what, Siobhan? I won't die either. I'll live on in this baby the way my grandfather lives in me."

We sat quietly. I opened the glove box and took out the tissues I kept there. We wiped our eyes, blew our noses, and didn't speak or make eye contact.

Being an unwed mother wouldn't be a cakewalk for her, especially in 1986 rural Texas. Unwed pregnant girls still dealt with being ostracized, whispered about, and judged. It was slightly better than when I was in high school, when a girl pregnant out-of-wedlock disappeared for a few months, telling everyone she was spending the summer at her aunt's house in Kansas, but really went to Edna Gladney's in Houston to have the child and give it up for adoption.

I was sure Paris being sixteen, unmarried, pregnant, and having terminal melanoma, would cause a completely new level of talk around Kingsland.

A sudden rap on the window startled us both, and I turned to see BZ standing next to the car, bending to look inside.

"Is everything okay?" BZ's brows were drawn.

He knew we'd been to the doctor and undoubtedly thought we had gotten bad news about Paris's condition. I'd thought we had, until Paris told me about her Grandfather. Now I wasn't so sure this wasn't the best news possible.

Paris looked at BZ and told him, "I'm going to have a baby."

If I'd had a camera and captured BZ's expression at that moment, I could have put it in a dictionary. A for adoration with a photo of Madonna and Child, B for beatific with a photo of Mother Theresa, C for cherub and a picture of a child angel and, D for dumbfounded with a picture of BZ's face when Paris told him the news.

BZ's face, after it relaxed from its state of astonishment, became a furrowed mass of concern. He went to Paris's side of the car and opened her door. He wrapped her in a hug, didn't say a word, held her for the longest time, and then said, "You are quite the little package, aren't you? One surprise after another. So, what now?"

Paris shrugged, "I'll have to figure it out, BZ."

Chapter Twenty-Five

Paris called her mother from the station and told her Dr. Hardwick wanted her to see another doctor the next day. She didn't go into detail on the phone. She said, "I'm not sure exactly. I'll know more tomorrow. Is it okay if I stay at Siobhan's another night?"

While I went out to cover a mini-Fiesta at a local pre-school, Paris waited at the office and went to lunch with Bud. He took her to Crumpets where, she told me later, "I think I ate everything on the menu, it was so good."

She told Bud about the pregnancy. She told me later, "I told Bud what my grandfather said to me about our ancestors. He told me he understood completely."

She hadn't expected Bud to be so understanding. She didn't know about Bud's great loss. I wondered if Bud felt he had ended when his daughter died. I'd never thought about me being the end of my grandfather, and I doubted my mother had ever considered such a concept. Her self-absorption wouldn't let her go very far away from things in her own immediate best interest.

When I'd finished my work for the day, Bud called me into his office. "Be back on Monday."

"I planned on being here tomorrow after we go to the doctor, Bud." I laughed.

"Paris needs you. She's afraid to tell her parents. She's afraid of what her parents are going to say. She's afraid of everything, even though she's not showing it now. She told me at lunch."

"That must have been some lunch," I teased.

"She didn't say it, but I listened between the words. She kept reassuring herself. 'I'm sure my parents will be okay with this,' she'd say. Or, 'I hope mother won't be too embarrassed.' Things like that. You go with her to tell her parents."

"Thank you, Bud. I'll be back bright and early Monday." I left his office, went to Paris, and she squealed when I told her I'd be able to go to Kingsland with her. She went right into Bud's office, and I could see her hugging him.

BZ came to my desk "Is she going to be okay?"

"I think so, BZ. We'll know more tomorrow. Bud gave me a few days off so I can go with her when she tells her folks. This isn't going to be easy, is it?"

He sighed, "I can't imagine what her parents are going to do," he finally said. "I asked myself what I would do if it was one of my girls. Every time I think about it, I get this sick feeling in the pit of my stomach, and I don't want to go there."

Paris came out of Bud's office, went to BZ and said, "Don't worry about me. I'll be fine."

We left the station, and on the way home, Paris asked,

"Can we go see Phyllis? I want to tell her. She's been wonderful to me."

"Don't you think you might want to wait until you tell Charlie and your mom and dad?" I asked her.

"Oh, gosh." .She grinned sheepishly. "I should, shouldn't I? But I'm so excited."

"Well, it's up to you." I hoped my voice carried enough of the remainder of my message, *wait until you tell your families before you tell everyone else in the world.*

"Okay," she agreed, "I won't say anything, but can we still go see her?" She brightened.

We stopped by the spa, and Phyllis was thrilled. "Group hug," she exclaimed when she saw us. We talked about everything except Paris being pregnant.

She told us she'd met Tristan's brother. "He's the only family he has left in the world. He's nice, but not nearly as handsome or accomplished as Tristan." She beamed as she said Tristan's name.

"Are you going to marry him?" Paris asked the question Phyllis and I had discussed about a dozen times in the past month.

"We've only been dating a few months," she told Paris. "It might be a little early to talk about getting married."

"A lot can happen in two months," Paris said, glancing sideways at me.

I nodded "True," and then shook my head as a reminder to her that she wasn't going to say anything.

We went to Tristan's with Phyllis. By the time we got back to my place, we were exhausted. That didn't keep us from talking for hours more. We spent a lot of time discussing Paris's concerns about how her parents were going to react to her decision to have the baby. She knew Charlie would be shocked but happy when the news sunk in.

281

"My parents will probably shit bricks, though."

I laughed at the crude image and shook my head at her, "You are full of surprises, Miss Potty mouth."

"It will be all right. I'm going to keep saying that. It will be all right, it will be all right, it will be all right," and she drifted off to sleep, repeating her new mantra.

The ob-gyn confirmed what we'd heard from Dr. Doom the day before. Definitely, Paris would be having a baby in mid-December.

"It's difficult to pin down first pregnancies," Doctor Becker told us. "And because of the cancer, we will want to see you more frequently than we typically see a first-time mom."

We left the appointment and Paris said, "I need to go home. You are coming with me, aren't you?"

"I wouldn't miss it for the world," I lied. I dreaded their reaction, too.

We got Paris's things from my condominium, then she followed me in her truck as we drove to Johnson City, where we stopped at the Dairy Queen for lunch and the ladies room.

"You know, Siobhan, Charlie will be getting out of class about the time we get to Kingsland. Do you mind driving the long way through Marble Falls so I can tell him about the baby? I really want him to be with me when I tell my parents."

We left Johnson City and drove straight up Highway 281 to Marble Falls. Traffic was light in the picturesque town on the lake. We stopped at the first traffic light and turned left at the second. School was letting out for the day and we joined the long line of vehicles waiting to pick up students. Paris saw where Charlie's Jeep was parked. She rolled down the truck window and pointed to it. I nodded and we waited.

I had a better vantage point than Paris did. I saw Charlie leaving the main building. I tapped my horn to get Paris's attention and pointed toward the walkway. Paris opened the door of the truck and stood on the running board. I could hear her shout, "Charlie, Charlie!"

The look on his face was exactly the look any woman would want to see on the face of the man she loved. He broke into a run, reached Paris's truck, and leaned in to kiss her. I could tell by his expression Paris told him about the baby. Charlie looked away from her toward my car, but it didn't register that I was in line behind them. He looked back at her, leaned inside the cab of the truck, and kissed her, very lightly. I saw Paris hold his face between her hands and then watched as her thumbs wiped away his tears.

The pick-up line began moving, and people behind us started to honk. That got Charlie's attention. He shook his head as he backed away from Paris's truck. She pulled forward and I followed. Charlie saw me and waved sheepishly. He got into his Jeep and followed us toward Kingsland on 143. Paris led the way and pulled over at the scenic overlook before the Kingsland city limits. She came over to me. I let down my car window.

"Yes, ma'am?" I asked.

"We'd like to talk for a minute," she told me, still glowing.

Charlie got out of his Jeep and walked toward me, hands in his pockets, head down, trying not to look too proud. His face betrayed his effort.

"Hi Siobhan," he said, grinning as only Charlie Garza could.

My mind raced. I wanted to give them privacy, but I didn't want to reach the ranch without Paris. I looked at my gas gauge "I'll stop at the Exxon and fill up," I said.

"Okay," Paris brightened. "We won't be long. We'll catch up with you."

They were at the Exxon before I finished filling my tank. They parked and came over to where I stood holding the nozzle. Paris spoke first.

"How much rent would you charge for your little house at the ranch?"

"I've never thought about it," I said, my brain firing a message for me to get more information. "Why?"

"Well," she grabbed Charlie's hand and clasped it to her. She looked up at Charlie, "You tell her."

"We are getting married." Charlie was certain as a clock chime.

"And," Paris said, "We want to know if you would rent the house at the ranch to us and the barn and corral for Charga?"

"I can do that," I answered. "But don't you think we ought to wait until we talk to your parents? That's why I came, isn't it?"

"But this is what we want," she answered, defiant as a toddler. I sensed a temper tantrum as she stamped her foot.

"Oh, Paris," I reached out and hugged her. "I want you to be happy. I want you and Charlie to do exactly what you want, but let's not go to your parents' home and start dropping all of this on them at once." I turned to put the nozzle back on the pump.

"I want to get married and live with Charlie and have our baby. I want to be normal." She began to cry.

"But you can't be, sweetheart." I wiped my hands on my pant leg before I stoked her hair.

"I can do a lot," Charlie protested.

"I don't doubt that," I said as a light rain began to fall.

We crammed into my little car to get out of the rain. I

started the engine and moved to where they had parked their vehicles.

"What do you think we should do?" Paris asked.

"I think," I said, "You tell your parents about the baby and let them feel the surprise. Tell them what you heard from Dr. Doom and Dr. Becker. Give them a chance."

"They aren't going to let us get married," Paris said. "My mother won't let me. She doesn't even want me to go to the store without her. I couldn't believe they let me go to the doctor all alone. If I hadn't said I was staying with you, they probably wouldn't have let me."

Watching her reaction, I picked up a clue. This afternoon was going to be rougher than I'd first thought. The mature young woman who'd dealt with dying in such a remarkable way was having a meltdown. I wondered if the pregnancy hormones were beginning to kick in.

It wasn't easy convincing them they should wait, but we finally reached an agreement to give Cardiff and Franklin a chance to absorb the news about the baby before they sprang the get-married idea on them.

They dashed through the sprinkling rain to their cars, and we caravanned our way to the gate of the Nash Ranch. I led, driving the caliche road not raising dust, thanks to the light rain dampening the dusty clay. The sun came out in full force as the house came into view and I took it as a good omen.

Franklin stood on the porch, watching the clouds. He ambled down to the gate, and held it open for us. Paris grabbed him and kissed him. Charlie shook his hand. Cardiff stood at the screened door, wiping her hands on her apron. She stepped on the porch. "Y'all are in time for dinner," she said.

Paris pulled me aside and asked, "Before or after?"

"After," I answered quickly and thought if we told them before, no one would eat a thing.

I forced myself to eat, but Paris and Charlie barely touched their plates. Cardiff kept questioning the meal. "Did I put too much salt in the gravy?"

"No, Cardiff. It's great! I reassured her and took a huge bite.

"Charlie, do you want a little more of this squash casserole? You loved it the last time I made it."

Charlie said, "Thank you." To his credit, he took the dish, scooped a large helping, and managed to eat it all.

Rome and India were telling us about something that had happened in the cafeteria at their school, and London tried to tell about something that happened in the cafeteria at his school, too.

Franklin said, "London, you don't go to school yet."

London insisted he did, "Yes I do. You just don't know about it."

We all laughed. He was the high point of our dinner.

I helped Cardiff clear the table. I'd been there so often and she'd gotten so used to me being around that she let me help put away leftovers. She called, "Rome, India, dishes."

Paris and Charlie came into the kitchen and Paris said, "Mom and Dad, Charlie and I need to talk to you about something. You come too, Siobhan."

We followed them to the front porch, where they had arranged the wicker porch furniture in a circle. The earlier shower had cooled the air, and I felt a slight chill. I shivered as I sat down.

"How about some coffee?" Franklin noticed and asked me.

I thought he'd had a great idea and I wanted to accept

the offer, but Paris took control, saying, "Can we talk first?"

Her voice shook when she spoke. Cardiff and Franklin sensed it too. Their faces registered alarm.

Cardiff blurted, "What did the doctor say?"

Franklin didn't say anything, but leaned forward in his chair. Cardiff reached her hand to him. They clasped hands, and their fingers intertwined.

Chapter Twenty-Six

Paris started speaking in her normal voice, but quickly she was talking through tears. "I'm, well we, Charlie and I are going to have a baby."

Crickets chirped, cicadas droned, and I heard moth wings flapping against the light bulb overhead.

Cardiff broke the silence. She stood and her first words were, "Shouldn't you end the pregnancy? Didn't the doctor say it would hurt you to go through with it?"

The thought horrified Paris. "An abortion? You want me to get an abortion!"

"Crap," Franklin interrupted. "Your mother didn't say anything about an abortion. She wants to know what the doctor told you." He gave Cardiff a harsh look. She sat back in her chair.

"He said I could even go into remission."

"For how long?" Cardiff leaned forward.

"He didn't know. He's going to research it and let me know. And the ob-gyn…" she began.

Cardiff interrupted, her eyes narrowed and she sounded accusatory. "So *that's* the other doctor he wanted you to see."

I scrunched further back in my chair. Charlie scooted his closer to Paris and put his arm around her.

Franklin looked at Charlie. "I thought I could trust you, son."

"It's my fault,*"* Paris cried. "I'm the one. I'm the one who's going to die; I'm the one who wanted to have sex. I wanted to find out what the big deal was. I didn't want to die without doing it. Charlie must have asked me a million times if I really wanted to. I wanted it. It was me, not him."

Franklin's skeptical expression made me think he wanted to say more. I could see him biting his tongue to keep from saying something even more hurtful.

Ireland had heard the raised voices and was standing inside the screened door. Cardiff noticed her. "Ireland, go on back inside. Everything is okay out here."

"Paris is crying," Ireland pointed out. Obviously, everything wasn't okay.

"We'll let you know," Franklin said, rising from his chair.

"But Paris," Ireland said.

"I'm okay," Paris reassured her littlest sister.

Ireland turned, not convinced, and went inside the house.

"So you're going to have the baby?" Cardiff asked.

"Yes, unless Dr. Doom says something different. If the baby isn't going to be all right, then we'll have to think about doing something else."

Cardiff nodded, "But what about you? What if he says this pregnancy will hurt you? What then?" She was teetering between anger and concern.

"Mother, really? What difference could it possibly make to me? We all know I'm not here for the long haul. Remember what you told me that Uncle Paul wrote on his letters from Nam? I'm short."

Cardiff sobbed, and Franklin put his arms around her. Charlie held Paris. I sat alone. Franklin looked at me. "What do you think, Siobhan?"

"I think it's amazing, a miracle. What could the chances be? Paris is going to have a lifetime of experiences. As much as all of us deny it, we know Paris doesn't have a full life ahead of her," I tried to be as gentle as possible. "Now, she won't leave this world as a child, but as a woman." I leaned forward, my forearms on my knees.

"What do you two want to do?" Franklin finally asked Paris and Charlie.

Charlie stood up and solemnly said, "With your permission, Mr. Nash, I want to marry Paris."

"Marry her? Get married?" Cardiff acted as if the concept was foreign to her.

"Why not?" Paris challenged, "Isn't that what people do when they get pregnant?"

Franklin attempted to make peace. "Wait, wait. We are still in shock. We need to talk about this in the morning. Let's sleep on it."

Cardiff stood and reached for Paris's hand, Paris turned her body away from her mother and clung to Charlie.

I took my cue, "I need to go," I said. "Is that okay, Paris? Are you all right now?"

She flung her arms around my neck and hugged me. "Thank you, Siobhan, thank you. For everything."

I left to drive home, my eyes on the lookout for deer on the road. When I got home, I planned to go right to sleep I'd call Bud in the morning. The way I'd left the Nashes, there was no reason for me to miss work. I had a feeling I'd be taking more days later if I needed to get the house ready for Paris and Charlie. I started making a mental list. The road would need grading and a layer of gravel added. Either that or I'd have to pay for car repairs every week. I'd have to run a phone line to the house. Paris would need a phone in case she had an emergency. I wanted to put in a water purification system, not that the well water wasn't good, but I didn't want anything to cause problems for Paris or the baby.

When I got home, the message light on my phone blinked at me. Bud left a message. BZ did, too. Both of them wanted to know how the Nashes reacted to the news. I called them both. They each thought the Nashes would react as they had. I told them Paris and Charlie wanted to rent my ranch house from me so they could live there. Like true friends, they both offered to help get the place ready for the newlyweds. I hoped Paris would call me in the morning and tell me everything had been better after I left.

I called Phyllis and asked her, "Want to help me with a bridal shower?"

"Sure, who is getting married?"

It was a natural question, but I didn't answer. Instead, I asked, "Want to help me with a baby shower?"

"So the bride is pregnant?" Phyllis started thinking. "I can't imagine who it could be. Wait. Tracy! She's gotten her claws into that good-looking doctor!"

"Nope," I said.

"Is it someone I know?"

"Yes, it's someone you know."

"I give up, spill. Give, who is it?"

"Paris," I announced. "And Charlie."

"No!" Phyllis was stunned. "She was just here yesterday. She didn't say a thing."

"She hadn't even told Charlie yet. It's my fault she didn't say anything. I told her he might like to know before the rest of the world found out.

"Do her parents know?"

"Yeah, I went out to the ranch with Paris this afternoon. I was there when she and Charlie told them."

I told the story for the third time, and Phyllis, too, said she would help me get everything ready for the bride and groom. She asked about what the doctor said and asked how a pregnancy would affect Paris's prognosis. I explained we were waiting for him to find out more, "But whatever he finds out won't matter to Paris. I've never seen Paris this happy," I told Phyllis.

"I was thinking when you came by the spa that she looked wonderful," Phyllis added, "Now I know why."

I promised I'd keep her posted about everything that was going on.

She said, "I think we can start planning a wedding shower. I'm sure they will agree to let them tie the knot."

We hung up, and I got ready for bed. The phone rang while I was brushing my teeth. I answered it anyway, expecting Phyllis calling with some creative idea for a shower.

"Miss O'Shaunessy," a man's voice asked.

"I'm not interested," I mumbled.

"Wait one minute; I need to tell you something. I'm calling from Maine. I am your mother's friend, Jorge," he'd said. "Blayne. . ." he said tenderly, and I paused to think how beautiful my mother's name sounded, ". . .told me I should call you if she passed."

"Passed?" The toothpaste leaked down my chin.

"She has been quite ill for many years," he said, his voice thick with grief.

"What happened? I mean, why? Her condition?" I was outside myself, watching as I tried to grasp what he'd told me. I grabbed a handful of tissue and wiped toothpaste from my face.

"It is very complicated. Perhaps you will be able to talk with her doctor when you come. It doesn't feel right for me to talk about her. I hope you understand. You are her next of kin. Do you want to make the arrangements for her?"

The noise that escaped me sounded like a combination snort-choke. I'd have been equally prepared to plan a funeral for any person off the street.

"Did she leave instructions?" I had no idea what she'd want.

"Yes," Jorge said. "The attorney has all of that. You can see him when you come."

I didn't want to "come." I had no desire to fly to Maine. I needed to be available to Paris. I needed to go to work. I, I realized how little emotion I felt. I wasn't thinking about my mother at all. She had kept herself a stranger to me. I could hear her voice on the phone message when I'd called to thank her for the money she'd given Paris. "This is Blayne. I'm in the studio working. Leave a message for me." I'd left the message, meant to write a letter to her but never had. I never heeded BZ's advice to call her and try to reconnect.

Perhaps that had been her attempt to reach out to me as BZ insisted. She'd tried too late. I'd hardened too much. In time, I might have softened. . .now, in actuality, it was unequivocally very much too late. I waited for the thought to penetrate.

"Are you there, Miss," Jorge asked.

"Yes," I answered. "I don't even know where my mother lives in Maine."

"The easiest way to get to New Brunswick is to fly into New Hampshire, rent a car, and drive here."

I thanked him for calling me, rinsed my mouth, and called the airlines. There was an available flight to New Hampshire the following day at two.

I called to tell Bud I would be out for about a week.

"I'm sorry for your loss, Siobhan. Don't worry about work."

I thanked him, feeling counterfeit because I didn't feel a loss, but I did sense regret inching around the edges of the limited vision I had of my mother.

After Bud, I called Phyllis to tell her. She wanted to close the spa and go with me to Maine. I insisted I could do this on my own and thanked her for the generous offer.

"I'm here if you change your mind," she said. "I hate for you to go alone. Should you call Graciella? She and your mother had been in contact, remember?"

I hadn't thought of that. I didn't know what Graciella's relationship with my mother had been, but I did know they'd talked recently. I decided to let her know.

I tried the company number I used the day I made the appointment to meet with Eloy and left a message for Graciella to call me.

The next morning I'd almost finished packing when she called me back. I told her what Jorge said and was surprised when Graciella said, "I would like to go with you, Siobhan."

We met at the airport departure gate and spoke only briefly about my mother's death. I told Graciella what I knew, and we filled the remainder of our trip with impersonal conversation about the journey ahead of us. We flew American to Dallas and changed planes to fly into Manchester-Boston Regional. We rented a Ford Tahoe and followed the directions from the rental car attendant. They matched those Jorge had given me the day before. We stopped at the Brunswick Diner downtown, as Jorge had instructed, and I called his number to tell him we had arrived. He promised to meet us there in twenty minutes.

After we ate, something good, I don't remember what, a man who I knew immediately must be Jorge came in and scanned the diners. He looked every inch the artist, his hair pulled back in a long ponytail, Rorschach-like stains on his oversized knit shirt and baggy khaki shorts, socks with his Birkenstock sandals.

I waved my hand, and he rushed to our table. "I apologize," he began, "The drawbridge was up, and I had to wait for the boat to pass."

I introduced Graciella, and he shook hands with us. His hands were rough.

"The clay," he apologized, flipping his hands to show how dry and cracked his art made them.

We paid our bill and followed his car through town and into the woods surrounding it. He turned into a small enclave of houses several miles outside of Brunswick and parked in front of a small clapboard house surrounded by a white picket fence. He started up the walk and motioned us to follow. When he opened the door, I hesitated at the threshold, feeling I was trespassing into a stranger's house, not entering the home where my mother lived.

Graciella followed me inside. The little cottage could have been home to anyone. The tables and chests were old pieces, not antiques, painted in soft shades of grey-green and soft blue. The sofa and chairs, covered in soft-hued floral chintz, felt warm and comfortable. It was a pleasant room. I could not picture my mother in it.

"Her studio," Jorge directed.

We passed through the kitchen to the back of the house where a wall of floor-to-ceiling windows allowed the north light to illuminate the room, every inch of wall covered with paintings she had done. It was then I discovered my mother used children as subjects in her work. Every piece contained at least one child, sometimes two or three, each one doing some child-like thing: two girls playing hopscotch, a baseball team of mismatched boys using bed pillows for bases, a seesaw balancing a boy on one end, a girl on the other.

I walked behind her easel to see what she had been working on and saw myself with Charga and Paris. She had taped a photo from the day of the auction to the top of her easel. Her final work had been of me.

"I sent it to her," Graciella said about the photo.

That was the moment I stopped hating my mother, and began trying to understand the woman who left me.

Chapter Twenty-Seven

Jorge made an appointment for us with my mother's attorney, and I discovered she had indeed made me the beneficiary of everything. She left instructions for her funeral, and those had been sent to the funeral home. She wanted her casket closed, a brief ceremony at the Bowdoin Chapel, and then graveside services at the cemetery adjacent to the college.

Her attorney solved the mystery surrounding her death. Jorge avoided telling me she ended her life by overdosing on prescription medication. The attorney suggested we make an appointment with her psychiatrist.

We did, and he told us my mother had suffered from severe manic depression all of her life and that the episodes intensified as she aged. He reassured me repeatedly it had nothing to do with what I feared had been my recent mistreatment of her.

Graciella said, "I knew she had this battle."

I was surprised. My questioning expression prompted

her to say, "She didn't want anyone to know. She didn't want me to tell you."

I tried to compartmentalize my feelings about my mother's death and felt myself slipping from anger into guilt, then to remorse and betrayal. A part of me felt very proud of my mother, the gifted artist I had just discovered. I got angry again when I realized I'd be dealing with this new guilt for the rest of my life.

The old Bowdoin College Chapel where she wanted her service was lovely. The carved alter had been adorned with sprays of summer flowers. I thought the tributes were from her friends in Maine, but when the dark-suited funeral director presented me with the visitor's book, I found florists' cards inside from my friends, too. Flowers had come from Bud and my friends at KWNK, the Nashes, BZ and Sylvia, Tristan and Phyllis. Even Eloy had sent flowers from his mother and himself. The rest were from friends and patrons of my mother. The local newspaper ran a story about her. *Blayne Siobhan Tabbard, the well-known local artist whose sensitive portrayal of children at play gained national recognition, has passed at age fifty-two.*

I had difficulty reconciling the image of the woman who so loved children that she spent her life committing their images to canvas with the woman who didn't send birthday cards to her own daughter. On the flight back home to Texas, I told Graciella how I felt.

"She couldn't take you back," Graciella told me. "She fell apart when your father died. That episode was the beginning of her sickness. Did you know she was often hospitalized?"

I had not known.

"Your grandfather was a good man, but he wouldn't let you go live with your mother when she got out of the hospital. She refused to stay on her medication. The doctors told him she would be unpredictable. He was afraid for you, Siobhan. Blayne told everyone she hated Texas and wanted to go to Europe to study art. Your grandfather feared her being there somewhere, losing reality *and* you in some foreign country. He said he would fight her in court if she tried to take you with her."

"Why didn't he tell me? Why did he let me feel she didn't want me all those years?" This new knowledge hurt me deeply.

"You know your grandfather," Graciella defended him. "He was a man of pride. Did he ever say terrible things to you about your mother?"

I shook my head. "No. My grandfather never talked much about my mother."

"If he had said, 'Your mother is a crazy woman', then what would you have done?"

"I might have..." I paused trying to imagine what I would have thought. "...felt sorry for her."

"Do you think you would have worried more about her? If he told you he didn't know where she was from one week to another, what would you have done?" She paused.

Knowing my grandfather, I could see why he ignored the truth about my mother. By not talking about her to me, he also prevented himself from missing his daughter. He tried to spare us both the pain caused by her illness.

When we got back to town, I thanked Graciella, not only for going with me to Maine but also for filling in the blanks of my life. I began to grieve, not necessarily for my mother. I didn't really know her. I grieved for what might have been my life if she had not been ill, if things had happened differently.

When I drove home from the airport, I dreaded going

into my empty house. I was very relieved when I found Phyllis's car blocking my driveway. She was sitting inside reading magazines, windows down, cool breeze riffling her hair. When she saw me, she waved, backed her car out of my driveway, and let me drive in first. She parked behind my car.

"How are you doing?" she asked as she took my carry-on from me.

"As well as can be expected." I answered as accurately as I could, for a woman who had only recently discovered information that contradicted everything she'd ever believed about her mother.

When we got inside my house, I collapsed on the sofa. Phyllis turned on lamps, opened shutters, and lowered the thermostat. She went to the kitchen, brought me a glass of ice water, put on the kettle for tea and came back to sit beside me.

I began to feel safe for the first time since I'd received Jorge's call.

"I've missed you," Phyllis said. "Not only while you've been gone, but I know I haven't been much of a friend since Tristan and I..." Her voice trailed off.

"Don't I know you're always only a phone call away? I'm happy for you and Tristan." I grasped her hand. I didn't need to say more.

"Tell me," she asked, "what happened in Maine?"

Her open-ended question allowed me to start anywhere and tell her anything, from the morbid details to the exact feelings I'd experienced. I began with the phone call. I got to the part about my mother's house, and I said, "I was shocked when I saw her work, Phyllis. The local paper called her a nationally prominent artist known for her sensitive portrayal of children. Can you believe that?"

Phyllis shook her head. Our hands clasped.

"And, you won't believe this. The painting on her easel, what she'd been working on, was of me with Paris and Charga. Graciella sent her the photo, and she had it taped onto her easel. She captured us perfectly."

I started sobbing. Phyllis put her arms around me and held me while I cried. She got up to get a box of tissues from my nightstand. We both took a couple and wiped our eyes. I blew my nose and kept crying. I couldn't stop.

Through my sobs, I told Phyllis my mother had taken every leftover prescription pill she had. "It wasn't accidental, Phyl she wanted to die. Maybe I could have done something. If I'd called again to thank her, if I'd made an effort, it might have been different."

My body shook. Every nerve fired. My whole belief system cratered. All of my life I'd believed my mother had the maternal instincts of a wild rabbit. I'd called her a drive-by parent. "Remember when she showed up at my twenty-first birthday party?"

The kettle shrieked in the kitchen and we both jumped at the sound. Phyllis stood up. "Let's make tea."

We went to the kitchen, and she started the tea leaves steeping. "My mother was diagnosed with manic-depression years ago. Do you think I might have been that way too? I mean by the way I reacted after the divorce?"

"No." Her answer was succinct. "From what I know about that disease, it doesn't go away, and you haven't been depressed since you snapped out of that phase of your life. I think you went to the ranch to decide who you wanted to be when you grew up."

"I'm still trying to figure that one out."

We sat quietly as the night sky darkened and streetlights flickered on. When I told Phyllis about the service and all the flowers and thanked her for the ones she sent, she said, "I wanted to be there for you. I was very glad Graciella went. If she hadn't offered, I was going to go."

I hugged her. "And you'd have left who in charge?" I laughed.

"This has made me realize it's time for me to train someone to run the place, so I can leave every once in a while."

"Something good comes from bad," I quipped.

"Yeah, like that's the good that comes from this," she shook her head. "I think the good from this, late as it is in coming, is that you finally got to know your mother."

"I don't know my mother," I contradicted.

"Yes, you do. You know her more than you have ever in your entire life. You know she loved you."

"And how do I know that?"

"The paintings. She never left you. You are in every one of them. I believe every brush stroke placed was in honor of you. That's the only way she could love you without hurting you."

I thought about the paintings hanging on the wall of her studio. They were sensitive, gentle portraits done in soft pastel hues. I especially like the one of the little boy looking up, holding a broken sand dollar in his chubby hands, tears flowing down his cheeks. She had to love children to paint them with such delicate precision. I could see love there.

"I need to go back and dispose of everything. I have to sell the house, find homes for the paintings, and take care of all of her things. She left it all to me," I told her. Then I whispered, "I am suddenly a very wealthy young woman."

We looked at the calendar inside of my pantry door and decided we would fly up to Maine and drive back in my mother's Mercedes. It would be a road trip extraordinaire.

At almost nine o'clock, Phyllis left me. She'd scrambled eggs, all I had in my fridge, and we'd eaten before she left. As she drove away, I flipped off the porch light, then went to the phone, and called to talk with Paris.

Franklin answered the phone, told me how sorry they were to hear about my mother, and then he called Paris to the phone.

"Siobhan, I'm so sorry," she said as soon as she held the receiver. "I'll always think of how generous she was helping us get Charga back."

"She had almost finished a painting of us," I said.

"Of us?" Paris was confused.

"It was the last thing she worked on before she died. It's beautiful. I can't wait for you to see it. Enough about me. How are you feeling? Are you okay? How are your parents doing?"

"Yes, I'd love to," she said, not answering my questions.

She confused me, but I caught on rather quickly. "Are they listening and you don't want to talk?"

"Yes, Friday will work for me," she said with a bright lilt. "Daddy, can I go spend the night at Siobhan's on Friday night?"

She invited herself for a visit and I didn't mind. It gave me something to look forward to for the weekend.

Bud told me to take as much time away from work as I needed. I decided I'd go back the following Monday. I needed to get myself glued back together; being with Paris, and helping her work through her new circumstances would do that for me. I needed to be distracted from my troubles, and nothing did that quite as well as helping someone else deal with theirs.

Paris arrived around eleven Friday morning, carrying

a huge duffle bag. I figured she planned to stay longer than one night.

As soon as she threw the duffle in the guest room, she said, "You have to help us elope. Charlie is coming when school is out. We can drive to Mexico and get married Saturday morning."

"Wait a minute." My pulse quickened. I sat down at the table, pushed out a chair for Paris, and said, "Let's talk about this for a little while. What's happening with your parents?"

"They don't think we should get married. They think I should stay at home, so they can take care of me."

She operated on fury fuel, and I'd never seen her so tense and angry. The gentle child I'd fallen in love with had disappeared. "This isn't you, Paris. What's happened to bring this on?"

"They don't understand. We all know how sick I am, even though I don't feel sick right now. They are controlling my life and me. I don't have time." She sounded panicky, "I want to live my life the way I choose, not how they want me to live it."

Paris's age and condition collided. I remembered being at the same stage and feeling the same way.

Teenagers want to be in charge of their lives, but there was an enormous difference between her situation and that of a typical teen. Her life was ending, and we knew it; we simply didn't know how much time she had left. Losing her was a certainty, and now, with her pregnancy thrown into the mix, an innocent child added to the picture, everyone's emotions were volcanic.

I knew her parents were focused on what was best for her, and I needed to reach Paris in a way that made her understand from their point of view. Then I'd have to get her parents to understand how Paris felt. Of one thing, I was certain. I was not driving anyone to Mexico!

Chapter Twenty-Eight

I reasoned with Paris and convinced her to drive to Kingsland to meet with her parents right away. We stopped at the Johnson City DQ and spent a few minutes walking up and down Main Street, talking about my mother. Paris was very curious about the way I'd felt when I was growing up without a mother. She wanted to know how I felt when my mother wasn't there for me.

"Do you think my child will think I left because I wanted to?"

"You won't have any control over leaving, and everyone will tell your child that." I tried to say it in a way that could help her see the difference between the way my mother left me and the way she would be leaving her child.

"But do children think that way? Or do they just feel the loss?"

Her astuteness always surprised me. Whenever I became comfortable talking to a sixteen-year-old, she would share her insights, and flabbergast me by the mature grasp of human nature she possessed.

I tried to think back to my feelings when I was a small girl wondering why I didn't have a mother like the other kids. "If I'd been told my mother was very ill and couldn't be with me, it might have made me feel it wasn't my fault that she left me," I admitted.

"But children don't understand death," she said. "I know. I went back and dug up my pet rabbit after we'd buried her because I thought she'd get back up and be fine. That was unpleasant." Her nose crinkled.

"Well, after knowing what I know now about my mother's mental health, I understand what my grandfather tried to do. He wanted to keep me safe. I also know my mother wouldn't have been able to care for me. In a strange way, I appreciate her staying out of my life the way she did. Since I didn't know, I felt I was missing something important. I thought if I had a mother, my life would be perfect. Now, I know those imaginings were completely off the mark. Even with all of the uncertainty of Grandfather's serial marrying, I had a total conviction that he loved me better than he did any of those women."

When we got back to our cars, she took the lead. We were about to turn off at Round Mountain, when we saw Charlie's Jeep heading south toward San Antonio. She chased him down and told him everything had changed. We formed a caravan again, and I followed them to the ranch gate. I asked if they'd hang back until I had a chance to talk with her parents.

"Let's go to Sonic," Charlie said, and they drove away toward Kingsland.

I headed to the ranch house, waited for the dust to settle, then got out of my car. Cardiff came out to the front porch to see who had driven up. She bent down and looked inside the car. Her brow furrowed in concern.

She rushed toward the gate, and as I opened the car door she said, "Where is Paris? She said she was going to stay with you?"

Before I could say a word, Cardiff started crying.

"Cardiff," I started to speak.

She interrupted me. "She's run off with him hasn't she? You came to tell me they've run off together." She glared at me as if she thought I had been complicit in the plan.

"No, Cardiff. They've gone to the Sonic." I paused. "We met up with Charlie on the highway." Then I added the truth. "They did want me to drive them to Mexico so they could get married. I refused."

She began to cry. "I'm sorry, Siobhan. It isn't fair to have this dumped on you. I know you are dealing with your mother's death. You don't need this right now."

"No one needs this, ever, Cardiff," I began. "I can tell this whole thing is taking a terrible toll on you, and on Paris, too."

"I don't know who my little girl is anymore. I feel as though I've lost her already." We walked up the steps to the porch, and she told me. "Everything was fine after the auction. She spent a lot of time out in the barn with Charga. She and Charlie used to sit out here with him every night. She and I talked about everything. Then she started getting more and more secretive and moody. Franklin and I blamed it on the illness, then when we found out she was pregnant, and the moodiness made more sense. I tried to talk with her about what we could do as a family to make her life happy until the," she paused, "end."

I nodded, understanding Cardiff's concern about her daughter. "I suggested the whole family go down to the coast or Six Flags or something, or go to New York or Disney."

"What did she think about that?" I already knew, but I wanted Cardiff to tell me.

"She said, 'Mother, I don't want to go away. I want to stay at home with Charlie and Charga, and take care of us.' Then she said, 'You are avoiding the fact that I'm not a child anymore. I'm having a child.' "

"But she will always be your little girl won't she?" I believed Cardiff would eventually realize what had happened between her daughter and herself.

Cardiff cried out, "She doesn't know how I feel. I'm losing my first-born child, my baby."

"So is she, Cardiff." I waited for the thought to soak in. "She's losing her first-born child, too, but in a different way. She's going to be leaving her baby behind. She is as worried about her baby as you are about her. You two are feeling very similar losses."

She looked at me; her face softened; understanding dawned on her beautiful face. "She really isn't my baby anymore."

"No, she isn't, and now she wants to be your friend. Can you think how you would be dealing with this if she was your friend instead of your daughter?" I hoped I was being as successful reaching her as I thought I was. "As inconceivable as it may seem to you, she needs a friend more than she needs a mother."

"What are you thinking, Siobhan?" She was searching my face for an answer.

"I think she and Charlie should get married." I knew it wasn't what she wanted to hear, but it was what I'd come to believe. "They asked if they could rent the house at my ranch in New Braunfels. I told them I'd think about it. Now,

I think it would be a great answer for them, but I won't agree if you can't support the decision."

Cardiff's expression changed. Her face smoothed as she listened. I could see her considering my proposal.

"They could be married and live like any normal young couple," I continued. "If Charlie's father agrees, and if Franklin and you can agree, you could all be planning a wedding instead of arguing, hurting, and sneaking around."

"What if something happens to the baby? We don't have any assurance the baby will even survive to term. What if they get married and then miscarry. Then what?" Cardiff slipped back to thinking of everything that could go wrong.

"Cardiff," I tried to be gentle with her, "Can we think this through? What if nothing goes wrong? What if the baby is born perfectly healthy and they've spent whatever time Paris has left in absolute marital bliss. Do you want to deny her that experience? Paris is dying; it's all we know for sure."

Cardiff nodded at me.

I kept talking. "Even if Paris goes into a pregnancy remission, it will not last forever. What, another six months?"

Cardiff listened, wiping her eyes and nose with a wadded pink tissue.

I went on. "So, we know she might have six months, if the baby goes to term. Then what? How long will she have? Another two months, maybe three. We are dealing with nothing but uncertainty from then on."

Cardiff said, "My point exactly."

I thought I'd lost the argument. "But look at it from Paris's point of view. She's a sixteen-year-old girl who is going to have a baby she won't be able raise. She loves a boy who loves her very much, but you want her to spend the last months of her life longing for him, wishing she could be with him and living a life like normal people. Why can't she?"

"Because she's too young," Cardiff pounded her fists on her knees.

That ticked me off. "She's too damn young to die is what she is." I matched Cardiff's emotion. "But she's not too young to have a child, and she's not too young to be married. I think what's happening for Paris is miraculous. She has a good reason to shelve concerns for your feelings and even her fear of impending death. This is how she copes. At first she focused on saving Charga, and now she's focusing on the baby she's carrying."

Cardiff said nothing. She seemed calm for a change.

I hated being harsh, but I wanted her to think beyond keeping her daughter at home. I plunged on. "We can do one of two things for her. We can force her to face the reality that she's dying, be damned and determined she face the facts. We can get a calendar and make her mark off the days every morning until she can't hold a pencil anymore."

I tried to check my emotions, but it was difficult. It wouldn't do any good to lose control with Cardiff. I felt I was walking a tightrope suspended between two fragile columns: Cardiff one, Paris the other.

Cardiff watched her hands as she unfolded and refolded the tissue she held. She smoothed the crumples as if she were systematically leveling all of her unruly thoughts. I felt she'd reached a tipping point. This was the perfect time to tell Cardiff what Paris told me about the conversation she'd had with her grandfather.

"Paris is happy because she is leaving part of herself behind, a legacy."

I rushed on while I felt she might be able to hear me. "We can give Paris a wonderful gift. We can give her the illusion that she will live forever. She knows she's dying. We don't need to keep telling her. The best gift we can give her is to move into the world she wants and love her there."

It was getting late. Dusk made hazy shadows. I'd said everything possible to change her mind.

"I love you, Cardiff, and I love your family. I hope you understand I'm not judging anyone. I promised Paris I would talk with you. I've been as honest as I can be."

"Thank you, Siobhan. You've helped me think about this in a different way. I'll need to think more about what you told me and talk with Franklin," she hugged me. "Thank you. You are a good friend to us and to Paris. You understand her, don't you?"

"I think it's because I love her. Not the way you and Franklin love her. I don't understand the connection myself, but from the first time I saw her swaying in the judging arena, I felt I'd known her all my life."

On the way out of the ranch on the caliche road, I saw a vehicle coming toward me. It was Franklin and the kids returning from the grocery store. We pulled up, driver side to driver side.

"Hey," I said as I lowered my window and looked up into the big truck.

All of the kids yelled "Hi," and wanted me to turn around and come back so they could visit with me.

"Not tonight," I said. "I've got to get back to town. I'll be back soon though."

We waved goodbye, and I drove toward the gate. When I got there, I saw Charlie's Jeep on the road outside the fence. He and Paris were talking quietly. They didn't notice me until I got out and opened the gate, and then Charlie jumped out and apologized for not doing it for me.

"That's okay, you can close it," I smiled at him and

backed my car up so they could drive through. I drove out, parked my car on the shoulder, and walked back to the passenger side of the Jeep where Paris sat.

"I had a long talk with your Mom," I told her. "She loves you. She loves you sixteen years more than you love this little thing," I patted her tummy. "Be gentle with you mother, Paris."

Charlie closed the gate and got back in the Jeep, his face looked more defiant than I'd ever seen it before.

"Please don't be angry," I begged them. "This is going to work out. Honest."

"My dad understands," Charlie told me. "He believes I have to be a man and be responsible."

"That's honorable, Charlie. However, you have to remember, the Nashes' situation is slightly different. They are losing their daughter. Try to think about how they feel. Put yourself in their shoes."

I didn't know if the two of them could empathize with anyone else. They were perfectly in tune with each other as young lovers are, and the rest of world was out of their galaxy. I hoped they'd try to understand her parents.

I slapped my flattened palm on the hood of his Jeep and walked back to the gate. I opened it wide enough to slip through and got back in my car. I said everything I could think to say. Now the Nash family had to work out how they would love one another from this point onward.

Chapter Twenty-Nine

Paris called the next day, "Thank you, thank you, thank you, Siobhan. We're getting married."

"I am so happy, Paris. I know you will be very happy." What else could I say?

"Will you be my maid-of-honor?" She asked in all seriousness.

I pondered the question. "I am so honored you asked me, but don't you think your mother would be more involved if you had your sisters and brothers in the wedding party?"

"I hadn't thought about that," she said. "I think it would make her happy."

In early May the wedding of Miss Paris Lee Nash and Mr. Charles Mendoza Garza took place at the gazebo down on the lake, Paris's favorite place. She wore a beautiful white silk dress and the sheer lace veil her grandmother and mother had both worn when they were married. Charlie wore a new dark blue suit and they both gave the impression of having dropped down from heaven to grace us with their presence.

Charlie appeared to have been born for this moment. His dark complexion looked swarthy against his crisp white shirt and he seemed mature and capable of handling anything. He assumed his new role as husband and protector with solemnity, standing with his hand on Paris's small waist.

She gazed up at him with complete trust and adoration. I only hoped they would be able to sustain their love through all that lay ahead.

Gathered were guests, family members of the bride and groom, and the new friends they made saving Charga: Phyllis and Tristan, Lannie White, the Gallagher's, Bud Johnson, Luis and his wife along with Pepe, BZ, Sylvia and the girls. Dr. Doom and Tracy came, too, but didn't stay late.

India was her sister's maid of honor. I'd made the right decision when I declined her invitation to be in the wedding party. India was serene in a long deep violet dress. Rome stood proudly as best man next to Charlie; he was wearing a new dark blue suit, too. Ireland dropped petals ahead of Paris's entrance, and precious London bore wedding rings on a satin pillow, walking slowly, taking his job very seriously.

Cardiff did her best not to cry as Franklin, the picture of fatherly pride, escorted Paris up the steps to meet Charlie. The Pastor from the nearby Lutheran Church conducted the ceremony. When he reached *until death do us part,* I heard a collective intake of breath. Everyone tried to forget the future.

I'd been there when they planned the ceremony. Charlie wanted the until death part taken out. Paris wouldn't hear of it. She cried when she told him and us, "Charlie I want you to go on after I die. We will part. I want that in there so you will know."

When the pastor presented the newlyweds, "Mr. and Mrs. Charles Garza," they faced the group of family and friends, and we could see the joy and love they had for one another and for each of us as well.

The day couldn't have been more perfect, cooler than usual for early-May in Texas. Seven round tables waited on the lawn, each draped in white. Centerpieces, ten narrow bud vases tied together in one bouquet by wide violet satin ribbon, was a festive touch. Each narrow vase, etched with *Paris and Charlie, May 8, 1986,* contained a violet-blue hydrangea blossom, designed to serve dual purpose, as centerpiece and party favor. Each guest could take a flower and vase home as a remembrance of the day Paris and Charlie married.

BZ filmed the ceremony and continued filming throughout the reception. He wanted Charlie to be able to remember this day for the rest of his life.

Tristan catered the reception dinner with a buffet of traditional Mexican dishes. We feasted on *empanadas, quesadillas, guacamole, camarones al gusto, arroz, borracho frijoles* and a *tres leche* wedding cake.

Paris's uncle and aunt, the talker from the spa, hired a limousine to take the newlyweds to a secret honeymoon location. We all knew Cardiff and Franklin had reserved the honeymoon suite at the historic Faust Hotel in downtown New Braunfels for them. It wasn't exotic, but it was perfect.

Charlie's father, Ramiro, such a kind man, hired a troop of Mariachis to play at the reception and Charlie's aunt Rosa brought a huge wedding bell piñata for the children to break open. Ireland completely wrecked the bell, whacking it with the white satin-wrapped bat until no one could recognize it. As the sweets scattered, the children dove to collect them and then reluctantly shared the candy with the other guests.

In the weeks following the wedding, Paris and Charlie settled into the little house at my ranch. As soon as Franklin and Cardiff agreed to the wedding, I'd gone to work fixing the place to make it inhabitable. I'd had the road graded and re-graveled, refurbished the barn and corral for Charga, had the house painted inside and out. I replaced all of the counter tops, re-faced the cabinets, and bought new appliances. I added new bathroom fixtures. They were necessary. The hardwood floors were an extravagance, but made the little house elegant. The inheritance from my mother couldn't have come at a more beneficial time.

My neighbor, Melvyn Gefers, did all of the work. He could do anything around construction and was able to oversee the licensed work that was required.

I will never forget Paris's face when she saw the house for the first time. She oohed and aahed over everything.

She and Charlie came with her mom and dad, and Phyllis and I helped them settle in. Phyllis and I had made our trip to Maine in early in the month, and packed up my mother's house and her artwork. I brought my mother's things to furnish the little cottage for Charlie and Paris. I stood back and watched Paris with my own absolute joy. When she opened the door to the second bedroom, the nursery, I held my breath.

Cardiff and I had decorated the nursery together. We'd chosen in the palest shade of lemon yellow we could find. The white furniture was a perfect backdrop for the custom-made accessories we got from a little shop in the same shopping center as Phyllis's spa. We selected fabric in yellow with Paris's favorite color, lavender. It came in several pattern ways, plaid, check, floral and stripe. We shuttered the windows to darken the room so the baby could nap, and I'd bought a new braid area rug to cover the hardwood floor.

One of my mother's paintings hung over the crib. It was the one of the little girl and boy on the seesaw. I figured that way, no matter what gender the baby turned out to be, we would be safe because the painting represented both. Cardiff and I were almost as excited as Paris and Charlie about the upcoming birth.

After we made sure everything was perfect for the newlyweds, we left them with an address book filled with the phone numbers of everyone who loved them, maps from the New Braunfels Visitor's Bureau and a New Braunfels telephone directory. For the first time in their lives, they were on their own.

It was the first weekend in December when I got the call from Cardiff. Paris and Charlie were on their way to the hospital. Paris had started labor, a little early, but not dangerously so. I got to the hospital before they arrived and happened to run into Dexter Hardwick just finishing his rounds. I told him Paris was on her way.

He stayed to greet her and Charlie, told them he'd be checking back throughout the day, and escorted them behind the swinging doors long before the nurses were ready for them. I waited until Charlie told me I could go back to see Paris but stayed only a minute. I wanted to be in the lobby when Cardiff and Franklin arrived because I didn't want Cardiff to think I was trying to take her place. I sat in the lobby on one of the rough fabric covered chairs; Charlie paced and wondered aloud why everyone was taking so long to get there. Finally, Cardiff, Franklin, and Ramiro arrived.

Everyone, except Franklin, took turns going back to

see Paris. After a couple of hours Charlie stuck his head out through the swinging door and said, "She's going to delivery!" He didn't look dark or handsome. He looked scared.

I went back with Cardiff, and we walked beside the gurney until they wheeled Paris through the double doors into the delivery room. We went back to the waiting area with Charlie. He needed us more than Paris did at that moment. We filled the time with conversation, asking about names they'd chosen for a boy or girl. Charlie wouldn't tell us what they'd decided.

Cardiff confided at one point, "I was in hard labor for over eight hours with Paris."

That terrified Charlie. He looked at his digital watch. "She's been in there for twenty-two and a-half minutes. I wish they'd let me be with her. Her doctor told me I have to wait out here."

About an hour later, Dr. Becker came out to announce to Charlie that he had beautiful baby girl. He suddenly became a bashful little boy, turned to shake his dad's hand, and surprised us all by putting his head on his father's shoulder to weep. It reminded me of the first time I talked to Charlie after Paris collapsed in the judging ring, when I'd seen him with his head on Charga's back. On this day, his tears were pure joy.

Charlie went back to be with Paris and to meet his daughter. Cardiff and Ramiro went back, too. I waited with Franklin in the small waiting room. Franklin, out of his element, seemed a little embarrassed to be in the part of the hospital so clearly the domain of women. He apologized, almost blushing.

"I know all about birthing four legged animals," he told me. "I've even pulled a few breech-borne calves out of their mother's womb."

I nodded, letting him know I didn't doubt his expertise in *that* arena.

"I don't want to see Paris until she's all cleaned up and everything." He twirled his hat on his hand.

"Franklin, it's a little less primitive in the hospital. I think you could go back now. It would mean a lot to Paris if you would."

Even though skeptical, he ventured with me through the double doors.

Cardiff met us, saying, "They are going to put her in the nursery. We can see her through the window."

Franklin wore a baffled expression. I guess because they knew one another so well, Cardiff knew what he was thinking, "They mean the baby, Franklin. Not Paris."

Cardiff led us down the corridor to the nursery window. The sign showed the visiting times, which would not start for another three hours.

"She'll be right here," Cardiff reassured us.

"How is Paris," I asked.

"Tuckered plum out," Cardiff sighed. "She's a trooper, though. They did a spinal, so she's not feeling it yet."

The window shades opened and a turquoise clad nurse held a tightly wrapped bundle up close to the window so we could see. The tiny pink cocoon wasn't much larger than a football. A tiny mouth stretched opened wide, then retracted back into a tiny pout. Her eyes were swollen slits lined with minute lashes. I swore she had tiny dimples, just like Paris. The nurse put her down in a clear Lucite bassinette and left her in front of the window for us to admire. A pink card stuck on it proclaimed *baby-girl Nash-Garza six pounds and one-half ounces, nineteen inches long.*

We watched her sleep. I'd never seen a more beautiful

newborn. Her fine dark hair wisped up from her clear olive skin. I could see she'd have Charlie's complexion and both parents' dark hair. I wondered what color her eyes would be. I hoped they'd be blue like Paris's. Her little lower lip now sucked under the top one, and she began to hiccup.

"Look, she's got hiccups," Franklin announced.

Ramiro said, "She looks like Charlie did when he was born."

Franklin disagreed. "She looks like one of the Nashes."

We saw Paris after she'd settled in her room, and we raved about her little girl. We swore she and Charlie had the most beautiful baby in the nursery. Paris couldn't wait to hold her daughter, but the hospital wouldn't allow an infant in the room as long as visitors were there.

I told her, "I'm only going to stay for a few minutes. I just came for a hug from you."

I bent to hug her slight frame and she whispered, "No, you get to stay longer. Don't tell Mom."

I thought I'd misunderstood, but Charlie took me aside and whispered, "Leave and come back in twenty minutes or so."

I said, "Goodbye, everyone. I'll see you soon." Then I went to the lobby gift store. I bought a newborn-sized long gown in the softest yellow fabric I'd ever felt and a lavender bunny, which was softer still. I felt a little guilty when I hid behind a display rack as Cardiff, Franklin and Ramiro walked by on their way out of the hospital.

I took my gifts back to the room, and Paris admired them, touching the soft bunny to her face.

"They are bringing her up. We want you to be here to hold her."

I was thrilled, but didn't understand why I'd received

this privilege.

"What are you naming her?" I had to ask.

Paris hadn't told anyone, the name they chose for their baby. When anyone asked, she'd said, "You'll see. Wait until after it's born, please."

I looked expectantly from Charlie to Paris and back again to Paris, hoping they would finally tell me.

"Heaven," Paris said. "We are going to name her Heaven." She said it in a voice as soft and caressing as cashmere.

I must have frowned, an unconscious reaction, but I couldn't remember having ever heard anyone naming a baby Heaven before.

"Don't you like it?" I could tell by her expression that it was important to her that I did.

"Of course, I love it," I reassured, smiling, even though I wasn't sure I did.

"That way," Charlie explained to me, "whenever she hears her name, she'll know that's where her mother is, looking down, and watching over her."

Chapter Thirty

When the nurse came in with Heaven, she handed her to Paris right away and then looked at me curiously. She was poised next to the bed, holding a small bottle with a slanted nipple.

"She's staying," Paris said, noticing the nurse's glance at me. She snuggled her daughter into the crook of her arm and took the bottle from the nurse's hand.

"Can I unwrap her first?" Paris asked as if she'd gotten a birthday present and didn't want to break some rule of etiquette by opening it too soon.

The young nurse smiled. "She's your daughter."

Paris laid the baby on her lap and gently untucked the blanket from its tight folds. She unwrapped the blanket from around her baby girl.

The nurse said, "I'll be back in about twenty minutes," and left the room.

Paris stripped the baby bare, kissed fingers and toes

and the bottoms of her tiny feet. Charlie sat beside her, stroking one diminutive arm, his adoring expression making him look more handsome than ever before.

"Why are her feet blue? Is she cold?" Charlie wanted to know, when he noticed tinges of color on the soles of her tiny little feet.

"No, that's the ink left from where they took her footprints when she was born," Paris explained. "So they won't mix-up the babies in the nursery."

Both Paris and Charlie admired their daughter. When Heaven began to cry, Paris re-diapered, rewrapped and snuggled little Heaven in the crook of her arm. She barely touched the bottle's nipple to the baby's pouting lower lip when Heaven grabbed it in her mouth and began to suck.

We all marveled at Heaven's brilliance at being so smart that she figured out how to eat only hours after being born. A few minutes later, Paris looked at me and said, "Siobhan, I want you to feed her the rest of this."

I pointed at myself, "Me?"

"Umhmm, you," Paris nodded.

I went to the sink and washed my hands before I let Paris hand Heaven to me. The transfer went easily and I sat, looking down at this most precious baby. When I looked back, tears were flowing down Paris's cheeks.

Charlie said, "Siobhan, the reason we want you to be here," his voice was deeper than usual, almost as if he were presenting a speech, "is we want you to be Heaven's mother."

"Oh, I'd love to be her Godmother," I crooned, looking at the tiny face.

Paris spoke in a barely audible whisper. "No, Siobhan. Charlie and I want you to be Heaven's mother when I'm gone."

I couldn't have been more shocked if they'd asked me

to fly out the window.

The nurse came to take Heaven back to the nursery. Charlie hadn't even had a chance to hold his daughter.

Paris asked, "A few minutes more, please?"

I walked Heaven to Charlie and put her in his arms. He held her and cooed, holding the bottle like a pro. I sat on the edge of the bed next to Paris.

"You didn't answer, Siobhan." She looked at me expectantly.

"Paris, I will do whatever you want me to, but what will your parents say? I think your mom has already planned to take care of her." I looked from Paris's face to my hands in my lap. They felt empty.

"I know, they won't understand it," she answered me. "But I don't want my parents to raise her. I don't want them to be her parents *and* her grandparents. You and I both had remarkable relationships with our grandfathers, and I don't want Heaven to miss having that."

"I...I," I stammered.

Paris put her hand on my arm to stop me, "Do you love her?"

As crazy as it sounds, I did. I fell in love with the tiny bundle as soon as she put her in my arms, the same way I felt about Paris. I wasn't thinking about how I could make it work out or whether or not I'd know what to do with a baby, a child, a teen-ager. All I said was, "Paris, are you sure?"

"I am positive," Paris assured me. "You are the one person in the world who will know what she's feeling. Your mother left you, and you know what that's like. You will know what to say to reassure her that I loved her and I didn't want leave her. You will never let her feel the way you did when you were growing up. You will never let her doubt how I loved her. You will be sure she understands I would have given anything to be with her to watch her grow. You can do that for her and for me, Siobhan."

I left the hospital in a turmoil of emotions. I wasn't looking forward to the inevitable confrontation with Cardiff and Franklin and Ramiro.

Our meetings, fraught with doubt about the practicalities, left us all drained. Cardiff and Franklin wanted to raise the baby as a member of their family. Ramiro had huge concerns about his young son being responsible for a child. He didn't want Charlie burdened with raising Heaven, alone, at his young age. He agreed with the Nashes. They should raise Heaven.

Paris changed their minds. She told them she wanted them to be free to be grandparents to Heaven. She made me promise, in front of them, that I would do everything in my power to be sure they were as important in Heaven's life as our grandfathers were to us. Charlie and I stood behind the chair where Paris sat holding Heaven tightly in her arms as she explained. We were a united front.

We found a family law attorney to draw up the papers, and while he admitted we had a non-traditional arrangement, it was legal. Charlie and Paris agreed that after Paris's death, I'd adopt Heaven and that Charlie and I would share full parental rights.

Phyllis giggled when I told her what Paris wanted. "You a mother? What happened to being the reigning anchorwoman?"

She was the first of many who teased me about the about-face my career direction took. My dream of being the next Barbara Walters wasn't so important anymore, perhaps never was as important to me as it had been to my grandfather.

BZ was supportive. He said, "So, we'll cover the news

with a papoose. I think it can be done."

Bud went even further. He told me, "Vesta Muniz's husband is being transferred to Colorado. I need a new morning show host. How about it?"

Since my friendship with Paris, I'd become much more introspective and aware of how much of my life had been spent worrying about how I looked, instead of concentrating on other people. I'd learned from Paris that everyone has a story, maybe not as dramatic as hers but an interesting one, nonetheless. Bud noticed, too. He told me one day, "You are good with people, Siobhan. That's a gift."

He knew when he gave me the show that I'd do a good job, and he knew the set schedule would make it easier for me to work around a baby's needs.

My neighbor, Melvyn Gerfers, the man who'd done the work on the ranch house, agreed to build a house for me. Within four months, I had a home of my own at the ranch, connected by a dogtrot to the original house where Paris, Charlie, and Heaven lived.

When Charlie and Paris got married, Charlie had taken his GED and left school. Now he worked part-time at Henne Hardware in New Braunfels and enrolled in classes at Southwest Texas University in San Marcos. He commuted to classes every Tuesday and Thursday.

Marla Gerfers, Melvyn's wife, kept an eye on Paris and Heaven whenever Charlie and I were both away. Our plan worked really well for about five months. I moved into my house only days before Paris started to decline. BZ noticed right away.

He'd been coming to make videotapes for Paris to leave for Heaven. They wouldn't let me watch him do the taping, but every time he finished with a session, he'd come out to me and cry, "I can't do this anymore. It's breaking my heart."

He kept coming, though, for one day each week until Paris was simply too weak to continue.

Dr. Doom started coming to the ranch to check on Paris, rather than have her go in to San Antonio. He'd bring Tracy, and we'd fix dinner and pretend everything was perfectly normal.

Paris told everyone about her decision to let me be mother to Heaven, and everyone respected Paris's wishes. It was Paris who started calling me Mamatu.

"Well, Mamatu," Dexter said to me when no one else was near, "It's beginning." His face was solemn. He didn't have to say anything more. I already knew. I nodded.

We called in a local hospice group. They managed her pain and kept her comfortable until the end. Six weeks later on a Sunday afternoon, Paris died. We had called all of her close friends and family when the hospice nurse told us the time was near. All of them came before the end. Everyone who loved Paris wanted to be near when she left us.

Charga alerted us that she had passed. He knew before the rest of us, started bawling in the pen out back. I'd left Charlie in the bedroom with Paris, her pale little body almost lost in the feather bed. The hospice nurse had gone to take a walk.

When I heard Charga bawling, I knew. I rushed inside and found Charlie kneeling beside the bed, holding Paris's hand. She was pale and still. Heaven slept peacefully beside her.

Lannie White wrote the most beautiful column about Paris. The headline was "Goodbye, Paris Nash." Lannie reminded her readers about the little girl who had brought so many people together when Charga won Grand Champion. She received hundreds of calls from people asking what would happen to Charga now that Paris was gone. Later in the month, she did a short column on Charga, too.

In the following months, Charlie and I consoled, or rather tried to console, one another. I worried about him. He only smiled when he held the baby. He kept to himself and put all of his energy into work and study. Every night he would take Heaven to the television and watch one of the tapes Paris left for her.

I watched the tapes, too. Paris told about her life, sharing who she was with the daughter who would have no conscious memory of her. I could tell she was using her own life experience to pass on life lessons to her child. The last minutes of the last tape still break my heart. She spoke both to me and to her little girl.

Paris said, "I have to go. I don't want to, but I don't have a choice. Mamatu, now it's up to you and Charlie to take care of precious baby Heaven. I love you all."

Eventually, Charlie began to show signs of being his same old self again. I'd watch him leave the house in the morning to go to work or school. He'd walk outside, stand next to his Jeep, take his fingers from his temple to his lips, and then touch his chest. It happened so often, I had to ask him what it meant.

"I figured out how I could go on," he told me, trying not to cry. "I thought I'd die, too. But, I promised Paris I would always take care of Heaven, so I couldn't die. I had to live. I figured the reason I couldn't be normal was that I felt guilty when I wasn't thinking about her. I felt like I was leaving Paris behind. I know it doesn't make sense."

I must have had a questioning face. "Go on," I encouraged him.

"So I made up this thing where I take her from my

mind and kiss her and put her in my heart to go with me. She's always right here," he tapped his chest.

Epilogue

Over the years since Paris's death, so much has happened. Tristan and Phyllis asked Heaven to be flower girl at their wedding. They asked me to be Maid of Honor and BZ was Best Man.

Tracy and Dexter were married and got divorced two years later. We all knew it couldn't last. Lannie's sister divorced the beer man because he cheated on her. Pepe, who stole Charga, joined the army and is now an air traffic controller at DFW. Luis is very proud of his son.

Rome married a girl he met at A&M. India married her high school boyfriend and has two children of her own. Ireland, the little people-pleaser, got in trouble with drugs in high school. We worry about her every day. London is a psychologist in Houston and specializes in grief counseling.

Lannie White is still writing her daily column. Every few years during Rodeo Week, she does an update on Charga and usually for a few weeks following each story, strangers drive up to the ranch and ask to see the steer. Invariably, they tell us about the money they collected to help save him.

Some of them bring their own children to see the steer they helped rescue from certain death. Many have lived their lives not eating beef.

Most people were surprised when Bud Johnson and I married, but then none of them had been in his office the day he told me about losing his precious Alyssa. I think Heaven helped fill a little of the space his daughter's death left within him. Heaven had called him "Budjohnson" since she'd learned to talk, but we all loved it when she decided on her own to call him Papatu.

I hosted the show at KWNK until we married. It worked out fine because Bud hired a new girl at the station, a little older than most new hires. She was good at feature stories and was a natural replacement for me.

Charlie never remarried. He dated a little in his thirties, but no other woman could compare to his first love. He has been an exceptional father to his daughter. He became interested in building while he watched my house take shape and changed his major. He got a degree in home building and now constructs custom homes throughout the Texas Hill Country.

Heaven's school years went smoothly until fifth grade when she decided she wanted to be known as Nash Garza from then on because she had her fill of angel jokes and boys teasing her about getting into Heaven. Everyone in the family still calls her by her given name, though, so she still has reminders that her mother is watching over her.

The story Heaven wanted to hear most often while she was growing up was about the day Charga won Grand Champion. She loved the part about her mother fainting and how I made sure BZ got it on tape, I guess because that was when her Mama and her Mamatu first met. We weren't sure how confusing our unusual living arrangement might be to her. She didn't think it odd that her parents lived in separate houses. For a long time she thought every child had two bedrooms and could pick which one they wanted to sleep in on any given night.

As Paris always wanted, Heaven dearly loves both of her grandfathers. Ramiro taught her to speak Spanish and how to ride a horse. Franklin still gives her practical advice in the same homespun way Paris's grandfather had given advice to her. She loves her Nana Cardiff, too. Cardiff never really recovered from Paris's death. She always comments when she notices something about Heaven that reminds her of Paris.

"You sound just like your mother when you laugh," she told her just the other day.

Heaven graduated from high school at the top of her class and received a scholarship to A&M. She's in the veterinary science program. In one of the videos BZ made, Paris talks about the promise she made to Charga. I don't know if that prompted Heaven's interest in the field, but most of her research is on the geriatric bovine. Charga is her very own well-loved research animal. He's probably still alive because of her care.

It's been over twenty-five years since I first saw Paris Nash and as I look out my window, I see across the field a girl walking beside a lumbering old steer. I cannot imagine how proud Paris must be of us all. I glance toward the clouds, take my fingers to my temple, to my lips to kiss, and touch them to my heart.

THE END

337

Made in the USA
Charleston, SC
29 November 2012